LOVE'S
REDEMPTION

By the Author

Healing Hearts

No Boundaries

Love's Redemption

Visit us at www.boldstrokesbooks.com

Love's Redemption

by
Donna K. Ford

2016

ISBN 13: 978-1-62639-673-9

THIS TRADE PAPERBACK ORIGINAL IS PUBLISHED BY
BOLD STROKES BOOKS, INC.
P.O. BOX 249
VALLEY FALLS, NY 12185

FIRST EDITION: JUNE 2016

CREDITS
EDITOR: RUTH STERNGLANTZ
PRODUCTION DESIGN: STACIA SEAMAN
COVER DESIGN BY SHERI (GRAPHICARTIST2020@HOTMAIL.COM)

Acknowledgments

According to *Child Sexual Abuse Statistics: Darkness to Light* (D2L.org), child sexual abuse is likely the most prevalent health problem children face with the most serious array of consequences. They estimate that about 1 in 10 children will be sexually abused before their 18th birthday. That is approximately 1 in 7 girls and 1 in 25 boys. According to a 2003 National Institute of Justice report, 3 out of 4 adolescents who have been sexually assaulted were victimized by someone they knew well. A child who is the victim of prolonged sexual abuse usually develops low self-esteem, a feeling of worthlessness, and an abnormal or distorted view of sex. The child may become withdrawn and mistrustful of adults, and can become suicidal. No child should ever suffer the devastating effects of child sex abuse.

Writing *Love's Redemption* was an emotional journey like nothing I could have imagined. In my counseling career, I have seen the terrible things that people do to each other and have witnessed the amazing spirit and determination of the survivors to overcome their personal tragedy.

It is my hope that *Love's Redemption* will be one more step in the right direction toward breaking the silence and giving voice to the survivors.

As I mentioned, this book was an emotional journey for me that led me through my own memories of abuse and the effects that impact who I am to this day. Healing and surviving is an ongoing process. My partner Keah has been instrumental in my acceptance of myself. Her patience and understanding leaves me without words. I am forever grateful for her love.

I would also like to acknowledge my editor Ruth Sternglantz for encouraging me to write this story and for accepting the tough stuff in stride. I am grateful to be a part of the Bold Strokes Books family.

I would like to give a special thank you to my beta reader Brianne. Her patience and watchful eye were exactly what I needed. And most of all, I would like to acknowledge the readers. You are the reason I put these stories on paper. I hope each book represents the astounding spirit of your journey to love freely.

For the Survivors.

To Keah, for being my light in the dark places.

CHAPTER ONE

R hea blinked rapidly and squinted against the sun, her eyes unaccustomed to the brightness. She peered out the window of the van and marveled at the people walking freely along the streets. The world had changed in the last fifteen years and left her behind. Her time in prison hadn't been void of technological and social advancements, but her exposure was limited. Most of these people barely noticed each other, instead focusing their attention on electronic devices they carried in their hands, or they talked into their cell phones. Maybe that would make it easier not to be noticed.

Rhea stepped out of the transport van at the bus station and pulled her backpack across her left shoulder. She tugged at the strap with her right hand so that her arm crossed her chest and held a little of the warmth inside her plain blue prison-issue sweatshirt. She had a long walk ahead of her, and she needed to get moving if she was going to reach her mother's house before dark.

She stopped and studied the square red-brick building where her fate had been settled fifteen years earlier. A bronze plaque still stood outside the Rhea County courthouse boasting of the building's legacy as the location of the legendary Scopes Trial. As a child she'd marveled that her small Tennessee town had such a profound history, but she never imagined that one day she too would be on trial in this very place. She looked upon it now as the place where her town and her family had betrayed her.

Rhea took a step back and bumped into two women walking past her on the sidewalk.

"Excuse me. I'm very sorry."

"Oh, that's all right, dear," the first woman said automatically.

Rhea glanced at the two women, recognizing their faces instantly. They'd been part of her mother's church group when she was a girl. The woman who had spoken to her was Clara Spencer, the church organist. She hadn't changed much in the time Rhea had been away. She was still short and plump, although her hair had changed from black to gray. The second woman was Mary Parson, a harsh woman with beady black eyes and a sharp tongue. She was also the sheriff's wife. Rhea dropped her head as soon as she caught Mrs. Parson scrutinizing her.

"Do we know you?" Mrs. Parson asked.

"No. I'm just passing through town. Excuse me again, ladies."

She hadn't expected anyone to recognize her. She barely resembled the young girl with long hair and plump, rosy cheeks she'd been the last time they saw her. Rhea gripped her backpack and hurried away, hoping they wouldn't figure it out.

"I swear that girl reminds me of someone, but for the life of me I can't remember who," Mrs. Parson said as she walked away.

Rhea groaned. The last thing she needed was for the town gossip line to reach her mother before she did.

The crunch of gravel under Rhea's feet reverberated up her spine with each step. The place that had once been her home stood in the distance like a ghost, haunting her with memories of lust, lies, deceit, and betrayal. She stopped at the front of the ornate porch and squared her shoulders to defend herself against the cold gray eyes of her mother, who stood at the top of the steps with her arms crossed like a shield of impenetrable armor. Lines creased the once flawless face, and small round glasses created a false barrier between Rhea and the woman looking back at her.

"Hello, Momma."

"Rhea."

Rhea swallowed against the lump of fear and anger growing in her throat. She'd known this would be hard, but she hadn't expected to feel so vulnerable. She'd agreed to return home temporarily until she had work and other accommodations, to avoid going to a halfway house. Now that she was here, she was beginning to question if that had been such a good idea.

"I wrote to tell you I was getting out."

"I read it. Your parole officer called here too. I told her this is no place for you. This is a small town and no one has forgotten what you did. No one wants you here."

Rhea gritted her teeth against the venom in her mother's voice. No, she didn't expect anyone to forget what had happened, and she understood that no one here cared why she'd done what she'd done. In a small town like this, these things just didn't happen...until they did.

"What about you, Momma?" Rhea already knew the answer but had to ask. In the fifteen years she had been away, she hadn't seen or heard from her mother or her younger sister.

"You can stay in the barn for a few days to go through your old things. I had Tommy put them in the storage room. You can take your old Jeep too, Molly didn't want it."

A fresh pain stabbed through Rhea when her mother mentioned her sister. Molly hadn't understood what she'd done and hated her for it. She had never believed Rhea was protecting her and, believing their mother's lies instead, she'd turned her back on Rhea.

Rhea nodded. She understood how hard it had been for her sister. It was easier for everyone to believe Rhea was the evil one than to face the truth of what her father had done.

"Thank you for allowing me to take the Jeep and stay here. I have a place arranged, so I shouldn't be in your way for too long."

"The sooner the better. It's hard enough around here without you stirring things up all over town. I don't want anyone thinking I brought you back in after what you did."

Tears stung Rhea's eyes. "I had to do it. I couldn't let him hurt her, Momma." Rhea was surprised she had spoken the words out loud, but she wouldn't make excuses or apologize for what she'd done.

"He was your father," her mother snapped. "He was a good man. You had no right to destroy his legacy and our family name. Those were private matters."

Rhea turned away from her mother for the first time, the words striking her like a slap to the face. She felt sick. This only confirmed that her mother had known what her father had done to her. She'd known and done nothing to stop him. Her father's position in the community and the family name were more important than her own daughters.

"Why didn't you do anything? Why didn't you stop him? Why didn't you protect us?"

"He was your father."

Rhea blew out a breath. There was no use trying, there was no way to get through to her mother. Image and prestige were more important than truth.

"And you are our mother," Rhea said with a bite to the words. "It was a mistake for me to come here. I'll be in the barn." Rhea slid her hands into the pockets of her jeans as she walked and pinched the skin of her thighs to stop the urge to scream at her mother. She thought the years had dulled the pain of her mother's betrayal, but the wound was just as raw now as the day her mother had testified against her in court. She couldn't believe she'd even tried to reason with her mother. Uncertainty plagued her, and after being free for only a day she didn't know how she was going to make it on the outside. She had been gone too long. Prison was all she knew outside of this little town that was her namesake. Her mother was right about one thing: there was no way she could stay here. Anything would be better than being here.

❖

Morgan looked up from the calf she was feeding to find her sister J.J. leaning against the gate. It was an ominous sign.

"Whatever it is, I'm not buying," Morgan said playfully. As usual her sister was up to something. She only showed up without calling when she wanted something.

J.J. smiled. "Is that any way to talk to your big sister?"

Morgan laughed. "Considering the sister, I'd say it's a definite yes."

"You wound me," J.J. said as she placed her hand across her chest and faked a pained expression.

The calf finished its breakfast and Morgan shooed it away with a playful pat.

"Tell me you're not going to try to talk me into some scheme of yours, and I'll take it back."

J.J. ignored the stab and changed the subject. "New calf?"

Morgan nodded. "I'm supplementing his feeding because the mother isn't producing enough milk."

"Any other new additions to the farm?" J.J. asked.

Morgan stood. "We both know you aren't interested in the animals or the farm, J.J., so why don't you just tell me why you're here. What are you up to?"

J.J. sighed. "You should hear me out on this one, Morgan. I could really use your help."

Morgan straightened. This must be serious. It wasn't like J.J. to ask for favors. "Are the kids okay?"

J.J. swiped her hand through the air as if brushing off a gnat. "The kids are great. Don't worry, it's nothing like that."

Morgan studied her sister's face and tried to measure the seriousness in the set of her jaw and the worry lines at the corners of her eyes. She had a feeling she wasn't going to like this.

"Okay, I'll listen, but no promises beyond that."

"Fair. Let's go for a walk and I'll tell you a story."

Morgan sighed as J.J. turned and walked out, leaving the gate open behind her. This had to be bad. J.J. wanted something and was stalling. Morgan dusted off her hands and followed J.J. and soon fell into step beside her. She walked in silence, knowing that if she waited J.J. out, she would eventually tell her what had her in a twist.

"You know you work too hard around here. You need some help," J.J. said in a casual tone.

Morgan wasn't buying her sister's sudden concern for her farm and figured this would eventually lead to the point of J.J.'s visit.

"Do you still have the small engine shop?"

Morgan nodded. "I have a few pieces I'm working on but nothing too overwhelming."

"But as summer comes on you'll have more work, right?"

Morgan stopped walking and looked at her sister. "Where's this going, J.J.?"

J.J. sighed. "I know someone who really needs a job and a place to stay. I was hoping you would hire her to help out around here."

"I don't need any help. I'm doing fine on my own."

"Yeah, and that's why the fence by the goat house is broken, the barn has three inches of dirt on the hall walk, and your gallery looks like it's been abandoned."

Morgan frowned. She didn't want to argue with J.J., but she didn't want some stranger barging in on her life either. "Maybe that's the way I like it."

"Come on, Morgan, won't you at least give this girl a try? She's really hard up and this would be perfect for her. You need help even if you don't want to admit it."

"Who's the girl?"

J.J. looked away and Morgan knew she wasn't going to like the answer.

"Well, I shouldn't really call her a girl. She's thirty-two years old and just needs a break. Hell, I'd hire her if I could. Maybe you could just let her work on a trial basis until you make up your mind. If things don't work out then we'll think of something else. Come on, Morgan, you could use the help. She could stay in Grandpa's old cabin and you would hardly even know she's here."

Morgan laughed. "That cabin isn't fit to live in right now, especially in winter. Anybody would be miserable living there. Besides, I gave up charity work, remember?"

"She won't be here for a few weeks. I'll help you get the place ready, and she can do most of the work herself. This is a win for you."

Morgan raised an eyebrow and scrutinized her sister. "You're going to help? What aren't you telling me, J.J.? Who's this girl? How do you know her?"

J.J. grimaced. "Promise me you'll try?" she pleaded.

Morgan blew out a breath. She always had trouble saying no

to her sister. "Okay, I'll give her a job and she can stay in the cabin. Now, what's the story?"

J.J. looked worried and wouldn't look Morgan in the eye. That was a bad sign and Morgan figured she was about to regret her agreement.

"She's one of my parolees."

Morgan gasped, but before she could protest, J.J. launched into her argument again. "Wait. You'll just have to meet her. She has a very troubled past and this is her one shot at a real life. I wouldn't ask if it wasn't important, and I believe in her."

Morgan's stomach twisted as if she was going to be sick. "You want one of your parolees to live here...with me? Have you lost your mind? You know I don't tolerate that kind of life. If you haven't noticed, I'm not in the business of saving people. I'm not fit for the job, or don't you remember the last time—"

"She's not like that." J.J. cut her off before she could finish. "She was just a child when she got into trouble. The only way she's going to make it is if someone gives her a chance."

"Yeah, what did she do?"

J.J. looked away again.

Morgan laughed. "Oh, this ought to be rich. What? Did she kill somebody or something?"

J.J. looked up in surprise.

Morgan took a step back, shocked at the truth. "No way." Morgan couldn't believe J.J. would seriously suggest she bring a convicted murderer to live on her farm. "Seriously, you actually want me to hire and live with a murderer? Wasn't what happened with Ashley bad enough? What do you think I can do?"

Morgan paced back and forth in front of her studio. Nothing could have prepared her for this. "What are you thinking?" she grumbled and sat down on the steps.

J.J. held her hands out toward Morgan with her palms up. "It isn't as easy as that. She was a child and someone hurt her. Everything I know about this case tells me she was backed into a corner and did the only thing she thought could save her. Before this happened, she was an honor student in her high school, class president, hell, she was even the freaking homecoming queen. Nothing in her history suggested she would hurt anybody."

"But she did," Morgan snapped. "There's always another way. I don't want that kind of violence around me."

J.J. sat down and put an arm around Morgan's neck. "Please, Morgan, do this for me. Trust me on this one. It's the right thing to do."

Morgan groaned and wrapped an arm around her sister. "I don't like it."

"I know."

J.J. tightened her grip. Morgan gave in but couldn't shake the feeling she was making a huge mistake. But J.J. was her sister and her weakness. If this was important to her, Morgan didn't really have a choice. She would try.

"When will she be here?"

J.J. bounced up and down, still holding on to Morgan with all her strength. "Thank you, thank you, thank you. She'll be here the first week of February."

Morgan leaned back and pinned her sister with her eyes. "You've got a lot of work to get done then if that cabin is going to be ready."

J.J. smiled. "Deal."

❖

Rhea lay awake in her makeshift bed in the hayloft, listening to the sounds of the night. It was too quiet and too dark. She imagined she could hear the voices of women murmuring, some angry, some crying, some whispering lost prayers to a God she no longer believed in. But the voices were silent on this, her first night of freedom. She sighed at the irony. She would never be free from the betrayal of her father or the judgment of a world who continued to punish women and children for the crimes of their abusers. Her mother was proof enough that her life was condemned. She had to find a way out of this place. Prison was better than this new hell.

Rhea rose with the first glow of morning light and sat in the loft looking out over the fields. The winter morning glowed with orange light as the sun slowly climbed the mountain and peeked its head above the ridge, seeming to set the trees ablaze.

Rhea watched her breath freeze into a puff of white against the chill, crisp air. She drew her legs up and rested her chin on her knees. This was the first sunrise she had witnessed in almost sixteen years and it was more breathtaking than she remembered. For the first time since she was seventeen years old she was hopeful. The sunrise was her reminder that she could begin again. She was renewed and her determination solidified. She promised herself she would build a new life. She would never again be a victim. She swore that every day she would make her own fate and never again let anyone close enough to hurt her.

She lifted her face and let the sun kiss her cheeks. Her skin tingled from the touch of warmth against her cool skin. The sound of movement below got her attention and she stood and dusted herself off. She still wore the prison-issue sweatshirt she had been given and decided the first thing she wanted to do was go through her old clothes. Surely she had an old coat, some T-shirts, maybe some old jeans she could still wear if they hadn't rotted away or been eaten by insects or rodents. She looked down at her sneakers and wiggled her toes. At least her boots would still fit. She had lost the softness of youth and replaced the supple curves of a girl with the hard, thin lines of a woman who never got enough to eat and spent her free time burning off pent-up energy with what exercise she could in her cell.

The barn was still dark, but Rhea didn't turn on the lights right away. She stood still and took in the smell of old hay and dust. Horses murmured in their stalls, sensing her presence. She envisioned the long corridor lined with stalls as she'd last seen it. The memory of the feel of the railing sliding beneath her palm made her hand itch. These were once comforts. She wanted to pretend for a moment that her life had been a terrible dream, but those were childish wishes and she was far beyond fairy tales.

She flipped on the light and blinked as her eyes adjusted to the sudden brightness. She studied the long hallway that was just as she'd remembered. It was as if time itself had stopped the day she left. Everything stood frozen in her memory as if she was holding her breath and she only needed to exhale and her life would begin again. She blew out her breath. *Let's do this.*

Three hours later Rhea heard a familiar voice murmuring in the distance and realized Tommy had come in to tend the horses. A moment later he was standing in the doorway, a sly grin on his face.

"Well, I'll be. All that time away and you're still the prettiest girl in town."

Rhea smiled. "Hi, Tommy."

Tommy nodded toward the box of things Rhea had been sifting through. "Ms. Daniels had me bring those things out here a while after you were sent away. I figured you'd be back someday, so I took care of a few things for you."

"Thanks." Rhea pointed to a box of dresses she'd put aside along with trophies, ribbons, her scholarship letter, and her high school yearbook. "I don't think I'll need these anymore."

Those things hadn't been real to her anyway. Her life had been an act, always pretending to be someone she wasn't, always working to hide her secret life. There was no more hiding for her.

Tommy pointed to a small box on a shelf. "The keys to the Jeep are in there. Ms. Daniels said you'd be taking it with you. I used it for small errands for the farm just to keep it running, and the tags and all are good too."

Rhea remembered the day her parents had brought the Jeep home for her sixteenth birthday. She had felt like she was walking on air because transportation was her ticket out, the first door opened to freedom. Even now a small thrill ran through her. That was one dream that would finally come true. She opened the box and slipped the keys into her pocket. She began to pack the few belongings she could use into a contractor bag she'd found in the tack room. It was fitting that her life had been condensed into one trash bag. She found her old seed coat and coveralls and her boots. The jeans were questionable but would have to do.

"I appreciate all you've done for me. Most people around here wouldn't care."

Tommy shrugged. "I suppose everyone has their own way of dealing with things. I knew you back then. You worked hard to please everybody. I believed you back then and I believe you now."

Tears stung her eyes. Tommy was the only one who did believe her. "Thank you. That means a lot to me, Tommy."

He nodded. "Well, I've got work to do. There's coffee in the office. Give me a yell if you need anything."

"Hey, Tommy?" Rhea called.

"Yeah," he said, sticking his head back around the corner.

"How's Molly?"

Tommy sighed. "Things were tough on her. She was real restless there for a while and gave your momma a hard way to go. She got herself into a little trouble here and there but nothing too serious. She wasn't into the books and school stuff the way you always were. But by the time she hit high school she had a plan and fast-tracked her way into the air force. She seems to be doing real good. But she doesn't come around but maybe every couple of years."

"Does she hate me?"

"Aw, now, that's hard to say. At first she was real hurt and mad. But as she grew up, I think she started to figure things out for herself. I'm not sure how she ever worked it out. She used to ask me questions about you and your daddy, but I didn't know much. I think she eventually just wanted to get away from it all."

Rhea took a deep breath and thought about everything Tommy had said. "The air force, huh?"

Tommy smiled. "Yep."

Rhea smiled, and a moment later, Tommy was gone.

She looked around at the mess surrounding her and decided it was a good time for a break. She dusted herself off and headed for the coffee. She smiled. Hmm. The air force, how about that.

By early afternoon Rhea had cleared through all her things and managed to salvage a few essentials. She had expected her boots to be rotten, but Tommy had kept them oiled and they looked better than the last time she'd worn them. She had a few pairs of jeans and some old shirts she used to wear when working around the farm. Her coveralls and coat were still in good shape, but she could have done without the smell of mothballs. Thanks to the crappy prison food and the exercise routine she'd stuck to so she didn't lose her mind, she was a bit smaller than she used to be.

Now the next order of business was food, and she still had to check in with her parole officer. Both would require contact with her mother. Rhea swallowed. She wasn't ready for the next round with her mother, but she couldn't put it off much longer. The sooner she took care of this business, the sooner she could leave.

Every step closer to the house filled her with dread. She climbed the steps to the porch and knocked on the door. She jumped back when her mother answered with a .410 shotgun in her hands pointed at Rhea's chest.

"Jesus, Momma, what are you doing with that thing?"

"Get back. You aren't stepping one foot inside this house," her mother barked.

"Okay. I wasn't going to come in. I just need to use the phone. I have to check in with my parole officer."

"I'll bring the phone out. You can wait in the yard."

Rhea dropped her head and backed off the porch. She didn't expect her mother to welcome her home, but the hostility was a bit much. Her stomach growled and was beginning to hurt. It was going on twenty-four hours since she had eaten and her body was protesting. Prison food wasn't something she craved, but her body was used to eating at the same time every day and wasn't happy she had already missed three meals. But after the reception she just got from her mother, there was no way she was asking for food.

Her mother stepped out onto the porch with the phone and a tray of bologna sandwiches and a pitcher of iced tea. Rhea's head was spinning from the contradictions in her mother. One minute she was ready to shoot her and the next she was bringing her lunch.

"What's all this?"

Her mother squared her shoulders and brushed a strand of loose hair from her face. "No one will ever say I let anyone under my roof go hungry."

Rhea noticed her mother had cooked the bologna until it was black, the way she had liked it as a child. One small victory, she guessed, or an olive branch perhaps. Rhea would never understand her mother, but for the moment she was thankful for her twisted hospitality.

"Thank you."

For just a moment the hard look in her mother's eyes softened. Her mother shifted on her feet and twisted her fingers together. "Just leave the phone on the tray when you're done. I'll get it later."

Rhea nodded and watched her mother retreat back into the house. She tried to imagine what her mother's life had been like. What could have made her accept the deplorable? Rhea sighed. She had loved her father too. That had been the one thing he used against her to keep the secret. Had he managed to garner the same hold on her mother?

Chapter Two

R hea shivered. She didn't remember it ever getting quite this cold in January. It had been raining all day and sleet was beginning to fall in heavy pellets that were quickly coating the trees and everything else in its path. She was nervous about setting out on her own in this weather, but the thought of spending one more night in the cold barn was enough to inspire her courage.

Tommy picked up the small box she'd put aside and set it in the front seat of the Jeep. "You sure you want to head out in this weather?"

Rhea looked out into the freezing rain. "I don't think I have much choice."

Tommy scuffed his boot on the ground. "Yeah. I guess I can't blame you. It's gotta get mighty cold up in that loft at night."

"Yeah. That's a big part of it." She paused, then confessed, "I think everyone will rest a little easier once I'm gone."

Tommy held up one finger, motioning for her to wait. "Before you go I have something for you."

Rhea watched as the old farmhand rustled down the hall and disappeared into the office. She was shocked at how old he'd gotten. She could remember him teaching her how to spit when she was five and showing her how to bridle a horse when she was eight. He had been the one to teach her how to bait a fishhook. Rhea warmed at the memories, thankful to have something good to take away with her.

Tommy came back carrying a large box. He slid the box into the back of the Jeep and gave it a pat before shutting the door.

"What's that?" Rhea asked.

Tommy shrugged. "I picked up some things I thought you might need until you can get on your feet. It's not much, but I reckon you won't starve." He pulled a knit cap and a new pair of gloves out of his pocket and handed them to her. "And you could use something on that bare noggin of yours too."

Rhea cleared her throat and fought back the tears that stung her eyes. "Thanks, Tommy. You didn't have to do all that."

He shrugged. "I know." He put a heavy hand on her shoulder. "I'm sorry I didn't know what your daddy was up to back then. I'm just sorry."

Rhea swallowed and nodded. "That means a lot."

He handed her a crumpled-up piece of paper. "That's my number if you ever need anything."

Rhea couldn't take any more and threw her arms around Tommy and hugged him. His heavy hand came down on her back in an awkward pat.

"Take care of yourself, kid, and don't let them get the best of you."

As she rolled out, Rhea stopped the Jeep in front of the house and peered through the freezing rain at the dim light that glowed through the windows of her mother's house. A figure passed in front of the window, and she could make out the image of her mother as she parted the drapes and looked outside.

Rhea held her breath, hoping for some hint of compassion from her mother. The curtain closed and the shadow of her mother faded. A moment later the porch light went out. Rhea choked back the sadness and disappointment. It was time to stop wishing for her mother's love. Love didn't exist. People just used others for what they wanted and disguised it as something else. Love wasn't real.

The heavy clouds obscured what little light was left in the day. She needed to get moving if she was going to make her destination before dark. She put the Jeep in gear and turned to the open road. Night would fall fast in this weather and she still wasn't used to driving. Uncertainty and fear stabbed through her and she stopped at the end of the drive. If she stayed, she wouldn't have to brave the weather or the night. But if she didn't leave, she would spend another night of bitter cold, haunting memories, and paralyzing self-doubt.

Rhea pulled onto the road. No fear was worse than that pain. She would face death itself not to spend another night here. She had at least a two-hour drive in this weather, but as soon as the view of her mother's house faded, the tight grip around her heart eased and for the first time in days she drew in a deep breath. She was relieved when she passed the sign signaling her departure from Rhea County. Some of the darkness slipped away only to be replaced by a new doubt.

All she had were some directions and an address her parole officer had given her. She had a job and a place to live. That was more than she had hoped for and she was eager to get started. She wasn't sure why her parole officer was helping her out, but she would take what she could get.

It was fully dark out now and the rain and sleet hammered against the windshield like rocks falling from the sky. It was as if Mother Nature herself was conspiring against her. The roads were twisted and narrow and the painted lines were barely visible in most sections of road.

It had been forever since she'd even seen a road sign and she wasn't sure she was on the right road. Rhea took the next right onto a deserted dirt track that was covered with patches of ice and pools of water. The rain had turned to heavy snow and sleet and the road was covered, making it hard to see the washed-out areas and deep gullies.

Rhea turned a corner, and before she could react, a tree fell across the road in front of her. The best she could do to avoid it was to jerk the wheel to the left. An instant later the Jeep slid off the road and came to rest against the bank of the mountain. The horn blared and no matter what she did she couldn't make it stop. Her seat belt was jammed and she couldn't get out. Rhea slammed her palm against the steering wheel in frustration. Great, what else could happen?

She peered out the windshield and squinted through the snow.

She was certain she could see light from a house just ahead. If she could just get out she might be able to get some help.

A minute later she saw a dark figure running toward her. Fear shot through Rhea and she became more frantic in her attempt to free herself. She couldn't defend herself and she couldn't run.

The passenger door opened and a woman with loose dark hair that clung to her face in wet waves poked her head inside. Relief instantly flooded Rhea, but her guard was still up. Just because it was a woman, didn't mean she was safe.

"Hey, you okay?" the woman asked.

Rhea looked at her and tried to keep the panic out of her voice. "I'm stuck."

The woman climbed halfway inside the Jeep and studied the problem. She put her hand on the seat belt and tried the release. The woman's hand brushed against Rhea's hip and she flinched and tried to move away. The woman pulled back and put her hands up, signaling she meant no harm.

"Sorry, I didn't mean to get in your space. This is quite a mess, isn't it?" The woman gestured to the mix of snow and sleet outside.

Rhea forced a light smile, but fear had her heart racing like a trapped rabbit.

"Looks like you could use a little help here. Do you mind?"

Rhea shook her head.

"Okay. Let's start by taking your foot off that brake."

Rhea looked down at her foot mashed against the brake pedal. She shifted her foot and it hit the floor with a thud.

The woman reached across the cab and turned off the engine. When she looked back at Rhea she was so close Rhea could smell the lingering hint of orange blossoms mingled with fire and ash. Her dark hair was covered by a knitted cap and strands of wet hair were plastered against her face, but that didn't hide the strong line of her jaw or the soft, pale skin of her face. There was tenderness in her eyes that calmed the storm of fear raging inside Rhea.

"You can let out the clutch now."

The woman smiled at her. The smile was calm and gentle and Rhea wondered if she was real or if this was one of those stories she read about where people insisted they had been rescued by angels. The woman placed her hand on Rhea's shoulder. The touch was soft and tentative but not threatening.

"Lean back and try the release again."

Rhea did as instructed and to her surprise the seat belt snapped open. The relief was instant and she fought back the flood of tears that threatened. "Thanks."

"You're welcome."

The woman pulled away allowing some space between them. "My name's Morgan Scott and this is my farm. Let's get you out of here and up to the house so we can dry out."

Rhea let out a sigh of relief. She wasn't lost after all. "You're Morgan Scott?"

"That's what I said."

Rhea extended her hand. It didn't matter how scared she was, politeness had been ingrained in her since the day she was born. "I'm Rhea Daniels."

Rhea didn't miss the hesitation or the brief frown that creased Morgan's brow.

Morgan took Rhea's hand. "You picked a heck of a time to show up. Were you trying to get yourself killed?"

Rhea didn't miss the disapproval in Morgan's voice or the lines that formed around the corners of her eyes as if she was trying to predict the sudden move of a snake. Morgan reminded her of the guards at the prison who challenged her every time she was moved to a new section or a new pod. It was a familiar language Rhea understood very well, and the protective defenses she'd developed over the years fell effortlessly into place.

"I said I'd be here. I'm here. You got a problem with that?"

Morgan appeared to consider this for a moment and then shrugged. "No. I guess you didn't order the weather. I'm just surprised to see you. I didn't expect you for a couple more weeks."

"Yeah, well, my last place wasn't working out and I was ready to move on."

Morgan dropped her gaze and slid out of the Jeep, her boots smacking against the muddy road with a squish. "Well, you're here now, so let's get out of here before we freeze to death. I'm tired of being wet."

"What about my Jeep?" Rhea asked.

Morgan glanced back at her. "Grab what you'll need for now. We'll come back down tomorrow and clear this tree out. There's nothing we can do tonight without making a mess and freezing our butts off."

Rhea considered her options and finally conceded that Morgan was right. At least Morgan hadn't turned her away. But she wasn't blind and she hadn't missed the distrust in Morgan's eyes. This wouldn't be much different than staying at her mother's. She'd been convicted on people's opinions before, not the facts. That was the thing with opinions, everyone had one.

❖

Morgan's house was warm and cozy, and despite her earlier distance and disapproval, she invited Rhea inside. Rhea glanced around the big open room. She might have traded one farm for another, but this was nothing like her mother's house. Her mother surrounded herself with expensive furniture, crystal, silver, and lace, all the things she thought made her look important. Morgan's house was the complete opposite. The room was comfortable with few furnishings and the decor was functional and somewhat industrial.

Rhea put her bag down and was drawn to the large hearth where the heat of the fire was strongest. She turned back to Morgan and noticed the footprints she'd left across the hardwood floor. She looked down at her feet and, to her horror, saw the mud clinging to her boots. She quickly took them off and brought them back to the mat by the door where Morgan had stored her own.

"I'm sorry. Do you have something I could use to clean this up?"

Morgan glanced at the footprints marking her floor and nodded to her right. "The kitchen's in there—I have paper towels by the sink."

Rhea hesitated. She was uncertain what to do. She was in a

stranger's home and suddenly she didn't know how to behave and the fear was quickly rising again.

"It's okay, I'll get them," Morgan said with a pat to Rhea's shoulder. "Go get warm."

Rhea still hadn't moved when Morgan came back into the room carrying paper towels and spray cleaner.

Morgan handed half the towels to Rhea and began cleaning up the mess. Rhea was stunned. Morgan hadn't been angry or ordered her to clean up, and she was even helping. Rhea got down on all fours and went to work.

Morgan sat back on her heels and inspected the floor. "See, good as new." She tossed the paper towels on the fire. "Would you like some coffee to help shake off that chill?"

Rhea was shaking, but it wasn't from the cold. She wasn't sure what she had expected. She hadn't thought about anything beyond getting out of prison and then getting away from her mother. It hadn't occurred to her that she had no idea what to do next. She'd spent almost half her life locked away like an animal in a zoo being told what to do every hour of every day. She didn't know how to be normal.

"Do you have any sweet tea?" Rhea asked.

Morgan smiled. "This is the South, isn't it?"

Rhea smiled this time and some of the fear slipped away.

"Come on, how about something to eat with that tea?" Morgan turned and walked back into the kitchen.

Rhea followed and tried to ignore the tension settling in knots between her shoulder blades as Morgan pulled a pot out of the refrigerator and put it on the stove.

"I'm afraid leftovers will have to do tonight."

The air quickly filled with the aroma of real food and Rhea's mouth watered. She'd eaten little more than bologna-and-cheese sandwiches for days and the smell of real cooked food almost made her weep. She shrugged her shoulders.

"If there's enough, I don't want to put you out or anything."

Morgan pulled two bowls from the cupboard and retrieved two spoons from a drawer. "It's no trouble and there's plenty." Morgan pointed to the island in the center of the room. "Sit. I'll only need a minute."

Rhea sat down and propped her elbows on the edge of the cold stone surface and watched Morgan. It was strange to be sitting in someone's kitchen, sipping sweet tea, and anticipating a hot cooked meal. She kept expecting to wake up and this would all be a dream, and she would still be locked up behind heavy stone walls.

She could tell by Morgan's initial reaction to her name that Morgan knew about her past, but since then, Morgan had been polite, kind, and welcoming. What was Morgan's game? Her polite hospitality reminded Rhea of how her mother used to host dinner parties when she was young, and how her mother always talked sweetly to the women who belonged to the Catholic Church although in private she condemned them for not being Baptist. Was Morgan simply being kind to the enemy? Whatever her game, Rhea was grateful for the warmth of the room, the refreshing drink in her hand, and a chance to be on her own.

Morgan filled the bowls, placed them on the island, and took her seat across from Rhea. The girl looked like she wanted to jump on the bowl of stew as if she hadn't eaten in days. A cold knot formed in Morgan's throat when she realized there was a chance that this was true. J.J. had said Rhea had been in prison for murder, but the woman sitting across from her didn't look like a killer. She tried to look tough, but Morgan guessed that was mostly distrust and fear. Rhea had a petite build and feminine features that softened her otherwise lean, toned physique that made her seem hard. Her dark hair had been cut close to the scalp in a buzz cut, but that didn't take away from the sloping line of her face and the glow of her piercing blue eyes. Morgan noted the almost perfect symmetry of her face, with a narrow straight nose and prominent cheekbones punctuated by a perfect dimple in each cheek. Rhea was beautiful.

Rhea finished her stew quickly and glanced toward Morgan's half-eaten portion. Morgan wiped her mouth with her napkin and picked up her coffee. "There's more on the stove if you want it, otherwise it'll be thrown out. I don't keep leftovers for more than two days."

Rhea looked down at her bowl and then to the pot across the room. She looked back up at Morgan and swallowed as if she was trying to figure something out. "Can I get you some more too?"

Morgan smiled. "Sure, just a little though."

Rhea filled Morgan's bowl and returned to her seat. This time she ate more slowly and Morgan was glad the ice had been broken. She didn't like Rhea's past, but she had agreed to take her in, and that meant she had to find a way to accept that there were some things she would never understand. So far Rhea hadn't turned out to be anything like what she'd expected, and Morgan had the feeling she shouldn't make any more assumptions without giving Rhea the chance to prove herself. Rhea had a hungry look in her eyes that said she shouldn't be underestimated. Morgan just hoped J.J. was right and she wouldn't end up regretting this.

Chapter Three

The cabin was small but had everything Rhea needed. She could tell Morgan had done some recent work on the place by the smell of new paint and sawdust that still lingered in the air. The bed was bigger than she was used to and the old-fashioned quilts were soft and heavy. Morgan showed her how to use the woodstove. She was warm, but the silence was too much and grated on her nerves like an itch in her brain. She lay awake listening through the silence. She hadn't made friends in prison and there was no one to miss, but at least she hadn't been alone there.

In the beginning, the night sounds had kept her awake, holding her in a tight fist of fear. Over time she had found a connection to the broken sobs, bargains made with God or the devil, the sounds of sex and violence, and plots and plans made under cover of night. She had stayed quiet and that had kept her alive. She knew drug dealers, mules, gang members, thieves, and murderers like her. Desperation was the one thing she found they all had in common. She rarely met anyone who hadn't made hard decisions in the face of what seemed like no choice or when the choice made was the lesser evil.

The women she'd met were hard because they had to be to survive. For most, prison was no different than living on the streets. They'd just traded one set of captors for another. But Rhea hadn't fit in there any more than she had on the outside. Her survival had hinged on her ability to figure out the game being played and the part she had to play in it. As a child she had learned to do her best to be perfect. She got good grades, did as she was told, even appeared popular with the other kids in her school. But none of it had been real. At least it hadn't felt real to her. Once in prison she quickly learned to be hard, to face a challenge head-on, and to never turn her back. Weakness wasn't a quality you could afford when everyone was seeking their own pound of your flesh.

This was the first time in her life that she didn't have to pretend. But without pretending, who was she? Rhea slid out of bed, pulled on her jeans and boots, and went outside. The snow had stopped late in the night. A thick layer covered the ground like icing on a cake and gave the air a luminescent glow. The first rays of sun glistened across the surface like diamonds scattered across the ground.

Rhea was restless without some direction or someone telling her where to go next. Routine was the one thing she could count on in prison and she felt lost and anxious without it. She needed to shake it off. She opened the door and closed it. Then opened the door and closed it again and thrilled at the freedom the small gesture represented. Would she ever get used to not having locks and bars dictating her every movement? She pulled on her coat and stepped outside. The crisp air stung her face and she took a deep breath, filling her lungs with fresh, clean air. Her boots crunched with each step through the fresh snow, which seemed oddly loud in the surrounding silence. She looked around at the open space before her and felt overwhelmed by the breadth of the world. The only boundary was the split-rail fence and the cobblestone wall that outlined the property. There was no chain link or razor wire, no one with guns preventing her from going where she pleased. She had the sudden urge to run, a surge of power so strong she was certain her heart would burst. So she ran.

The cold air burned through her lungs and her legs ached from the pounding of her boots on the frozen ground. Out of breath, she stopped at the top of a hill that overlooked the farm. She imagined what the fields would look like in summer when the wildflowers danced on the breeze. Rhea wiped her face and was surprised that her cheeks were moist with tears. The idea of crying now was absurd. She hadn't cried in years. She began to laugh and was convinced she was losing her mind. Her laughter died slowly, replaced again by the silence and crushing knowledge that she was alone.

She turned in a circle and took in the world around her, longing for something to connect to, something she could hold on to that would give her a place in the world. A flicker of movement to her right drew her attention to the small barn at the edge of the field closest to the main house. Morgan walked out with two large bottles under her arm, and a young calf trailed behind her. Morgan sat on a stump and began to bottle-feed the calf.

This small act of tenderness struck a chord and Rhea watched Morgan closely. There was something about Morgan that was different. She didn't carry the hard edge of pain that most showed in the depths of their eyes and the line of their lips. Morgan lived by different rules. Her eyes were soft and caring, her voice firm but guiding, her body strong but gentle.

The last thought shocked her. What was she doing thinking about Morgan's body? When had she even noticed something like that? Morgan was certainly unusual and there was no doubt she was the only person Rhea had to rely on right now, but since when did she care what someone looked like? Morgan was her boss and there was nothing else to it. Rhea sighed. It was time to go to work.

❖

Morgan looked up from the calf she was feeding to see Rhea walking toward her. Rhea smiled sheepishly and stuffed her hands in the pockets of her coat. She looked nervous. Morgan wasn't ready to start sharing her space or her animals with someone and she resented the intrusion. But she had to admit she was curious about the girl. Rhea carried herself with confidence as if daring the world to challenge her, but when her guard was down uncertainty and fear lingered in her eyes like a haunted soul. What kind of pain could put such a tortured look in the eyes of someone so young? She had no idea what prison was like or what things had happened in Rhea's life to send her there.

"Good morning, I didn't expect to see you so early. Is everything okay with the cabin?"

Rhea nodded. "The cabin's perfect, I just wanted to go for a walk. Do you need any help?"

"Thanks, but I'm pretty much done here."

Rhea shifted from foot to foot and Morgan wondered what she wasn't saying. Rhea looked like she could jump out of her skin at any moment, but Morgan waited her out. She gathered up the bottles and spread hay for the calf.

Rhea finally broke. "So what do you want me to do around here?"

Morgan took a deep breath and looked around before meeting Rhea's gaze. Her eyes looked questioning...uncertain...nervous.

Morgan shrugged. "What do you want to do?"

Rhea frowned and considered the question. "I don't know. You're the boss. You get to tell me what to do."

Morgan smiled. She guessed Rhea was used to people telling her what to do, and it would be easy to dump the chores she didn't like on her, but something told Morgan that wasn't the way to go.

"Well, I guess I could, but I'd still like to know what you want to do. This will work out better for both of us if you aren't miserable, and I know I prefer to do what I like. When I do what I like, I get more done. I figure you're no different."

Rhea shrugged. "The thing is, I don't really know what I like. What are my choices?"

Morgan grimaced. "That's a long list." Maybe if she played her cards right she wouldn't have to see much of Rhea and she could get on with her work. Maybe this could work out for both of them. "Why don't I just show you around and point out things as we go. There's the farmwork, some small-engine work, the farrier work, and the gallery. I'm sure you'll find something along the way."

Rhea pushed her hands deeper into her pockets. "So you just want me to tag along and then I get to choose?"

Morgan shrugged. "Yep, that's the plan." She paused to reconsider. "Of course whatever's left over, we'll have to split."

Rhea smiled. "I can do that." Morgan had surprised her again and some of her defenses fell. Morgan wasn't like most people she had encountered, and this was the first time someone hadn't tried to control her. Everyone always had a game they were running, some kind of manipulation to get something from you. But Morgan was different and Rhea couldn't find the hook. When she looked into Morgan's eyes she couldn't find the tell, some shift of the eye that would alert her to Morgan's game. Morgan's eyes were sincere and Rhea wasn't sure what that meant. Maybe all this open air was getting to her. No one was that good. But if Morgan was going to give her a chance, she was going to take it.

Rhea studied everything Morgan pointed out to her. She was eager to please and wanted to earn her place. She wasn't looking for a handout, and just because Morgan had been generous up until now, didn't mean she didn't have a price.

The farmwork was pretty routine and she could handle the chores, but it wasn't her favorite work and reminded her too much of home. *Home.* The word didn't fit, but she didn't know any other word to describe the place where she grew up. Home, family, trust, honor...those were all words that didn't belong in her world.

The small engine shop was where she was most comfortable, but it only took a quick look around the place to see Morgan didn't focus too much attention there. The small shop was no bigger than three horse stalls wide, and the place was a total wreck. Tools lay willy-nilly around the room as if forgotten wherever they were last used. Oil stains and dirt marred the floor and the place reeked of gasoline and oil. If she was going to work in here, things would have to change, and that meant a lot of cleaning.

Rhea ran her finger through a sticky glob of goo on the worktable and made a face.

"What?" Morgan asked.

"I take it this is one of those areas where you don't enjoy your work."

Morgan glanced around the room as if unaware of the chaos in front of her. Rhea was certain this wasn't normal for Morgan.

Everything else she'd seen around Morgan said she was a woman of routine and order, but not this room.

Rhea picked up an oil-stained rag and held it out to Morgan. "Looks like you're trying to burn the place down. I didn't peg you as a firebug."

She meant the statement as a joke, but the glimmer in Morgan's eyes dimmed and her smile faded.

"No, of course not, I would never—"

"Relax, Morgan. It was a joke."

Morgan didn't have to say anything. Her reaction was all Rhea needed to be reminded that she was the ex-con and that was exactly how Morgan saw her.

"You're right. I don't particularly like the mechanic stuff, but it pays the bills."

"Okay." Rhea pushed on. "I can help you out in here, but I'd like to clean things up a little."

Morgan shrugged. "It's all yours. You know what you're doing?"

Rhea squared her shoulders. She figured Morgan was going to flinch away every time she mentioned prison, but she learned a long time ago not to run from someone else's fear. Rhea had worked hard to earn her tech certificate in the vocational classes she was offered in prison and she was proud of her skills.

"Yeah. I know what I'm doing."

"All right then. We'll work on these later and see what you can do. We have one more stop to make."

Rhea followed Morgan to a building closer to the house that looked like an old general store. Antique metal signs were nailed to the front of the building advertising Phillips 66, Castrol Oil, and Coca Cola. Rhea stopped and ran her fingers along the rough iron gates that guarded the large wood doors. The metal had been worked into the pattern of wild ivy so delicate that it was as if it would come to life at any moment and wind its way around her hand.

Morgan slid a key into the lock and pulled the gates open. She held her breath as Rhea studied her work. It was like this every time someone saw her studio for the first time. It was like having her life, her emotions, the essence of her soul on display, and she waited with bated breath for judgment to be passed.

Rhea stepped inside and walked around the room. She brushed her fingers lightly against the metal statues and studied every detail of the curves and welds that made each piece unique. She turned to Morgan, her eyes bright and unguarded.

Morgan's heart stopped. Rhea looked so innocent, like a child discovering something new in her world. The stern crease in her brow was now smooth, giving Morgan a glimpse at her youth. The tension usually present in her body softened, and in that moment Morgan felt like time stopped. She held her breath and hoped Rhea understood her work was more than cold metal.

Rhea spread her hands out at her sides and gestured around the room. "You did all this?"

Morgan nodded, still speechless. She was awestruck at the glimpse of the tender side of Rhea and the person Rhea could have been if she had made different choices.

"These are incredible."

"I'm glad you like them." Morgan didn't want to move. She didn't want to do anything to lose this moment. She didn't know what it meant, but there was something special in the unguarded smile creasing the corners of Rhea's lips. Morgan felt as if she'd been given a gift. She was confused about why it mattered so much, but it just felt good.

"I'm a blacksmith. Most of my work is with metal."

"I've never seen anything like this. So if I take on more of the chores and the small-engine work, that'll give you more time to do this stuff, right?"

Morgan nodded.

"All right then." Rhea glanced out the door. "Before we get started, can we get my Jeep out?"

Morgan nodded again. "Sure. I'll get the chainsaw."

Rhea stepped outside and Morgan was relieved and disappointed that they were moving on to less personal business.

She would never get used to showing someone her work for the first time, but she was always grateful once she had. Rhea was no exception, but Rhea had made her feel like her work was special. Rhea had no expectations to blur her vision and impression of the art, and her expression had said everything Morgan needed to hear. A needling warning reminded her to keep her distance. Rhea might seem harmless, but Morgan already knew better. She'd learned the hard way that people didn't change, and once a line had been crossed it was easier to cross the second time. And she couldn't afford any more betrayal or disappointment in her life.

❖

Morgan wielded the chainsaw like it was a butter knife as she cut through the gnarled branches of the old pine with precision and what appeared to be little effort. Rhea grabbed the discarded limbs as soon as they broke free and moved them to a pile in the back of Morgan's truck. Once the road was clear, Morgan shut off the chainsaw and stowed it in the truck. Rhea watched her move around the Jeep, surveying the damage.

"Your Jeep's in remarkable condition for its age. It looks like it could have been driven off the lot yesterday."

Rhea shoved her hands in her pockets. "Well, it was kind of stored for me while I was away."

Morgan looked away. "Well, it's a nice one."

"Thanks," Rhea said, not missing the slight stiffening in Morgan's shoulders. "What do we do now?"

"I don't think it's stuck too bad. You're not on your side and all four wheels have contact. Let's try four-wheel drive first and see if she'll drive out."

Rhea hesitated. "Do you want to do it? I'm still getting the hang of driving."

Morgan stared at her as if considering something. "No, you go ahead. You can do it. All you have to do is take it slow."

Rhea climbed into the Jeep through the passenger door and

slid into the driver's seat. She put the key in the ignition and took a deep breath. Her hands were shaking, and she was certain she was about to make a complete fool out of herself. She pushed in the clutch, put her foot on the brake, and held her breath as she started the ignition. So far, so good. She adjusted the lever to put the Jeep in four-wheel drive and sighed when a symbol appeared on the dash showing the four-wheel drive was engaged.

"Nice and easy now," Morgan said, a few feet in front of the Jeep.

Rhea let out on the clutch a little too quickly and her heart jumped when the Jeep lurched forward and died.

"It's okay. Just take your time and feel the clutch engage," Morgan encouraged.

Rhea sighed and shook out her hands. This time she did as Morgan said and felt the slight pull when the clutch engaged, and she let off the brake and gave it a little gas. The Jeep shifted and started to move forward.

"Start to turn the wheel to the right," Morgan instructed.

Rhea was more riveted to Morgan's instructions than to the road ahead of her. Morgan's encouragement began to bolster her courage and she was almost excited. The Jeep climbed out of the ditch with little effort and a moment later she was on the road again. Rhea was elated. She'd done it.

"Great job," Morgan exclaimed and patted the side of the Jeep. "I knew you could do it."

Rhea rolled down the window. "Thanks for that. That was awesome."

Morgan flashed Rhea a full toothy smile. It was the first time Rhea had seen her smile since they'd met, and it was as if the sun had broken free of clouds. Rhea liked the smile and the idea that she had somehow been its cause.

"Doesn't look like there's any damage. Let's get her up to the house and take a look."

Rhea nodded. She waited for Morgan to get in her truck and followed her to the farm.

Morgan motioned for her to pull into an open area next to her as she stepped out of the truck, still smiling. "Come inside, it's time for lunch."

Morgan hadn't put it as a question, so Rhea followed her inside, careful to remove her boots at the door this time.

"I didn't ask how you slept last night. Was everything okay with the cabin?"

"Sure, everything was fine." Rhea would have thought anything was better than prison or her mother's barn.

"It still needs some work, but like I said last night, I wasn't expecting you till next week. The windows still need to be resealed, and a few glass panes need to be replaced, and I was going to check out that old General Electric refrigerator. It's been in there since the 1950s and I haven't had a chance to make sure it's working properly."

"No problem. I think I can do most of that myself. If I need some help I'll let you know." Rhea stood at the counter uncertain what she should do next. "What do you need me to do?"

Morgan nodded to a cabinet above Rhea's head. "You can get out the glasses and pour the tea. I'll have these sandwiches ready in a minute. I hope you don't mind tuna fish sandwiches."

Rhea's stomach rumbled. "No. That's great, thanks."

A couple minutes later, Morgan settled on a stool in front of Rhea and picked up her sandwich. "So, what do you think of the work so far? Thought of what you want to do?"

Rhea was grateful for the easygoing conversation. She knew Morgan had been less than happy she'd shown up at her door last night, and she didn't seem too thrilled to see her this morning either. But both times Morgan had warmed up to her after a while and had a way of making Rhea feel at ease.

"I'd like to do the small-engine work, if you don't mind. I can help out with feeding and cleaning up and I'm pretty handy with a hammer and nails. I noticed you needed some repairs as we walked through today. Of course anything else you want me to do is fine too."

Morgan smiled. "That sounds like a great place to start. I

probably won't be around much. I'm usually out on a farm call or working in the studio. I wander around the farm at all hours of the day and night, so don't think anything of it. I like to work when the mood hits me, so that pretty much means you set your own hours. I don't care when you work as long as the work gets done and the animals are well cared for."

Rhea nodded in understanding. Morgan was giving her room to prove or disprove herself and maybe even hinting at her need for space. "Not a problem."

"Good," Morgan said, taking a bite out of her sandwich. "Now eat up. I want to see what you can do with those lawn mowers before the day is out."

Rhea smiled and took a huge bite, filling her mouth until her cheeks bulged.

Morgan laughed. "I said eat your food, not inhale it."

Rhea took a drink of her tea and finished her food. So far she was having a great day. It was the first time she'd smiled in forever and Morgan was good company. Rhea drew in a deep breath, suddenly filled with a fierce desire to prove herself to Morgan. She could get used to a life like this, and she didn't want to do anything to mess that up.

❖

Rhea carried the last of the iron and steel in from the truck and stacked it in the room where Morgan showed her she did her welding. Morgan was in the studio putting together an order for a client and had left Rhea to work alone. Lost in her work, she was startled by the chug of a diesel engine that came to rest outside the studio. Rhea went to the door and watched Morgan walk to the entrance just as the truck door slammed shut. A bull of a man with a round bald head and caterpillar eyebrows stomped up to Morgan. His scowl left no doubt of his disposition. His left cheek bulged with the full plug of tobacco clenched between his cheek and teeth. He stopped at the door and spat at Morgan's feet.

"Hello, Jeff. What can I do for you today?"

Rhea stepped closer so she could see the man more clearly. The instant he moved into view, the hair on the back of her neck stood up. Whatever this guy wanted, he wasn't selling Girl Scout cookies.

"You got those gate latches ready for the Miller barn?"

Morgan nodded. "I do. Come on in and I'll get the bill."

Rhea slid behind a sculpture of a large grasshopper as Jeff walked through the studio. She wasn't sure why, but she didn't want him to know she was there. She had the urge to run out the door while he waited for Morgan, but the big man turned and spotted her before she could get away.

"Who the hell are you?"

Rhea clenched her teeth and glared at him.

"Jeff, what would your momma say if she saw you being rude like that?" Morgan said.

The big man cut his eyes back to Morgan and sneered. "I reckon she'd be damned disappointed I talk to the likes of you at all, Morgan, but this job left me no choice. Get those damned latches so I can get the hell outta here. I've no interest in you or your little skank."

Rhea growled and took a step toward the man.

"Rhea," Morgan called, "would you mind going into the back there and getting that crate off the bench? It'll be marked with a horseshoe."

Rhea took a deep breath and did what she was asked. She wasn't used to backing down from anyone, and she didn't like how this guy talked to Morgan, but the last thing she needed was to get fired or, even worse, get a parole violation.

"Yeah, sure, I'll do that."

Rhea didn't want to leave Morgan alone with this creep, but Morgan seemed unfazed. She scanned the room and located the box Morgan wanted and hurried back out. She expected the guy to get his stuff and go, but Morgan opened the crate and unpacked every item. She inspected each piece in front of the big man.

"Any problems, Jeff? I wouldn't want you to find issue with any of the pieces once you get back to the site."

Rhea gave up a silent cheer and congratulations to Morgan in her cunning. Obviously Morgan was used to dealing with him and had anticipated a problem.

"They're fine," he grumbled.

"Good. I'm glad you're pleased. Now if you'll sign this, stating everything is in order, we can settle up."

"You trying to accuse me of something?" The big man leaned across the counter in an obvious attempt to intimidate Morgan.

Morgan smiled. "Of course not. I know that sometimes things happen during transport, and I just want it to be clear I'm not responsible for damage once an item has been picked up. I'm sure you understand that, Jeff." Morgan handed him a pen.

Jeff snatched the pen from Morgan's hand and signed the paper. He grabbed the box and stormed out.

"What a jerk," Rhea said, relieved to hear the truck pull away outside.

Morgan sighed. "He isn't a very nice man, I agree."

"Why were you so nice to him when he talked to you that way?"

Morgan shrugged. "Why would I rise to his anger? I choose not to be a part of his hate."

Rhea glanced toward the door. "I wanted to clobber him."

"Violence isn't the answer," Morgan said and turned to face Rhea. "His hate and anger are consuming him and I have no interest in adding to his pain. It's my choice whether I let his anger become my problem."

Morgan walked out without another word. Rhea scrambled to figure out what had just happened. What did she mean *add to his pain*? Surely Morgan wasn't that soft. If so, she was certainly in for a world of grief. People would be lined up outside her door, waiting to take a piece of her. But not Rhea. She wasn't afraid of a fight and she was nobody's doormat.

CHAPTER FOUR

Morgan stopped her ATV along the fence line at the back of her property and peered through the morning mist. She watched Rhea run along the ridge in the distance, her stride determined and strong. She reminded Morgan of a young deer reveling in the birth of a new day. Sadness fell across her like the dark clouds of a stormy night when she imagined Rhea locked away in a prison, unable to see the sun, unable to run free across the fields.

She hadn't seen Rhea in three days. The incident with Jeff had upset Morgan more than she had realized, and since then she'd been avoiding Rhea. She'd been pushing Rhea away, punishing her for things that had nothing to do with that day in the studio. Morgan watched Rhea disappear over the ridge and regret crawled across her skin like hot metal dipped in water. She gave Rhea a little time before she followed the fence line to the cabin. To her surprise she found more than one place that had been recently mended. Rhea had been busy, and Morgan felt more than a little guilty for neglecting so many of the chores lately. She hadn't meant for Rhea to do *all* the work.

Rhea stepped out onto the porch when Morgan stopped the ATV in front of the cabin. Morgan caught her breath at the sight of Rhea in a pair of faded blue jeans worn threadbare, work boots, and an equally faded flannel shirt. Morgan allowed her gaze to trail up Rhea's body and lingered on the soft mounds of breasts perfectly framed beneath the thin fabric. Rhea had rolled the shirtsleeves up to her elbows, exposing the pale skin and firm muscles of her forearms. She looked thinner. Morgan chastised herself. She hadn't done a very good job helping Rhea settle into the farm. Had she even had food to eat? Morgan let out a long breath. She had taken a lot for granted with Rhea.

Morgan smiled and stepped off the ATV. "Looks like you've been busy—the fence looks good. I'd been meaning to get to that for weeks now. Thanks."

Rhea shifted uncomfortably on her feet and stuffed her hands in her pockets. "That's what you hired me for, isn't it?"

Morgan's smile widened at Rhea's sudden awkwardness. She caught the defensiveness in Rhea's tone. Her guard was up. Morgan couldn't blame her after how she'd behaved the past few days.

"You've finished all the repairs I had pending at the shop too. You know you don't have to work around the clock, right?" Morgan kept her tone light and playful and hoped she could melt some of the ice shimmering in Rhea's liquid blue eyes.

A faint smile lifted the corners of Rhea's mouth. Morgan shifted as her head grew light from a familiar but surprising stir in her belly. She would have to be blind not to notice how attractive Rhea was, and she wasn't blind. Morgan tried to focus on the reason for her visit and drew her eyes away from the curves of Rhea's body to Rhea's mouth. Those soft lips, that smile could be her undoing.

"I have to go into town for supplies today. Would you mind tagging along? I have some feed to pick up at the Co-op and some heavier pieces of steel, and I could use your help."

Rhea looked uncertain and Morgan thought she was going to say no. Morgan took a step onto the porch and pulled her wallet out of her back pocket. She handed Rhea three crisp one hundred dollar bills.

"Here's your pay for the week. You've worked hard and I figure you could use some supplies around here."

Rhea looked down at the money. "It's too much. I can't take that."

Morgan was confused. "Rhea, I've seen the work you've done

and the money you've brought in at the shop this week. Trust me, for what you've done so far, this is barely minimum wage."

Rhea frowned. "Really?" She reached for the bills, her fingers sweeping across Morgan's hand as light as a butterfly landing on a flower. Morgan's skin warmed, and her stomach fluttered at the faint touch.

Rhea pulled her hand away, and her brows furrowed as if she was trying to figure something out.

Morgan went on as if she hadn't felt the energy pass between them. "Yeah. And trust me, it won't go very far. You'll see. What do you say, you up for a little trip to town?"

Rhea smiled again and nodded.

"Good. I'm out of milk and almost everything else. I hope you're okay with a little grocery shopping while we're out."

Rhea's eyes brightened, and her nod was more earnest this time. "That'd be great."

Morgan kicked herself again for not realizing Rhea needed food and the basics. How had Rhea managed the last few days without their usual lunch and dinner? Rhea was living up to her end of the bargain, and it was time Morgan got on board and started giving Rhea a chance.

❖

Rhea leaned against the counter at Hoskins Drugstore and Soda Fountain. Her mouth watered as she waited for her first chocolate milkshake in fifteen years. It was the first time she could remember feeling happy.

The waitress set the large glass in front of her full to the rim with thick chocolate topped with a cloud of fluffy whipped cream and a plump cherry nestled on top. She placed a spoon and a straw on a napkin on the counter next to the glass.

Rhea licked her lips in anticipation of the sweet heaven in front of her. She chose the spoon first and scooped out a mouthful of the whipped cream. It melted on her tongue, coating her mouth with creamy richness. This was even better than she had expected. She scooped out a spoonful of the chocolate and closed her eyes as the full, rich flavor flooded her mouth with bliss. In that moment the world could have exploded around her, and she would have died a happy woman. This was by far the best moment of her life.

Halfway through the milkshake she switched to the straw and allowed the thick chocolate ice cream to melt a little more as she watched the cherry sink to the bottom of the glass.

She heard the bell ring above the door and a dark shadow blocked some of the sunlight streaming through the giant storefront windows. Rhea's shoulders stiffened and the tiny hairs at the back of her neck prickled as someone walked up and leaned over the stool beside her. Rhea shifted uncomfortably and chanced a glance at the newcomer. She clenched her jaw the instant she recognized the man. It was Jeff, the man who had been so rude to Morgan at the studio.

Jeff ordered a cup of coffee and turned to Rhea. "Hey, aren't you that girl I saw over at Morgan's place?"

Rhea nodded. She shifted her eyes just enough to keep him in sight without encouraging any small talk.

"Sorry about calling you a skank. That wasn't right. Morgan and me have some bad blood between us, and I lose it a little when she's around."

Rhea toyed with her straw. "Sure."

Jeff turned to face her with one arm against the counter and leaned toward her. "What's a pretty lady like you doing with the likes of Morgan Scott anyway?"

Rhea fished the cherry from the bottom of her glass with her spoon. It didn't take a rocket scientist to figure out this guy's game. She wasn't stupid and she wasn't in the mood to play.

"She's my boss."

"Your boss, huh?" Jeff ran his finger along the side of Rhea's arm.

Rhea flinched and jerked her arm away as a dull pain lanced through her as if he had drawn the tip of a knife across her bones.

The sensation traveled to her fingertips, and she reflexively closed her hand into a fist.

Jeff laughed. "Trust me, sweetheart, you need to watch yourself with Morgan or you'll be doing more for her than shoveling shit and mending fences, if you know what I mean."

Rhea blinked in irritation and tried to reel in the spark of anger that made her cheeks burn. "No, I'm afraid I don't. Why don't you enlighten me?"

Jeff smiled and blew across the top of his coffee cup, filling the air with the rancid smell of tobacco and black coffee.

Rhea's stomach soured, and she pushed the last of the milkshake aside.

"Morgan's the kind of woman who thinks she can have what belongs to a man." Jeff reached his hand toward Rhea as if to stroke her cheek.

Rhea threw up her arm and slapped his hand away. "What the hell do you think you're doing?"

Jeff laughed again. "I'm just being friendly, there's no need to get in a twist."

Rhea stood and moved away, putting the stool between them. She didn't want this creep to touch her again. She put her money on the counter and told the waitress to keep the change.

"Come on, honey, don't run off so soon. I thought we could get to know each other a little better. What's your name? What was it Morgan called you? Ray, wasn't it? That's a man's name."

Rhea moved to go, and Jeff grabbed her arm, preventing her from leaving. Rhea met the big man's gaze for the first time, and panic hit her the instant she saw the lustful look in his eyes. She'd seen that look before. She'd been prey to that hunger almost every night when her father came to her room. The sour smell of him and the burning whiskey on his breath were sometimes bad enough to make her vomit.

Rhea grabbed Jeff by the balls and gave his nuts a twist. "Don't touch me, you fat fuck!"

Jeff yelled, "Let me go, you stupid bitch."

The waitress gasped and moved away.

"What's wrong, Jeff? I thought you wanted to get to know each other a little better. You touched me first. I guess that makes this consensual."

Jeff's face was death-white now. "Let go," he groaned.

"The only thing you need to know about me is that if you put your hands on me again, you'll lose them."

The bell above the door rang again, and Rhea let Jeff go but didn't take her eyes off him.

"Hey, Rhea, you about ready to go?"

Rhea didn't back down but at last let her eyes follow the sound of the familiar voice. Rhea had never been so happy to see anyone in her life as Morgan strolled up beside her as if she didn't have a care in the world. Her body was relaxed and she moved with confidence, her shoulders back, her head held high, and a little swagger in her step. She winked at Rhea as she sidled up next to her as if sending Rhea a message.

"Hello, Jeff. I see you're still having trouble making friends."

The big man glared, and Rhea imagined she could hear the grinding of his teeth as his jaw clenched.

"Shut up, Morgan. I don't think anyone invited you to the party."

Morgan shrugged. "Too bad, I'm sure the conversation was riveting. I'm sorry to break things up, but Rhea and I have some things to do. It's good to see you again, Jeff."

Morgan held out her hand and gestured for Rhea to walk ahead of her.

Rhea sighed and stepped away, never taking her eyes off Jeff as she passed.

"You know, one of these days you're going to stick your nose where it doesn't belong and someone's going to put you in your place for good," Jeff growled.

Morgan smiled. "Have a nice day, Jeff."

Rhea walked beside Morgan in silence. She didn't understand how Morgan could be so nice to that jerk.

They were half a block away before Morgan broke the silence. "You okay?"

Rhea shrugged. "Sure. I can handle assholes like him."

Morgan frowned. "I'm sure you can, but that doesn't mean their words and actions don't hurt."

Rhea glanced over at Morgan. She still didn't show any tension in her body, and there was only the slightest dip in the tone of her voice to betray her emotions.

"You're one to talk."

Morgan smiled this time. "Just because I choose not to let him see the wounds doesn't mean they aren't there. But if I play into his anger, things only get worse for both of us."

Rhea shook her head. Her own anger still simmered just beneath the surface and she wanted nothing more than to shut that prick's mouth for him. "Someone needs to knock that plug of tobacco down his throat and let him choke on it."

Morgan stopped and looked at Rhea. Her frown was so deep with disappointment that Rhea flinched.

"How does that help anyone? Beyond that, how many people does it hurt? You can't go around forcing people to do or be something just because you don't like them," Morgan said.

Rhea wasn't sure what did it, maybe it was putting up with Jeff and his degrading attitude, maybe it was the disappointment in Morgan's eyes, but something had struck a nerve, and she was beyond angry now. "Yeah, well, I'm not going to let anyone treat me like their property. Sometimes if you don't fight back, everyone loses, Morgan."

Rhea turned and stormed away. She needed to cool off before she said something that would really get her fired. She wasn't even sure who she was angry with the most, Morgan for her passive, fantasy view of the world, Jeff for his chauvinistic, degrading attitude, or her father for ruining her life.

Maybe Morgan was right. Maybe she wasn't any better than the men who had hurt her. Maybe all she knew was pain. How was she ever going to make it in the world if she couldn't be more than a victim? Rhea ducked down an alley and threw up behind a Dumpster. Everything was spinning out of control. She was only safe when she was alone in her cabin, and she longed for the silent solitude of the farm. She couldn't afford to mess things up with Morgan. She didn't think she had the strength to start over, and she couldn't go back to her mother. She had to get it together and make things right.

❖

Morgan wasn't sure this thing with Rhea was going to work out. She wanted to believe that Rhea could make a change, but her sudden outburst of anger was scary. Morgan needed to talk to J.J. Maybe they needed to reconsider some things and work something else out for Rhea. There were times when Rhea's guard was down, and Morgan forgot about Rhea's past, but most of the time she was wound so tight, Morgan thought she might snap. What was she doing taking in an ex-con anyway? She shook her head. That wasn't fair. Rhea wasn't just an ex-con. Rhea was strong, independent, hardworking, smart, and beautiful. She'd been through a lot, and she wasn't going to have a chance in the world if no one saw beyond her past to all the good she had to offer, and that included Morgan.

Morgan turned the corner to find Rhea leaning against the side of her truck. Her arms were folded across her chest, but there was no sign of the anger that burned so fierce earlier. Morgan keyed the locks and got in the truck. Rhea opened the door and climbed in beside her.

"I'm sorry about what I said back there. I shouldn't have taken everything out on you like that."

Morgan wrapped her left arm over the steering wheel and leaned forward to see Rhea better. "I'm sorry too. I didn't mean to discount your feelings like that. Jeff can be a lot to handle. I'm sorry I upset you."

"Yeah. Thanks." Rhea picked at a loose thread in a hole in her jeans. She wasn't used to anyone apologizing to her, and Morgan's sincerity caught her off guard. She took a chance and asked the question that could change her life. "You going to make me leave?"

Morgan sighed. "Honestly, I thought about it. But I don't think we're there yet. So if you still want to stay, the job's still yours."

Rhea let out a long heavy breath. "That's good then."

Morgan knew she'd overreacted earlier. What was it about Rhea that had her so jumpy? She could take all kinds of crap from people like Jeff, but the minute Rhea stepped on her toes, she'd been ready to pull the plug on the deal. Maybe she needed to heed her own words. Who was she helping and who would she hurt by continuing to hold Rhea's past against her…or was it her own past that kept getting in the way? She had no business trying to help anyone turn their life around. She'd tried that with Ashley, and it had cost her everything. She couldn't allow that to happen again.

Morgan sat back and started the truck.

Rhea's next words were soft, almost timid. "He said you two have some bad blood between you. What did he mean?"

Morgan clenched the steering wheel with both hands. There it was. She didn't like to think about Ashley and she never talked about her.

"That was a long time ago. We were little more than kids."

Rhea nodded. "Yeah, I get that, but that doesn't mean we aren't still paying for the things we did back then."

Morgan cringed. She guessed Rhea knew better than anyone that there were some things that you never stopped paying for. "It isn't as dramatic as it sounds. He doesn't like who I am. That's how it's always been, and I don't see that ever changing."

Rhea bit her lip. "It's hard sometimes to tell the difference between love and hate," she said quietly before she turned to stare out the window, as if seeing images from the past. "You don't have to hate someone to hurt them and sometimes you love the person you hate the most."

"Is that what happened to you?" Morgan wanted to understand Rhea. She had a gut feeling that Rhea had the heart of a bull and wouldn't back down from a fight. Morgan was all about heart, but the fighting she could do without.

Rhea pulled her gaze away from the flickering images outside her window and met Morgan's eyes. "Yes."

Morgan swallowed. "What did you do?"

Rhea pressed her lips together and turned away. It was a long time before she answered. "You're right. There are some things I can't change. I can't force someone to be what I want them to be. But I did what I had to do."

Morgan's hands tightened on the steering wheel. "Do you regret it?"

Rhea considered her answer. This was one of those conversations that had the power to change a person. To Morgan's credit, this was the first time she had asked her about prison or what she'd done to get there. Most people would have asked on the first day. Maybe Morgan thought she already knew enough and had made her judgment already.

"I spent almost fifteen years trying to answer that question. No matter how I play things over in my head, the end is the same. So no, I don't regret it."

"Do you think what you did was right?"

Rhea laughed. "Sometimes there is no right, only a list of wrongs. Like I said, I did what I had to do."

Morgan didn't say anything, but the tight set of her shoulders reminded Rhea of the tension that she learned to read in the gang members just before someone got jumped. It was time to duck and cover. She didn't think Morgan was a physical threat, but something was brewing, and Rhea wanted to be ready.

"So Jeff knows something about you that he doesn't like, and he judges you by it, right?"

Morgan nodded.

"Kind of like you knowing something about me and judging me by that."

Morgan shook her head. "It's not the same thing, and I'm not judging you."

Rhea laughed. "Keep telling yourself that, but I don't think it's possible not to judge by the information you're given. Your problem is not having the right information. You don't know me, Morgan." Rhea leaned back against her seat and closed her eyes. Morgan was her boss, her ticket to starting over, and she didn't need to add to her problems by pissing off the one person who had given her a shot.

Rhea pictured the courtroom, her mother, neighbors she'd known her whole life, people she'd gone to church with every Sunday, even a few of the staff from her school. Everyone looked at her with hatred and disgust. No matter how many times she'd explained herself, told them what her father had done, no one believed her. No one cared about the truth. They believed what they wanted to believe based on what they'd been allowed to see. It didn't matter how many times she told the truth, no one believed her. Why would Morgan be any different?

❖

Morgan pushed her cart through the aisles and mentally ran down her list. Why didn't she write these things down? Grocery shopping wasn't exactly her favorite thing to do, and the last thing she wanted was to have to come back any sooner than necessary. She passed Rhea staring at the ice cream like a child at the candy counter. She looked into Rhea's basket and was surprised by how little was there.

"What's wrong?"

Rhea blew out an exasperated breath. "I don't know what to get. I can't believe how expensive everything is and I'm not sure I remember how to cook. I mean, I can make a sandwich and open a can of beans, but beyond that I'm a little lost."

Morgan laughed. In that moment she forgot all about Rhea's past and her own doubts and fears. In that moment she wasn't looking at a convicted felon or a murderer. Rhea was just a woman. She was lost and needed help and despite the frown furrowing her brow and the glint of fear and frustration marring her face, she was incredibly beautiful. Morgan's heart skipped, a sensation she tried to ignore.

Rhea laughed uncomfortably and the soft reverberation made Morgan's heart skip again, and this time the sensation was enough to take her breath. "Well, I don't think it's necessary to buy the whole store at once, but I think you'll need a little more than ice cream for dinner."

Rhea's shoulders eased, and she smiled up at Morgan.

"Want some help?" Morgan asked.

"Please."

Morgan had an overwhelming sense of relief, as if she'd been offered a lifesaving gift. Despite her rough start and no resources, Rhea had never once asked for help. Having her ask now was like turning a light on in the dark.

"What do you like?"

Rhea looked lost. "I don't know anymore."

Morgan's chest tightened. What kind of life could leave someone not even knowing what they liked to eat? "Okay. Let's start with something easy. How about spaghetti?"

Rhea's eyes brightened, and Morgan's heart broke at the innocence that was suddenly so apparent in Rhea's eyes. How had she not seen this before? Rhea had the body and mind of a woman who had seen the cruelty of the world, but she still had the heart of a child. What had it cost Rhea to hide the purest part of herself?

"What else do you miss?"

Rhea looked stunned. She licked her lips as if tasting something that lingered at the edge of her tongue.

"French fries. And maybe some chili with cheese melted on top."

Morgan smiled. It was worse than she thought. Rhea must have been a fast-food junkie as a teenager. "I think I have an idea to get you started, and we can build you up to some *real* food."

Fifteen minutes later, Rhea's cart showed improvement, and Morgan was at least satisfied she wouldn't starve to death in the next week or two.

Morgan pushed her cart to the checkout counter, and Rhea took her place in line behind her.

"Hello, Reverend Scott, it's so nice to see you," the woman

behind the register exclaimed as Morgan began to unload her items onto the conveyor belt.

"Hello, Mrs. Picket. It's good to see you too, but you know I'm not a reverend anymore."

"Oh, codswallop. I don't care what those stuffies in the church said, you're still the reverend to me. We don't see you around nearly enough. I've missed you. Things just aren't the same since you left."

Morgan's face slowly moved from a rosy shade of pink to a faint purple, and Rhea wondered if she was about to have a stroke. What was this woman talking about? She had definitely called Morgan *reverend* and Rhea's curiosity was piqued. Was Morgan some kind of priest? She thought back on how she had handled Jeff earlier. Was that priest-like? Rhea was confused about what little she knew about Morgan. Well it certainly explained her rose-colored view of the world. Rhea listened with intense interest as Morgan tried to skirt the woman's inquiries and more than colorful opinions of the church.

Outside Rhea helped Morgan load their groceries into a bin she kept in the back of the truck.

"Why did that woman call you *reverend*? Are you some kind of priest?"

Morgan didn't look at her, but Rhea saw her stiffen. What didn't Morgan want her to know?

"I used to be."

"How does that happen? How do you stop being a priest? Did you lose your faith or something?"

"No," Morgan snapped. She wiped her face with her hands and drew in a deep breath. "I was stripped of my duties with the church. That doesn't mean I lost my faith in God."

Morgan's sharp tone stung, and Rhea was surprised to find that, for whatever reason, she cared about what Morgan felt. She was well aware of the cruelty people could inflict on each other when they used God as a weapon. Her parents had been very good at it.

"I'm sorry. I didn't mean to hurt you. I'm just trying to understand. I don't believe in God, so I guess I wasn't thinking about how that would sound to you."

Morgan was silent for a long time, and Rhea was beginning to wonder if she was ever going to speak to her again. "Why'd they do it? Why'd they say you couldn't be a priest anymore?"

Morgan sighed. "I was involved with another woman, and I had performed several same-sex unions without the permission of the church."

Rhea caught her breath. "Wasn't that part of your job?"

"Usually, yes, but the church was opposed to same-sex marriage."

Rhea had an unsettling feeling of disappointment. "Where's your girlfriend then?"

A muscle jumped in Morgan's jaw. Rhea could tell Morgan was upset and considered letting the issue go. Whatever the story, this wound still hurt.

"I don't have one."

"But—"

"It's getting late, and I'd like to get back to get the feeding done before it gets much later. Is there anything else you need while we're out?"

Morgan's clipped tone and abrupt dismissal effectively stopped Rhea's questions. There was definitely a story there, and part of her wanted to push. After all, Morgan had asked about her past, and now that the tables were turned she didn't like it. But despite her curiosity, regret stirred in Rhea's belly. This was the first time she'd seen Morgan unsettled, hurt even, and she didn't like it. Maybe Morgan understood more about betrayal than she thought. The idea churned in Rhea's stomach, and she decided to go easy. She considered what she'd learned about Morgan since they'd met, and realized Morgan didn't leave the farm much except for business. She spent all her time working in her studio or on the farm. Maybe she wasn't the only one trying to lose herself in the safety and comfort of solitude.

CHAPTER FIVE

The next day Morgan followed the trail from the back of her house through the woods to the spring-fed stream that provided water to her farm. It was where she went when the world got too close. It was the place where she allowed nature to ground her and remind her that there was still some good left in the world. Her heart was heavy after running into Mrs. Picket at the store. She wasn't sure why she hadn't wanted to explain things to Rhea. It wasn't like it was a secret, but she hadn't wanted to explain what had happened to Ashley. That was a wound she was afraid would never heal.

She climbed up onto a large granite rock that overlooked the crest of a waterfall. The stone was cold despite the warm sunshine, and the cold bite grounded her to the moment. Morgan took a deep breath and lifted her face to the sun. She closed her eyes, focusing on the feel of warm sun on her skin, the soft breeze that rustled the loose strands of her hair, and the sound of the water churning through the granite and earth like a herd of blundering boar. Morgan smiled at the thought and realized for the first time how appropriate it was to describe a stream as a babbling brook. Who knew water had so much to say?

When the tension began to ease in her shoulders, she let out a long breath and began to pray. She believed that her conversation with God never ended, but it was in this place, when she put aside all the chores, all the worry, and the demands of life, that she felt the most comforted.

A branch snapped close by and Morgan opened her eyes, her

halted words left lingering on the air. She looked around, expecting to find a curious squirrel or a mink.

"Sorry," Rhea called from an adjoining trail. "I didn't know you were here. I didn't mean to scare you."

Morgan was surprised to see Rhea. She still wasn't used to having someone around all the time. But despite her earlier trepidation and irritation, she warmed at the sight of Rhea. "It's okay. There's room for both of us."

Rhea joined Morgan on the rock. "I heard your voice. Were you praying?"

Morgan nodded.

"Why?"

Morgan was confused by the question. "What do you mean?"

"Well, people usually pray when they want something or want to change something bad that's happening to them. I was curious which it was with you," Rhea said.

"It isn't like that at all. Of course I pray about things that are happening in my life, but I mostly pray for guidance, understanding, or forgiveness. For me, prayer is like having a conversation with an old friend."

Rhea fidgeted with a stick she found on the ground. "Does it ever do any good?"

"I don't know what you mean."

"I used to pray when I was a kid. As far as I can tell, no one was listening."

"Hmm." Morgan thought about what Rhea said. "I think sometimes we expect things to happen the way we want them to, and when that doesn't happen, disappointment gets in the way of our seeing the answer when it comes."

Rhea frowned. "Next you'll try to tell me that everything happens for a reason. I don't buy that. I can't see how there could be any benefit in children starving, earthquakes that swallow cities, families, homes. What is the purpose behind war and cancer?"

Morgan turned to Rhea. "These are terrible things that exist in our world. Many of them we have the power to change, some we don't. I don't think there is some divine purpose behind suffering.

I think that God suffers when we suffer. I think God is there as a comfort. It comforts me to know that no matter how hard things get, I am never alone."

"Like a friend?"

"See, you get it."

"So why do you think God let you get kicked out of the church?"

Morgan closed her eyes and took a deep breath. "I wasn't kicked out of church. I'm just not a priest anymore. People have free will and the ability to make their minds up for themselves. We are a bit like children having to learn things the hard way. Sometimes we make mistakes, sometimes we learn from them, and sometimes those mistakes hurt other people."

Rhea tossed the stick aside. "So you're saying we just blame God for the bad things that happen."

"Sometimes, yeah, we do."

Rhea thought about that for a while. "I'm sorry I upset you earlier. I can tell this is something that bothers you."

Morgan slid her arm through Rhea's and squeezed. "I shouldn't have snapped at you. I guess I'm still learning to deal with my own mistakes."

Rhea was surprised by Morgan's touch. She wasn't used to anyone showing any kind of affection toward her. Her skin warmed, and she was pleased that Morgan was comfortable enough with her to be close. She wanted to make things right with Morgan. "I have a way of pushing people's buttons sometimes. I'm sorry. And thank you for helping me with my groceries." Rhea sighed. "There's so much I have to learn. I never imagined things would be this hard."

Morgan leaned her head against Rhea's. "We never do." She pulled Rhea closer against her and watched the ever-changing water. "I'd like to help you. At the very least I'm a good listener. Everyone needs someone."

"You don't."

Morgan laughed. "Of course I do, even if I'm too stubborn most of the time to admit it. Look how much I need you."

Rhea jerked and looked at her with surprise. "You need me?"

Morgan smiled. "Since you've been here, I've seen just how

much help I did need. I was too afraid to let anyone close to admit that I was overwhelmed with all the work to do here."

Rhea frowned. "Oh."

"Having you around has made me realize how lost I'd become. Losing the church was only part of it. But since you've been here, I've had to look at a lot of things differently. It's very brave of you to start over here the way you have. In some ways you're showing me how to start over too."

Rhea didn't think of herself as brave, but hearing Morgan describe her that way made her feel proud. She laced her fingers over Morgan's hand wrapped around her arm. "Thank you for that."

Neither of them spoke for a long time. Rhea sat still, noticing each point where her body made contact with Morgan's. There was none of the usual fear and pain that plagued her when she was too close to someone. Morgan made her feel safe. Morgan's hand was warm wrapped around her biceps, and Rhea could feel Morgan's breast pressed against the back of her arm. Rhea's stomach fluttered as if a rabble of butterflies were swarming in her belly. The sensation was exciting and she tightened her hand on Morgan's wishing the feeling would never end.

Too soon, Morgan shifted and moved away. "I guess I better get back if I'm going to get any work done today."

"Oh, okay." Rhea was disappointed. She'd liked being here with Morgan and she wasn't ready for reality to wipe it all away.

"Would you like to have dinner with me tonight?" Morgan asked as she dusted herself off. "I can show you some simple things you can cook at home. Maybe you can try something new."

Rhea was excited to get a chance to talk with Morgan more. "Sure. That sounds great."

Morgan smiled. "Great."

Rhea felt Morgan's smile touch her somewhere deep inside. Her heart lightened and her own smile grew.

Morgan reached for her hand and pulled her to her feet. "Let's get going then, the chores are waiting." Morgan slid her arm around Rhea's shoulder. "Last one done does the dishes," Morgan teased.

Rhea laughed. "Deal."

❖

Rhea stood on Morgan's porch, staring at the door. It wasn't like she hadn't eaten with Morgan before, but tonight felt different. She had finished her work and chores and took the time to go back to the cabin and clean up and change her clothes. She had cleaned up her boots and put on her best old shirt. She bit her lip and knocked. A couple of minutes passed before Morgan opened the door. She smiled at Rhea.

"Hey, come on in. I was just getting started on dinner."

Morgan wore a fresh pair of new blue jeans, a crisp white button-up shirt, and a pair of black boots. A thick black belt circled her waist, adorned with a dark metal buckle in the shape of a Celtic knot. Rhea felt the odd fluttering in her stomach when she looked at Morgan and her face grew hot. She was glad Morgan hadn't seemed to notice her blush.

Morgan placed a bundle of spinach on the table, with a heap of mushrooms, peppers, and an onion. Next to that she had a large sirloin on a cutting board.

"You're just in time. You can cut the onion."

Rhea laughed. "What happened to letting me choose what chores I want to do?"

Morgan smiled. "Sorry, you're out of luck this time. But to be fair, if you cut the onion, I'll help with the dishes."

Rhea grinned. "What makes you think I lost our bet? I finished my chores early."

Morgan looked thoughtful for a moment. "That's the thing about being your own boss. I left work early today."

"That's not fair."

Morgan shrugged. "What can I say? I cheated."

Rhea laughed. "I'm going to remember that."

Morgan slid a cutting board over to Rhea and started slicing the meat.

"What are we cooking?"

Morgan smiled. "Fajitas."

Rhea's mouth watered. This was going to be a real treat.

Morgan placed a large pan on the stove. Moments later the room was filled with the smell of cooking meat and spices.

"Here, you finish this while I warm the tortillas." Morgan placed tortillas on a flat pan and heated them on the stove.

Rhea was swept up in the cooking and was enjoying the time with Morgan. They worked seamlessly together as they moved about the room. This was fun.

"This smells so good. I can hardly wait to taste it," Rhea said as she filled a large bowl with the steak and vegetables.

Morgan smiled as she set the table. It was nice to have Rhea there. "I'm glad you're here. I love to cook, but I hate to cook for myself. It seems like such a waste of time. When I do cook, I usually make enough to do for a couple of days so I don't have to bother for a while."

"Well, you can use me to get in your fix anytime you want."

They sat down to dinner and Morgan was pleased by how easy it was to be with Rhea. It was the first time they had spent any amount of time together without some kind of issue creating tension between them. "You didn't seem to know what foods you wanted to try, so I took a risk with the fajitas. I hope you like it."

"Oh, I can already tell I'm going to love it. Prison food wasn't something I enjoyed. Most things didn't have much flavor at all. I can say that food has been one of the things I've enjoyed most about being out."

Morgan refused to flinch away from the topic of prison. She wanted to know more about Rhea. "What did you miss?"

Rhea watched Morgan fill a tortilla with meat and vegetables and dress it with sour cream and lettuce and cheese. She filled her own tortilla as she thought about her answer.

"I missed being outside. It was like never getting a full breath of air. But what I thought about most of the time was my little sister."

"I didn't know you had a sister."

Rhea smiled. "Molly. She was eleven when everything happened. That was the last time I saw her."

Morgan stopped chewing and starred at Rhea. "That's rough. I can't imagine not being able to see J.J."

Rhea nodded. "You know, it's kinda weird that your sister is my parole officer. She's been really great with me. I don't know what I would have done if she hadn't arranged for me to be here."

"Where were you staying before?"

"My mother's farm in Rhea County. I wasn't exactly welcome there."

Morgan frowned. She didn't know the circumstances behind why Rhea went to prison and wasn't sure how much she should pry. "Do you miss home?"

"No," Rhea answered abruptly, "I hated being there. That isn't my home anymore. I don't think it ever really was. This place feels more like home to me than any place ever has."

Morgan smiled. "I'm glad you like it here. I like to think that this is your home too." Morgan was surprised by how true those words were. She was surprised by how much Rhea had become a part of her farm, her life.

"Thank you. Thank you for giving me a chance."

Morgan covered Rhea's hand with her own. Rhea's hand was cold. She wrapped both of her hands around Rhea's. "Are you cold? Your hand is like ice."

Rhea shook her head but didn't speak. She looked at Morgan with a curious expression.

"What?" Morgan asked.

Rhea's mouth went dry. She stared at her hand clasped in Morgan's tender grip. The sensation was unusual. It went beyond her usual discomfort to something sweet, something that went deeper than her skin. The tension in her muscles eased and Rhea allowed the warmth of Morgan's touch to warm the cold, hardened places in her heart.

"Let me go put another log on the fire," Morgan said, letting go of Rhea's hand.

"I'm really okay. My hands are almost always cold."

"Well, I'll stoke the fire anyway. Then I think you have some dishes to do."

Rhea grinned. "I thought you were going to help with that."

"Hmm, I might."

Rhea gathered the dishes while Morgan worked the fire. She washed the glasses first and handed them to Morgan to rinse and dry. Morgan stood so close Rhea could feel the brush of Morgan's arm against hers as they worked. Each dish she handed Morgan was like a stepping stone leading her closer to Morgan. She was beginning to care about Morgan, and she wasn't sure how she felt about that. All she knew in that moment was that the connection felt good.

Morgan put away the last of the dishes and folded the dish towel across the sink. "Want to go for a walk?"

Rhea shrugged. "Sure."

The temperature had dropped with the setting of the sun, and Rhea shivered when the cool night air hit the exposed skin of her face and neck. She pulled the collar of her coat up and pulled her knit cap over her head.

"Are you warm enough?" Morgan asked.

"I'm okay," Rhea answered, stuffing her hands into her pockets.

Morgan stopped at the edge of the stone wall that trailed around the property. She hopped up on the wall and looked up at the wide open sky littered with stars.

"Have you ever noticed that the sky is darkest and the stars the brightest on the coldest nights of winter?"

Rhea shook her head. "No. But I can see it now."

Morgan smiled. "What do you see when you look up there?"

Rhea shrugged. "I don't know. What do you see?"

"Sometimes I think of the stars as memories or what remains of people who have already moved on. Mostly they make me think of possibilities. There are so many things out there we know nothing about, things we can only dream of. If the stars can exist, heaven can exist, and there is no end to what we can do and become."

Rhea considered this. "I guess I've never really thought about it before. But I like that idea." Rhea studied the stars and tried to see things through Morgan's eyes. She liked the way Morgan put hope and goodness into everything. She had a way of making Rhea dare to dream. A northern wind blew across the field and Rhea shivered.

Morgan slid her arm around Rhea's shoulder and rubbed her hand up and down Rhea's arm. "Come here," she said as she pulled Rhea against her. "You're cold. Do you want to go inside?"

Rhea held still against Morgan, relishing the feel of Morgan's arm around her and the magic in the stars above her. "Maybe in a minute. It's hard to go inside when it's so beautiful."

"I know what you mean."

Morgan put her other arm around Rhea, encircling her with her warmth. It had been a good day. She realized she could enjoy someone again. Maybe some of her wounds were healing after all. She watched Rhea gaze up at the stars. She looked young and innocent in the faint glow of the moon and stars. Her cheeks were red and her pale skin took on an ethereal glow against the night. Morgan felt something stir inside and she was drawn to Rhea. Morgan brushed the feeling aside and pulled away. "I think I better call it a night. Morning will come early." She took Rhea's hand and pulled her to her feet. "Come on, I'll walk you home."

CHAPTER SIX

Rhea jerked awake at the sudden pounding on her door. She couldn't move. She choked in a breath and struggled for another as if a large, rough hand held her by the throat and choked her until the life threatened to leave her. She blinked her eyes and tried to focus on the clock beside the bed, anything not to see the hungry lust in his eyes as the weight of him bore down on her. There was no use fighting anymore. He was too big, too strong, and no one would help her if she screamed.

The pounding came again, and Rhea's vision cleared. She was alone in the room, but fear still gripped her muscles, and she struggled to shake off the helplessness. Someone was at her door, and she had to get up. She had to move. At last the bondage of sleep released her and she sprang from the bed like an animal from a cage. She moved so fast her back slammed against the wall behind her. She grabbed her jeans and her boots. She didn't have to look for her money because she never took it out of her pockets, and the new knife was clipped to her boot. It made it easier to have everything ready just in case she needed to get away fast. She pulled on a flannel shirt over her T-shirt as she raced down the hallway to the door.

"Who's there?" Her heart was pounding, and she was breathing as if she had been running for miles. She braced herself next to the door and tried to regain control of the fear coursing through her blood like a wildfire.

"It's Morgan, I need your help."

Rhea twisted the deadbolt and jerked the door open. Morgan was soaked from her waist down and caked in mud. A thin line of blood oozed from her nose and had been smeared across her right cheek. Rhea's fear intensified, and her gut twisted when she thought of Morgan hurt. Before she could think about what she was doing, she stepped close to Morgan and gripped her arms. "What's happened? What's wrong?"

"One of the Galloway calves is stuck in the mud down at the pond. I can't get him out, and if we don't do something soon, he'll drown."

Relief flooded Rhea as she realized Morgan wasn't in danger. "Okay, what do you need me to do?"

Morgan grabbed Rhea's hand and pulled her toward the ATV that sat idling in the yard. "Come on, I need you to help me rig a sling around him and pull him out with the Gator. I'll hold on to him and make sure he's not too bound up. We don't want to break his legs or worse. I tried to dig him out myself, but he just kept sinking."

Morgan's voice was frantic. Rhea had never seen anything shake her usual calm reserve, but Morgan was different with the animals. Morgan treated each one as tenderly as if they were her children, and Rhea was stunned by the desperation she heard in Morgan's voice. Rhea didn't want to think of what it would do to Morgan to lose the calf like this, but she was afraid of just how far Morgan would go to save him.

As soon as they reached the pond, Morgan grabbed a rope out of the ATV and handed it to Rhea. "Come on, we'll tie him first, then you can secure it to the Gator."

Rhea followed Morgan into the soupy cold water. The mud was thick and the suction threatened to pull her boots off with each step she took. Morgan went to the calf and held his head up. He was clearly exhausted and his wide brown eyes were wild with fear. Morgan pushed up on his chin and rested his head on her shoulder as she tried to pull the mud away from his knees and free his legs.

Rhea could barely force her arms under the calf to pull the rope around his body to make a sling without her head going into the water. Morgan was submerged to her chest now, and Rhea was afraid if the calf broke free he could drown her with his thrashing. This was no small calf—this was a half-grown steer.

"Let him go, Morgan, I'm going to pull him out."

"No, I have to manage his legs. I'll watch him. I'll be okay."

Rhea started the ATV and slowly moved forward until there was tension on the rope. "Okay, here we go." Rhea inched forward, her head turned so she could see the effect on the calf and Morgan.

"Hold it," Morgan yelled.

Rhea let off the throttle and waited. Morgan disappeared. Rhea was about to run back to the water when Morgan's voice rang out.

"Try again."

The battle to free the calf only took a few minutes but felt like an eternity. They worked as fast as they could and slowly separated mud from calf. The constant flood of adrenaline was all that kept Rhea going, and the fatigue was beginning to show as Morgan's hands shook, and her voice trembled from the cold. Rhea wasn't sure how much longer Morgan could keep up this fight.

"Here he comes," Morgan yelled.

Rhea kept pulling the calf and watched with wonder as his front legs suddenly sprang from the water and slapped down again as he used what little strength he had left to free himself. Rhea was still pulling and half dragging the calf through the mud. An instant later he was free and stumbled onto the grassy bank. Rhea killed the engine and sprinted to the calf. She needed to get the ropes off before he found another way to hurt himself. Luckily he was too tired to fight her, and with Morgan's constant care, he trusted her to help.

Morgan dragged herself out of the mud and collapsed onto the bank. As soon as Rhea was sure the calf wasn't in danger anymore, she moved to Morgan. She fell to her knees beside Morgan and leaned over her.

"Are you okay?"

Morgan was gasping for breath, and her chest heaved with each intake of air. Mud and grime coated her face, and her hair stuck to her cheeks and neck. She was a total mess, and Rhea had never seen anyone more beautiful in her life. She reached out a hand and brushed a muddy strand of hair off Morgan's cheek. The sun was up now, and the morning glow bathed Morgan in golden light.

Morgan nodded. "I just need to catch my breath." Her teeth chattered as she spoke. She opened her eyes, and Rhea caught her breath. It was the first time she had noticed the burst of gold and green in Morgan's milky brown eyes.

Rhea's gaze slid to the perfect curve of Morgan's lips and a new panic swept over her. "God, Morgan, your lips are turning blue." Rhea laid her palm against Morgan's cheek. Her skin was deathly cold. "Shit. We've got to get you out of these wet clothes before you freeze to death."

Rhea grasped Morgan's shoulders and sat her up. She gripped Morgan's coat and pulled it off her shoulders and slid her arms free. "Christ, you're cold." Rhea tugged at the waistband of Morgan's jeans. "Get these off."

Morgan's hands clasped Rhea's before she could undo the button of her jeans. "I've got it. Take care of the calf."

"Not until we get you inside and warm."

"That sounds good."

Rhea took Morgan's hands and pulled her up.

"The calf," Morgan urged with single-minded intensity, "we need to get him to the barn. We can't just leave him here."

"Never mind the calf. Go on and get inside. I'll take care of things out here." Morgan gripped Rhea's arm and swayed on her feet. "Christ, Morgan, go already." Rhea questioned whether she should leave Morgan alone, but there was no way Morgan would leave the calf in his vulnerable state. It was the only way she could think to get Morgan to go inside and get warm, but her guts churned with uncertainty, and she had the overwhelming need to take care of Morgan.

"Okay, just get him inside the cowshed with some food and water and put some straw on the ground. He'll be all right as long as he gets his strength back and warms up a bit."

"Right. I've got this, now go." Rhea looked down at the hand holding hers and had the sudden urge to tighten her grip and not let Morgan go. She squeezed Morgan's fingers slightly before sliding her hand from Morgan's. "I'll come to the house when I'm done and let you know how he's doing."

Morgan smiled at her and the praise in her eyes made Rhea's skin ripple with warmth that spread through her body into her core until she was trembling. She didn't know what was happening to her, but at that moment she would have done anything to hold that gaze one moment longer. It was as if everything in her life had been leading up to that moment of gratitude and tenderness, and for the first time in her life, Rhea belonged, her life had meaning, and she mattered.

How could she feel more joy from one moment, one look, one smile, than she had ever felt? Why did Morgan's approval mean so much? Perhaps it was just the unusual kindness Morgan had shown her when no one else had. Maybe she was just overreacting to stress. But she wanted more than anything to see Morgan. She needed to know she had done the right thing by letting her go alone. She needed to see for herself that Morgan was okay.

Rhea shook her head and coaxed the calf into the barn. She flashed back to the look in Morgan's eyes when she'd first opened the cabin door. Morgan had looked so wild and vulnerable, so unlike herself that it had frightened Rhea. But beyond everything, Morgan was beautiful.

When did she start thinking of Morgan that way? Was that what people felt when they felt safe with someone? When they felt trusted or accepted? Rhea struggled to get her head back on task. She had to stop daydreaming and get the job done or the next look Morgan gave her wouldn't be a happy one. It had become important to her to please Morgan, and that scared her. She didn't want anyone to hold that kind of power over her again. But this was different, and Morgan was her boss, not her father. Could she care about someone without losing herself? Could she take that risk?

❖

Morgan stripped off her clothes and left them in a muddy heap on the porch before going inside. She was chilled to the bone and the sun-kissed air was warmer than her wet muddy jeans, and there was no point creating another mess to clean up. A wall of warmth hit her the instant she stepped inside. She covered her chest with her arms and tried to hold the warmth against her body as she headed straight for the shower. The hot water stung her sensitive skin, and she slowly increased the temperature until the heat of the water and the steam in the room became a blanket of warmth. The water streamed down her face, washing away all traces of the filth that had caked her body only moments before. The water healed her aching muscles and soothed the fear until her trembling subsided. She couldn't wait for a steaming cup of coffee. Maybe that would be the elixir she needed to feel human again.

Morgan smiled. She didn't know what she would have done without Rhea's help. She wasn't used to relying on anyone, but this had been one time when she was grateful Rhea had been there. Rhea had been patient and caring when most people would have thought she had lost her mind by going into the water in those frigid temperatures. Not only had Rhea helped her, she had gone into the water with her.

She dried herself off and toweled her hair as she opened the bathroom door. Rhea stood in front of her with her hand poised to knock. Morgan gasped and took a step back, holding the towel loosely in her hand. "Oh God, you scared me."

Rhea's sharp appraising gaze traveled over her body. Morgan's nipples tightened and she shivered but this time it wasn't from the cold.

"Are you okay?" Rhea asked. Her voice was strained and a muscle at her jaw pulsed as she clenched her teeth.

Morgan tried to speak, but the intensity in Rhea's appraisal had ignited an inner fire that made her insides burn, and she was temporarily stunned. She hadn't had a woman look at her that way in a long time, and the sudden rush of desire left her speechless.

"Morgan?"

Morgan stepped back and tried to register what was happening with rational thought. She jerked. To her horror Rhea still wore her wet clothes. She had been out in the chill air tending to the calf while Morgan had been inside getting warm. "Come here, you've got to be freezing."

Rhea looked down at her muddy clothes and then to Morgan. "No. I just wanted to check on you. I'll go back to the cabin and get cleaned up. I didn't mean to barge in, but you didn't answer the door when I knocked. I called out, but you must not have heard me."

Morgan took Rhea's arm and pulled her inside. "I'm sorry, now get in here, you're letting all the heat out."

Morgan quickly shut the door when Rhea shuffled inside. She frantically tugged at Rhea's coat and glided her hands across her shoulders and down her arms as she pulled the coat off. Rhea flinched and stepped back. Her eyes were wide with fear.

"I can do it."

Morgan realized her misstep. "I'm sorry, I shouldn't have... I'm sorry." Morgan moved away. She suddenly realized she was still naked and hastily wrapped the towel around herself. "Take off your clothes and your boots. I'll get you something warm and clean while you shower. I want to know all about the calf, and I desperately need a cup of coffee."

Rhea stammered. "Morgan..."

"Get in the shower," Morgan ordered.

Rhea sighed and pulled off her boots.

Morgan shut the door and let out her breath. What just happened? She had been completely naked in front of Rhea and tried to undress her. Had she lost her mind? Morgan pushed away from the door. She had to get dressed. What was she going to say to Rhea now?

Morgan retrieved a pair of sweats and a T-shirt she thought Rhea could wear and cracked the bathroom door. Steam filled the air and she tried not to imagine Rhea naked under the spray of the jets.

"Here are some clothes for you to wear. Just leave yours on the floor, and I'll wash them with mine. Come to the kitchen when you're done. The coffee should be ready by then."

Morgan shut the bathroom door and hurried down the hall. What was she doing? She'd felt Rhea's gaze on her body as clear as if she'd been touched. She'd been aroused, and oh God, she couldn't believe she'd tried to undress Rhea. The poor woman had looked terrified. What was happening to her? Had the cold done something to her head? Morgan bowed her head. *Dear Father, please help me. Give me strength and show me the way.*

Morgan put the coffee on to brew and sat at the island. Once she stopped moving she realized how tired and hungry she was. Breakfast was a good idea.

Rhea walked into the kitchen, her hair still wet, and her skin pink from the heat of the shower. Her feet were bare, and the sweats Morgan had given her were a bit too big for her small frame. The T-shirt was too big too, and Morgan's eyes were drawn to a line of muscle along Rhea's neck that trailed down to a prominent collarbone. She imagined the feel of the tense muscle under her mouth.

Morgan glanced away. "Feel better?" she asked.

Rhea returned the smile but looked nervous, as if she didn't feel comfortable in her own skin.

"I thought we could use something to eat. I know you didn't get breakfast."

"You don't have to go to any trouble," Rhea said.

Morgan could tell Rhea was uncomfortable, and she thought she knew why. They'd been working together for weeks now, and just when she thought they were getting used to each other, Rhea would pull away again. After she had practically mauled her, she couldn't blame Rhea for being distant. She hadn't meant to, but she had crossed a line.

"I'm sorry about earlier. I didn't mean to make you uncomfortable. I shouldn't have touched you like that."

Rhea put her hands on the counter and looked down as if she was studying the pattern of the granite. When she looked up there was none of the usual distrust or defensiveness that kept everyone at a distance. At that moment Rhea was completely open and exposed. She trembled.

Morgan's hand closed over hers, and she flinched but didn't move her hand away this time. She needed Morgan to understand her. "It hurts."

Morgan swallowed and tightened her fingers around Rhea's hand. "Did I hurt you? Rhea, you have to forgive me. I wasn't thinking."

Rhea shook her head. "No. You didn't hurt me." She took a deep breath and tried to figure out how she was supposed to explain something she didn't understand herself.

"What hurts, Rhea?"

Rhea moved her thumb across the back of Morgan's hand. "Touch. When someone touches me, it hurts. It's as if my skin remembers the pain and every time someone touches me, it hurts."

Morgan looked confused.

How could she make Morgan understand what she was talking about? Maybe she should leave it alone, but she couldn't stand the look of fear she'd seen in Morgan's eyes when she'd pushed her away. She needed Morgan to know she hadn't done anything wrong.

To her relief Morgan spoke first.

"So, my hand on yours right now is hurting you?"

Rhea nodded slowly as if the movement was a whisper. She was afraid of what Morgan would think of her. "It isn't pain like hitting your thumb with a hammer or getting a cut. The pain is inside. You touch my hand and it's like the nerve endings light up and the pain sparks under my fingernails, in my elbows, down my spine, and it radiates all over. Soft touch or repetitive touch is the worst. It's like nails on a chalkboard, only I feel it on my bones."

Morgan stared at their linked hands as if expecting to see an injury there. "I'm sorry. I didn't know."

Morgan started to move her hand away, but Rhea closed her fingers around it in a subtle request that she stay. Morgan squeezed back, amazed by the softness of Rhea's touch.

"I didn't want you to think it was you. I barged in on you when I shouldn't have, and then I pushed you away when you tried to help me. You must think I'm crazy."

Morgan's mouth had gone dry, and she ran the tip of her tongue across her lips as disbelief and anger swelled in her heart. How could someone have hurt Rhea this way? She wanted to do something, anything to take the wounded look from Rhea's eyes.

"What happened to you? What caused this?"

Rhea shook her head. "I'm not sure that's a story you want to hear."

"I do," Morgan answered. "You can talk to me. You don't have to carry this alone."

Rhea sighed. "My therapist told me that physical trauma can leave flesh memories and because of my past my skin is hypersensitive to touch. It's like a defense mechanism, kind of a weird fight-or-flight response."

Morgan swallowed as a new wave of grief swept over her. She wanted to understand, and something told her Rhea needed that too. "So all touch hurts you?"

"As far as I know, yes. Some places are more sensitive than others, but I'm always aware that it's there."

"That's so sad," Morgan whispered.

"Most of the time it isn't an issue. I just wanted you to know so you wouldn't be afraid of me."

For the first time in weeks, Morgan was reminded of the reason Rhea was there. She still didn't know much about what Rhea had done, but she was beginning to understand that there were horrors in Rhea's past she couldn't begin to imagine.

"Thank you for telling me. I can't imagine this is easy for you to talk about."

Rhea let out a long breath. "It isn't easy to explain a lot of things."

Morgan waited and hoped Rhea would tell her more, but she could see Rhea had gone as far as she was willing. Morgan gave her hand a gentle squeeze before letting go. "I don't know about you, but I can't wait another minute for that coffee."

Morgan turned back to Rhea with two steaming cups and was disappointed that Rhea had retreated to the other side of the island, her expression once again closed. "Thank you for everything you did this morning. I would have lost the calf without your help. I'm really glad you're here."

Rhea smiled. "You're a little crazy, you know."

Morgan laughed. "So I've been told."

Rhea pursed her lips before a mischievous smile curled the corners of her mouth, and Morgan felt some of the tension pressing in on her heart ease.

"I guess that makes us quite the team then."

Morgan lifted her coffee to her lips and smiled at Rhea over the cup. "I guess it does." She considered the statement and was pleased to realize it was true. It was nice to have someone to rely on. It was nice not to be alone.

❖

Rhea lay on her bed and stared at the ceiling, thinking about Morgan. She'd been thinking about her ever since she'd walked in on her in the shower that morning, and she didn't understand why. She'd seen women naked in the shower before. It had been almost a daily occurrence in high school after gym class, and then in prison there was never any privacy for anything. But she'd never looked at a woman the way she'd looked at Morgan.

Morgan's body was hard with long lean muscle, carved sharp edges along her arms and thighs. Her stomach was flat and rigid with cords of muscle that rippled when she moved. Rhea hadn't been able to look away from the gentle curves of Morgan's hips or the soft swell of her breasts. Her brain had yelled for her to run, but her body refused to move, as if she was frozen in a dream. It hadn't been until Morgan touched her that she'd snapped awake, and the old instinct to flee made her push Morgan away.

Morgan hadn't been threatening. She'd been trying to take care of her. Rhea remembered the way Morgan's nipples had hardened under her gaze and her stomach tightened and tension grew until a dull ache throbbed between her legs. She pushed herself to get up. She needed to do something to get her mind off Morgan and the aching loneliness she felt.

Rhea went into the bathroom and looked at herself in the mirror. She studied the differences in her body compared to Morgan's. Morgan was taller with broad shoulders, a thin waist, and narrow hips. Rhea took off her clothes and studied herself. She had never really looked at herself before. Morgan's stomach had been hard with ripples of muscle that bunched when she moved. Rhea prodded her own stomach with her finger, surprised by the tightness under the soft layer of tissue. Her arms were sculpted with generous mounds of muscle but not the chiseled lines that clearly defined Morgan's arms.

She studied her breasts and frowned. They were fuller and heavier than Morgan's had been. The image of Morgan's nipples repeated in her memory and the ache in her loins came again. Rhea brushed her fingers lightly over her breasts and imagined Morgan's hands touching her. Her nipples hardened instantly and she gasped at the charge of hunger that suddenly erupted within her.

"No. This can't be happening." Rhea grabbed her clothes from the floor and dressed quickly. Her boots were still wet, so she slid into the tennis shoes she'd been given when she was released from prison. She had to get out and clear her head. She was clearly confused by everything that had happened over the last few weeks and needed to get her head straight.

She slammed the door on her way out, grabbed the porch rail, and swung herself over. She hit the ground at a full run, determined to burn the memory of Morgan's body out of hers.

❖

Morgan looked up from the drafting table and the drawings she had been studying when she heard the bell above the door chime. She groaned playfully when she saw J.J. walking toward her.

"What did I do this time?"

J.J. laughed. "Can't you just be happy to see me?"

"No. I wouldn't want you to think I like you," Morgan teased.

"You love me and you know it."

Morgan wrinkled her nose and stuck her tongue out at her sister.

J.J. laughed. "How are things going with Rhea?"

Morgan tossed her pencil onto the table and leaned back in her chair, folding her long arms over her head. "Things are good. She's been a big help."

J.J.'s eyes widened in surprise. "Really?"

"Yeah, really. What did you expect?"

"Nothing. It just isn't like you to admit that I was right."

Morgan smiled. "Yeah, well this time is different. Rhea has been great. I'm glad she's here."

J.J. shifted and began to fidget with her fingernails. Morgan recognized when her sister was avoiding something and braced herself for what was coming next. "Spit it out, J.J."

J.J. sighed. "How are *you* doing?"

Morgan tensed. She knew where this was going. "I already told you, things are good."

"I'm not talking about Rhea, I'm asking about you."

It was clear what J.J. was getting at, and she didn't want to have this conversation again. "I said, I'm fine. I don't have to be a part of the church to be okay. I have a lot of other work to do."

J.J. frowned. "I know you stay busy, and I know you still do a lot for the community, I just don't know if you take time to take care of yourself. You still don't come around, and we miss you."

"What do you want from me, J.J.?"

J.J. sighed. "I just want to know you're okay. What happened with Ashley was—"

Morgan put her hands up. "Stop."

"Come on, Morgan. Talk to me."

"There's nothing to talk about. She's gone. I've moved on the only way I know how. What do you expect from me?"

J.J. took a step closer. Morgan couldn't stand the pity in her eyes when she looked up at her.

"Oh, sweetie, I'm not trying to hurt you. I just don't want you to feel you have to do this alone. We still love you. I miss having my little sister around."

"I love you too, but the Ashley issue is off the table. I don't want to talk about it. Everyone wants me to move on, but no one wants to let it go."

"Okay. I'm sorry. I just never see you and I worry."

Morgan shook her head. She couldn't stay mad at J.J., and having her apologize only brought more guilt. J.J. was just worried about her, and she hadn't given her any reason not to be. "Thanks for looking out for me. I promise I'll come to you if I need anything, but I really am okay."

J.J. smiled. "Sure." She took a step back and looked around the studio. "The place looks better."

Morgan nodded. "I have a lot more time to work now that Rhea has taken over some of the other duties."

"Is she around? I need to do a home check while I'm here."

"Aha, I knew you didn't drive all the way out here just to see me."

J.J. put her hands on her hips the way she used to do when they were kids, signaling a lecture was on the way. "Let's just say two reasons to drive out to the middle of nowhere is good motivation." J.J. paused. "Besides, this way I get paid mileage."

Morgan laughed. "That's more like it."

"So, where do you think I can find her?"

"My guess is the workshop. Turns out she has a knack for restoring old tractors. She's been working on the old International Harvester Farmall I had stuck in the back."

J.J. eyed her suspiciously. "You really like her, don't you?"

"Sure. It was a little rough at first, but things are great now. I enjoy having her here. She's a hard worker and keeps to herself. What's not to like?"

J.J. stared at her as if she was studying a puzzle.

"What?"

J.J. shook her head. "Nothing. I just thought of something." J.J. waved Morgan off. "It's nothing. Do you mind if I go see Rhea for a while?"

"No. Go ahead." Morgan could see J.J. was concerned, and she regretted the months she had pushed her family away. "Hey," Morgan called out before J.J. closed the door, "would you like to stay for dinner?"

J.J. smiled. "Sure. That sounds great. Thanks." She tossed a wave in the air on her way out the door. "I'll catch up to you when I'm done."

Morgan smiled. She hadn't expected the church to turn on her, and she hadn't expected to lose Ashley. For a long time she had shut down and wasn't sure she would make it through. But J.J. hadn't given up on her, and it was time she started being a part of this family again.

CHAPTER SEVEN

One day tumbled into the next and before she knew it, it was late March and Rhea had been at Morgan's farm for two months. They had fallen into an easy routine. Rhea took care of the repairs and looked after the farm while Morgan worked in her studio and did the farrier work. So Rhea was surprised when Morgan asked her to go on a home call.

Rhea climbed into the truck and shut the door with a resounding thud. "Where are we going?"

Morgan started the truck and smiled. "Road trip."

"Yeah, which hat are you wearing today, farrier or artist?"

"Actually, today is your job. I got a call from a farmer friend about a 1947 Ford 8N. He's had it stored in an old barn for the last thirty years and wants to restore it. If it looks good, you'll have enough work to get you through till the summer business picks up."

Rhea was shocked. The work on the Harvester had gone well, but she hadn't expected to take on tractor restoration as a full-time job.

"Are you sure about this? I mean, this could be a complete rebuild. I've never done one. What if I can't do it?"

Morgan shrugged. "Let's just give it a look. If it's something you don't want to do, we'll pass on it. But if you like it, I'd like to take it on."

"Wait, you're going to leave this up to me?"

Morgan laughed. "Of course. I wouldn't ask you to do

something you weren't comfortable with. You know what you can handle better than I do. But for the record, I think you can do it."

Rhea thought about what Morgan was saying. She understood the logic, but she was uncomfortable with Morgan counting on her to do this. What if she screwed it up? She didn't want to disappoint Morgan. "What if I decide to move on before the job's done? What then?"

Morgan frowned. "I guess I hadn't thought of that. Are you planning on going somewhere?"

Rhea shook her head. "No, but that's a long time and things can change. Are you planning on keeping me around?"

Morgan drew in a sharp breath as if something had pained her. "I guess I was. I thought we had a deal. I thought things were working out."

Rhea wanted to believe Morgan meant what she said. She wanted to stay. The time on Morgan's farm was the only time in her life she'd felt safe, like her life was her own.

"Yeah, I like it here. But sometimes things change and there's nothing we can do about it."

Morgan's mood shifted as quickly as the change of the wind. Rhea recognized the look of pain in the lines of Morgan's mouth and heard it in her silence, as thick as morning fog.

"Hey, I'm sorry. I didn't mean to be a spoilsport. I guess I'm not used to the way you treat me. I get a little defensive when I start to think I owe someone something."

"No. You're right. Sometimes things do change, people leave. But that doesn't mean we stop moving forward, making plans, and taking risks."

"Did she leave you?" Rhea asked without thinking.

"Who?"

"Your girlfriend."

Morgan gasped.

Rhea waited, but Morgan didn't answer and she wouldn't look at her. Her skin had gone pale and she tugged at her lower lip with her teeth.

Rhea was about to give up when Morgan answered. "Her name was Ashley. And yes, you can say she left. She died."

"Oh, man. I'm sorry." Rhea didn't know what to say next. She had opened Morgan's wound and was watching her bleed. Why had she done that? She'd learned to see people's weaknesses in prison, but she hadn't meant to hurt Morgan. She just wanted to know why she was so different. Hell, most of the time she didn't even know how to relate to Morgan. Morgan was *good*. The kind of good Rhea thought only existed in fairy tales and children's stories. Pain was something she could relate to, and she realized now she had jumped on the question to cover her own insecurity. But hearing Morgan's sadness was different than listening to the stories in prison. She felt sad when she saw Morgan hurt. What touched Morgan somehow touched her too.

Morgan slowed the truck and pointed ahead. "Look."

Rhea peered through the glass. A young fawn stood on wobbly legs in the middle of the road just ahead of them.

"Why isn't it moving? It's going to get hit by a car," Rhea said as panic rose up in her throat.

"It can't be more than a week or two old," Morgan said.

Morgan slowly drove past the deer, but it didn't move. It just stared at them through the window. Morgan stopped and put the truck in reverse and backed up until the fawn was standing just outside her window.

"Isn't it a little early for the deer to start birthing?"

Morgan shrugged. "Easter is early this year. I guess this little one is too."

Rhea held her breath and stretched her neck to see the small deer watching her.

Morgan rolled down the window. "Hey, little one. You need to move on, it isn't safe here."

The fawn didn't move. It just looked back at Morgan, its big brown eyes innocent and trusting.

Morgan shut off the truck and opened her door.

When Morgan climbed out, Rhea scooted across the seat to see what was happening. To her amazement Morgan kneeled in front of the deer, reached out a hand, and stroked its face as if she was petting a dog.

Chills ran up Rhea's spine. She had never seen anything so pure and innocent in her life. The deer looked at Morgan as if it was trying to tell her something. There was no fear in its eyes as Morgan gently stroked its muzzle and down its neck.

A car approached from the other lane, and Morgan held up her hand until the car stopped. She looked back down at the deer and whispered something Rhea couldn't hear.

The deer glanced at the cars beginning to stack up and then looked back to Morgan. In a flash the deer jerked its head up as if listening to a call in the distance. It turned and walked to the edge of the road and disappeared into the woods.

Morgan climbed back into the truck as Rhea pushed herself into her own seat. Rhea was mesmerized. A faint smile lifted the corners of Morgan's mouth and her skin was glowing, and there was no hint of the pain that had struck her moments before. Joy radiated from her and Rhea could feel the energy vibrate between them.

"How did you do that? How did you just walk up to a wild animal like it was your pet?"

Morgan smiled. "I don't know." She shivered. "Man, that was amazing." She turned to Rhea and clasped her hand. "Could you feel that?"

Rhea was shocked by the sudden touch and the electricity that passed between them. Her skin tingled and she felt her heart flutter. She nodded. "Yeah, I did. I'm still not sure I believe it."

Morgan opened the glove compartment and took out a deck of cards. She quickly flipped through them until she found a card with a picture of a deer. "Native Americans believe that animals bring us messages." She handed the card to Rhea. "Here, see for yourself."

Rhea took the card and read aloud. "*Deer, symbolic of compassion, generosity, and unconditional love. The deer represents living for the greater good. If the deer crosses your path, the message may be a reminder for you to be gentle with yourself.*" She swallowed and looked back to Morgan. "So does this mean you're some kind of saint or something?"

Morgan laughed. "No, but maybe the compassion was for me, not the deer. And maybe I needed to be reminded that I loved Ashley even if her choices hurt me."

Rhea stared at the card in her hand and frowned. She didn't believe the spiritual stuff like Morgan did, but something had happened back there with that deer. She had seen it. She had felt it. And now she was more confused than ever.

"Is this because you're a priest?"

Morgan smiled and shook her head. "I doubt it. Besides, how do you know the message wasn't for you?"

Rhea was stunned. "No way. Not me."

"Why not?"

"Because I don't believe in God anymore. I don't buy into that spiritual stuff."

"How do you explain it then?" Morgan asked.

Rhea didn't have an answer. "Maybe it had rabies."

Morgan laughed. "I don't think deer get rabies."

Rhea slapped the card back onto the deck and tossed them into a cup holder. "Whatever."

Morgan smiled and turned down a narrow gravel road. "We're here. Are you ready to see your next project?"

Rhea recalled the way Morgan had touched the deer's face. She had been reverent in her touch as if she had been holding an angel in her hands. Something stirred in Rhea and settled the angst that always bubbled beneath the surface. She wasn't sure what amazed her more, the deer or Morgan. There were so many things she didn't understand. Maybe she would stay through the summer. "Sure. I've got nowhere else to be."

Morgan smiled and patted Rhea's shoulder, resting her hand there a moment as they walked up to the house. The warmth of Morgan's palm seeped into Rhea's skin without pain, and when Morgan moved her hand away, Rhea missed the warmth and comfort of her touch.

Morgan smiled reassuringly when Rhea stopped at the bottom of the steps. Rhea's heart fluttered, her skin tingled, and she had the desperate urge to reach for Morgan's hand. She trusted Morgan. She watched Morgan move, listened to the sound of her voice, and watched as the old man's face lit up in a smile when he saw her. Rhea knew the feeling. She wanted to drink in the tenderness of Morgan more than she wanted to draw in her next breath. Morgan made her believe she could stay.

❖

"Hey, let's stop in town for dinner, my treat," Morgan said cheerfully.

She'd been smiling since they cinched the tractor onto the trailer and shook hands with the old farmer. Rhea had to admit she was excited about the project. The old tractor called out to her. She knew what it was like to be locked away and forgotten, and she believed if she could give the old Ford new life, there was hope for them both.

"Sure. Do you think the tractor will be okay?"

"Not a problem. We can go to Sassy Ann's." Morgan grinned. "We can park in front and sit next to the window so you can keep an eye on your new baby the whole time."

Rhea smiled. "You think you know everything, don't you."

Morgan cocked an eyebrow. "No, but I'm learning."

Sassy Ann's was busy, but just as Morgan had said, she parked in front and found a table next to the window. Rhea was a little uncomfortable being around so many people, but she told herself she would be okay as long as she was with Morgan.

Halfway through the best burger of her life, a hand clamped down on the back of her chair.

"Hello, Morgan, Rhea."

Rhea jumped and the hair on the back of her neck stood on end.

"Hello, Jeff," Morgan replied in a monotone.

Rhea didn't speak. She looked up at the big man and did her

best impression of calm when what she really wanted to do was slap his hand off her chair.

He smiled down at her with a toothy grin. Rhea grimaced at the bits of tobacco and remnants of food still stuck in his teeth. Didn't this guy own a toothbrush?

Jeff ran his hand over his crotch. "I thought you might be interested in better company tonight. How about you and I go down to the VFW and do a little dancing, have a few drinks, and see what happens."

Rhea fought back the urge to gag. The thought of Jeff putting his shovel-sized hands on her was repulsive. "No, thank you, or did you forget how things ended the last time?"

Jeff glanced at Morgan and sneered at Rhea. "Trust me, honey, what I've got in mind is a whole lot better than anything Morgan can do for you."

Morgan cleared her throat.

Rhea shifted her chair so she wasn't pinned by the table. "Like I said, no, thanks."

Jeff set a beer on the table. "Have a beer. I can at least buy you a beer."

Rhea shook her head. "I don't drink."

Jeff laughed. "Sure you do."

Rhea lowered her voice to just above a growl. "Look, man, I'm trying real hard to be nice here, but I'm not interested in what you're selling."

Jeff sniffed as if he got a whiff of something he didn't like. "Well then, have a good night." He reached for the bottle and knocked the beer over. Cold liquid gushed across the table and into her lap.

Rhea jumped up from the table as ice-cold liquid soaked through her jeans. She threw her hands outward to keep her balance, her glass of water still clutched in her hand. As she jumped back from the table, her ice water was flung into Jeff's face.

He wiped his face with his giant hand as water dripped from his chin and soaked his shirt. "You bitch!"

"Hey, it was an accident," Rhea said as she used her napkin to blot off her pants.

Two waitresses bustled around the table with towels and did a good job of keeping Jeff at a distance.

Morgan handed some cash to their waitress. "Come on, Rhea, let's go."

"Rhea?" a man behind them asked. "Rhea Daniels?"

Rhea clenched her jaw as dread ran across her skin as if she'd been showered in ice. This would not be good.

A tall, skinny man approached Rhea. He squinted at her as if trying to see the face of a girl in the woman before him. He had gray hair, bushy black eyebrows, and small dark eyes. Rhea didn't recognize him.

"Holy hell, it is you. When did you get out? I thought you'd rot in jail for killing your daddy. Damn shame. I can't believe you get to run free after killing a damn good man."

Morgan put her arm around Rhea and pulled her through the door. "Come on, Rhea, get in the truck."

Rhea was moving on autopilot. She couldn't breathe, and she was having trouble figuring out what just happened.

Morgan slammed her door and hit the locks. "Who was that guy?"

Rhea shook her head. "I don't know," she whispered.

"Are you okay?"

Rhea's head hurt, and she felt like she'd been kicked in the gut. She shook her head. "I don't know."

Morgan's heart raced. The adrenaline coursing through her blood was enough to make her feel like she could run all the way back to the farm. She felt like she was running for her life, but it wasn't her life those men had questioned. Right now all she could think of was getting Rhea home. One moment they had been joking, and Rhea had been smiling one of her rare radiant smiles that melted Morgan's heart, and the next they were in the midst of pandemonium. Rhea had killed her father? Morgan pinched the bridge of her nose and pushed against the questions clouding her mind. That was the past. Right now she needed to look after Rhea.

Morgan didn't slow down as she veered onto the old dirt road leading to the farm. She didn't let up until she was outside the barn. Rhea hadn't said a word all the way home. Morgan stopped and killed the truck. Rhea didn't move, so Morgan came around and opened her door.

Rhea looked dazed. Her eyes were unfocused, and she didn't seem to realize where she was.

"Rhea, sweetheart, come on, let's get you inside."

Rhea complied, but as soon as her feet hit the ground she ran to the edge of the barn and vomited. Morgan waited until the retching stopped and the sobs began before she approached Rhea. She scuffed her boots on the ground as she moved so Rhea would know she was there.

"Rhea?"

Rhea held one hand out keeping Morgan away and pressed her other palm against the side of the barn as if the rough lumber was all that held her together. Morgan stepped closer and put her hand against Rhea's back. Tension vibrated through her muscles like electricity through a live wire. She trembled at Morgan's touch but didn't pull away.

Morgan wanted to put her arms around her and tell her it would be okay, but she couldn't. Rhea was too fragile to comfort. All she could do was wait and be there when she was ready. "Let's go inside."

Rhea sniffed and let her hand fall to her side. "That guy said my daddy was a good man." Rhea turned to Morgan, but her eyes were distant and clouded with pain. "How can that be?" Rhea slid to the ground and hugged her knees to her chest and began to rock back and forth.

Morgan kneeled on the ground in front of her and waited. Tears streamed down Rhea's cheeks like rivers, and her voice quivered when she spoke.

"It was my seventh birthday the first time he came into my room at night. I was asleep and woke up to his cold hand under my nightgown. I didn't understand what was happening. He told me I had to be a good girl. I cried. I begged him to stop. I told him he was hurting me." Rhea bit her lip as her chin quivered. "He never stopped."

Morgan clasped her hands over Rhea's as her own tears began to flow. Her heart broke for the child Rhea had been and the woman she had become. Everything was clear now. Morgan struggled against her own rage at what had been done to Rhea and marveled at the strength Rhea had shown to endure such a devastating betrayal.

Rhea looked into Morgan's eyes as if she was seeking absolution. The desperation in her voice ripped through Morgan like shards of glass. "How does that make my daddy a good man?"

Morgan swallowed. "It doesn't."

"Do you believe me?" Rhea asked, her voice shaking with fear and hurt.

Morgan couldn't imagine anyone hadn't believed what had happened to Rhea. That was another betrayal she had suffered. "Of course I believe you."

Rhea let go and thrust herself into Morgan's arms. Morgan held onto Rhea with all her being. Nothing in her life had ever been more important than holding on to Rhea and giving her the comfort she needed. Morgan rocked her and held on as tight as she could without hurting Rhea.

"I'm sorry he did that to you. I'm so sorry he hurt you."

Rhea melted against her as tremors rocked her body and she told her story. "I thought I was going to go off to college and get away. I was finally going to be free of him. I went out with some friends one night and came home late, and I saw him coming out of my little sister's room. All those years, I thought it was just something wrong with me. It had never occurred to me that he would hurt her. She was only eleven years old and I knew what he would do to her. I couldn't let that happen. He saw me standing there, and I could see it in his eyes that he knew that I knew. He didn't say anything—he just laughed and walked away."

Morgan closed her eyes and found it hard to breathe. Her chest was tight with rage and fear and hurt for Rhea. She bit down on her tongue to fight the urge to cry out.

"I heard him go into his study, and I knew he would drink himself to sleep there. So I waited. I shot my father in his sleep. Even then I was too afraid to face him."

"It's okay, Rhea. You're safe now," Morgan whispered against Rhea's hair.

"No one believed me. No one ever believed me."

"I believe you. You're safe now. I believe you." Morgan held on until Rhea pulled away.

Rhea sat up and let her head fall back against the barn and gazed into the night sky. Morgan looked up. It was a clear night and every star in the heavens had shown up to witness Rhea's confession.

❖

Rhea's scream sliced through Morgan like a knife piercing her flesh. Morgan jumped to her feet and ran from the cabin's kitchen to Rhea's bedroom. Rhea was curled up in the fetal position, crying into her pillow. Morgan slid onto the bed, wrapped her arms around her, and pulled her close. Rhea's hair was damp with sweat and tears stained her cheeks. Morgan didn't want to think of what nightmares Rhea was reliving.

"Shh," Morgan cooed as she rubbed Rhea's back and held her head against her chest. She held on until Rhea quieted and her body relaxed against her.

Morgan leaned back and stretched out on the bed beside Rhea. She wrapped herself around her, protecting her with her body. It was hard for her to imagine the hard, brass woman so vulnerable and broken. But Morgan knew no matter how much armor Rhea shrouded herself with, the child within was still hurt and afraid and nothing could undo that pain.

Rhea's fingers curled into a fist and gripped Morgan's shirt. She burrowed against Morgan, clinging to her like a life preserver. Morgan leaned her head against the headboard and tightened her arms around Rhea.

She knew she was walking on thin ice, and if she wasn't

careful she'd start to care too much. She'd thought she could save Ashley. She thought that with enough love she could fill the emptiness that plagued her and guard her against the addiction that stalked her. But in the end she hadn't been enough and the addiction had won.

Morgan loosened her arms and slid away from Rhea. She couldn't afford to let the same thing happen again. She'd do whatever she could to help Rhea, but she had to draw a line. She couldn't get too close. She couldn't survive that depth of loss again.

Morgan stood at the door and watched Rhea until she was certain she was sleeping soundly. She didn't think Rhea would remember much about the evening and was certain she wouldn't be comfortable waking up with Morgan in her bed. But no matter how much she told herself it was better for them both if she put distance between them, she still had a hard time walking away. She wouldn't leave, but she couldn't stay. She slipped out of the room, letting each step erect a barrier between them, resolving to herself that she wouldn't go back.

She walked onto the porch and took a deep breath of chill night air. She rested her elbows on the porch railing and looked up into the starry night. "What do you want from me? I don't know what it is you want me to do."

Morgan knew it wasn't her place to question why such horrible things were permitted to happen in the world. She didn't believe it was God's will that children were abused, that women were beaten by their partners, that people died from hunger, or a million other terrible things that happened in the world every day. She understood that with free will came choice, and with choice there would always be pain and suffering. But that understanding was no comfort to people like Rhea who had been violated and betrayed beyond anything she could fathom.

"Show me the way. I will trust in you to guide me. But I am scared. I don't want to fail again. Please show me the way."

❖

Rhea jerked awake. She was in her room, in her bed, surrounded by her things. She took a deep breath and rubbed her face. Her eyes were swollen and her skin was raw from crying. She took another deep breath and remembered the events of the night before. She closed her eyes again. She didn't want to relive that nightmare. What would Morgan think of her now? She didn't want to leave, but now that people knew who she was, things would be a lot harder. Morgan would have a hard time getting work once word got out that she had a convicted murderer living at her farm.

She winced at the stab of pain at the thought of what this could do to Morgan. Morgan had believed her. She had comforted her. Rhea blew out a breath. She had waited sixteen years for someone to do that. Morgan had held her without judgment or blame.

Somehow she had let her guard down, and for the first time she hadn't been hurt as a result. How could she run away now? Where would she go?

Rhea pushed herself out of bed. She pressed the heels of her hands against her temples and tried to stop the pounding headache that beat against her skull. Despite the pain in her head and salt scratching against her eyeballs, there was a new lightness in her heart. Telling her story had been like taking off a heavy pack that had been strapped to her back. She felt like herself, whoever that was. She wasn't pretending and she wasn't hiding anymore. She was standing on her own choices and living by her own values.

Rhea stopped midstep as she came into the living room. Morgan was asleep on her couch. She had one of the old quilts pulled up to her chin and had her coat draped across her feet. Rhea shook her head in disbelief. What was she going to do with this woman? It was as if all the good Rhea had looked for in the world was rolled up in Morgan.

Rhea sighed. If Morgan wanted her to stay, she wouldn't have the strength to leave. She would move heaven and earth to repay Morgan. She retreated to the bathroom to wash away the tearstains on her skin before slipping into the kitchen to make coffee.

As she expected, it didn't take long for Morgan to stir once the smell of coffee filled the air.

"Hey," Rhea said as she set a mug on the coffee table in front of Morgan.

Morgan smiled and rubbed her eyes. "Hey." She sat up and cradled the cup of coffee in her hands as if it held the elixir of life. She inhaled deeply and groaned. "Ah, that smells good."

Rhea smiled and sipped her own coffee. She sat back in a rocking chair and studied Morgan. "What are you doing here?"

Morgan's eyes widened. "I'm sorry. I didn't want to leave you alone last night, and I hoped you wouldn't mind if I crashed on the couch."

Rhea softened. "Thanks. Sorry I dumped everything on you last night. I guess I was just tired of carrying it all around by myself."

Morgan ran her thumb back and forth over the rim of her mug. "I'm glad you told me. I can't imagine what all this has been like for you."

Rhea nodded slowly, acknowledging the gravity of her situation. "People aren't going to like me being here now. It won't take long for word to get around, and that could hurt your business."

Morgan stared at Rhea thoughtfully as if she could see inside her soul. "Maybe. But it wouldn't be the first time I've dealt with scandal. I think I can handle it."

"You don't know that. Maybe I should start considering other arrangements."

"Other arrangements? You mean leaving?"

Rhea tried to sound cool, but inside she was terrified. Leaving wasn't just an option—it was a probability. "It might be better for both of us if I moved on. You don't need this kind of trouble."

Morgan sat forward and rested her elbows on her knees. Her expression was serious, and Rhea braced herself for what Morgan would decide.

"It's going to be like this wherever you go. Eventually someone will learn about your past, and you'll have to face those judgments. You can either spend the rest of your life running, or you can stay here and work through it. A lot has changed in fifteen years. People know more about child abuse now than they did back then. Give them a chance to understand."

"It's not that easy."

"No. I imagine it isn't. But those are your choices. It's up to you." Morgan drained her coffee and set the mug down with an air of finality. "Besides, you have a tractor to rebuild."

Rhea shook her head. She couldn't believe Morgan was willing to stick this out with her. She wouldn't find that offer in many places. It would be hard to start over, and she was still on parole. It wasn't like she had a free ticket or a clean slate. Maybe Morgan was right. Maybe she needed to stick it out.

"Okay, I'll try, but no promises," Rhea said.

"I'm not asking for any," Morgan replied with a serious note in her voice.

Rhea took a deep breath of relief and thought about everything Morgan had said. Something stood out to her. Morgan said this wouldn't be the first time she had dealt with scandal. What did that mean? Was she talking about losing her priesthood? Or was she talking about Ashley? Or was it something else? Morgan had given her bits and pieces of her life, but none of the details. What else was there to the good-hearted ex-priest who thought love could save the world?

Morgan pushed her hands through her hair and sighed. "Well, I need to see to the animals. You sure you're okay?" It had been a tough night, and she had no idea what was going through Rhea's mind. Rhea's raw emotion and instinct to flee had not only scared her, it had shown her just how deeply people could hurt one another. She hadn't trusted Rhea when she first came to the farm, and she knew that others would come to worse conclusions once the word got out that Rhea had been convicted of murder.

"I'm okay. I'll catch up with you in a bit."

Morgan nodded and smiled. "Thanks for the coffee."

Rhea opened the door. She spoke just as Morgan was about to step outside. "Thanks for staying with me last night. You didn't have to do that."

Morgan hesitated before meeting Rhea's eyes. "I was glad to do it. I'm glad you trusted me." Morgan swallowed hard. "You aren't alone anymore."

Rhea smiled and dropped her gaze. "Thanks."

Morgan wanted to brush her hand along Rhea's cheek, reassure her things would be all right, but knew she shouldn't. It was her instinct to protect Rhea, to want to help her discover a different life, but she had no idea how that would happen. She had always jumped into things headfirst without thinking of the cost, and she had always paid a heavy price. Warning bells were blaring in her mind, but the memory of the anguish on Rhea's face was enough to push her to ignore the danger to herself. No one had ever stood up for Rhea. It was time someone did.

Morgan stepped away and sketched a wave in the air as she retreated. Something told her Rhea would need a little time after everything that had happened, and if she was honest with herself, she could use a little air. Holding Rhea had stirred a cacophony of emotions. She had wanted to soothe her, protect her, grieve with her, rage with her, but there had been a moment when things had shifted. She had become acutely aware of how perfectly Rhea fit against her. She could smell the gentle hint of mint and orange and wild mountain air when she pressed her check against Rhea's hair. Rhea's breath brushed against her skin and a ripple of desire had coursed through her.

Guilt forced its way to the front of Morgan's awareness. She couldn't believe she could even consider the simmering attraction when Rhea was in so much pain. But it had been Rhea's vulnerability that had completed the formula of desire. Rhea was undeniably beautiful, strong, witty, smart, and talented. It was Rhea's willingness to show her weakness, her raw emotion, that had shown Morgan the depth of her strength. Rhea's willingness to trust after what she had been through was incomprehensible, but there she was, allowing herself to be held, comforted, and even touched.

Morgan's heart raced. That was her pattern, wasn't it? She was drawn to damaged women, someone she could save. Well, she wasn't in that business anymore, and she needed to get her body to understand that. Rhea was off-limits. She needed a friend, someone she could trust, and that was exactly who Morgan planned to be for her.

CHAPTER EIGHT

Morgan picked up the phone as her cell began to play "Trouble" by P!nk. "Hey, J.J., what's up?"

"Hey, Morgan, how are things going up there?"

"Good. Why?" Morgan asked as a knot formed in her gut.

"I got a call from the Anderson County sheriff's department. The sheriff up there says he's received several complaints this week about Rhea. He says the folks there in Andersonville aren't happy to find out they have a convicted murderer living in their town."

Morgan's hand tightened around the phone. "So what did he want?"

Morgan heard the frustration in J.J.'s sigh as her breath rattled through the cell connection. "Nothing yet. He just wanted to let me know he wasn't happy about the flak he's receiving. He understands Rhea isn't doing anything wrong by being there, but he made it clear he wouldn't tolerate any problems in his town."

Morgan closed her eyes against the dull pain that pressed against the back of her eyes.

"Morgan?"

"Yeah."

"What happened? I know something had to trigger this mess."

Morgan sighed. "We ran into someone who recognized Rhea. Let's just say he was a big fan of her father and didn't take too well to her being out."

"Damn, that's rough."

"You don't know the half of it," Morgan said through gritted teeth.

"So I take it she told you about her dad…what happened?"

"Yeah, she told me."

There was silence on the line. She could almost hear the thoughts in J.J.'s brain. Morgan waited.

"Are you okay?" J.J. asked.

"I can't say I'm happy about any of this, but give it a little time and people will get over themselves."

"I don't know, Morgan. I don't like this. The sheriff made it sound like people are considering something drastic."

"What does that mean?" Morgan barked. "What are they going to do, send out a lynch mob?"

"Hell, I don't know, I wouldn't put it past some of those backwoods Bubbas."

Morgan thrust her hand into her hair and pulled at the strands in frustration. "Look, Rhea is doing a good job. She hasn't left the farm in a week, and these folks will just have to figure things out for themselves. You know how gossip is around here. But whatever they're saying, Rhea hasn't done anything to give anyone a reason to worry."

She heard J.J. sigh. "Okay. Just be careful. I don't want you getting caught up in anything. Let me know if you have any problems."

"Yeah, I'll do that." Morgan ended the call. Her mouth had gone dry, and her hands were shaking. It had been the same when the church pushed her out. There had been constant whispers, blatant disdain, threats, and the daily phone calls from people telling her she was an abomination. That had been the worst. People she cared for, people she thought of as friends suddenly treated her like she was a danger to their values and beliefs, despite most knowing her for her entire life.

She braced herself for the madness to begin again. That was how she'd started doing so many different jobs. It was a way to make ends meet. She looked out over the studio and hoped the customers she had would trust her to run her own business and wouldn't care who she paid to change the oil and spark plugs in their lawn mower. How much would it take before Rhea gave up and left?

She had watched this town drain the life out of Ashley to the point where she wouldn't leave the house, until finally something broke. Ashley knew the farm had been Morgan's family home, and she would never want to leave. So in the end Ashley hadn't asked her to go. She gave in, gave up, and walked away. By the time Morgan had gathered the courage to fight for her, it had been too late.

Morgan shuddered. A warning voice whispered in the recesses of her mind. *People don't change.* She clenched her jaw. Ashley had changed and she had worked for years to prove it. Ashley hadn't failed. She had lost hope when she lost the church, her family, and her friends. *I wasn't enough and I didn't fight hard enough to save her.* Morgan drew in a deep breath and resolved not to let the same thing happen to Rhea.

❖

Rhea listened to the rain hammer against the tin roof of the workshop. She sat on the floor and studied the diagram of the Ford engine. There was something soothing in the rhythmic thrum of the rain and the smell of dirt and grease from the old tractor. She ran her fingers across the diagram and cataloged the parts laid out on the floor in front of her. There was so much more going on than just a bunch of parts, grease, and gasoline. The tractor had lived a life of purpose, and the scars were evident in its faded red paint, the rust eating at its bones and the remnants of some long-ago crop in a faraway field caked in its crevices like wrinkles etched in skin.

She had removed the old nests of mice she found under the engine cover. The rodents had done a number on the electrical and hoses, but those would have needed to be replaced anyway. Something thudded against the rear wall of the shop, and Rhea jumped. She stared at the wall, her heart thundering in her chest, and her skin crawled as if every cell in her body had gone on alert.

After a few minutes of silence, she shook herself. She was used to all sorts of noises coming from the animals in the barn, but nothing should have been able to hit the wall of the shop. She glanced at the clock. It was two in the morning. Rhea listened. She tried to make out any sounds that stood out against the hammering of the rain on metal but didn't hear anything out of place. She licked her lips and convinced herself she was being paranoid. There was no way anyone would be out in this weather, in the middle of nowhere, at this hour of the morning. Maybe Morgan was stirring about, checking the animals again.

Rhea rubbed her hand across the back of her neck and sighed. That could be it. She'd seen Morgan out all hours of the night walking the land, checking the animals, or spending all night in her studio. Rhea often wondered what kept Morgan up at night and how she found the energy to do so many things. Rhea was daydreaming and was surprised to find her thoughts had drifted to the gentle sound of Morgan's voice and the calm resolve that was always so clear in her eyes. Instantly the tense muscles in her shoulders began to relax as if she had been lulled into a peaceful dream. How did that happen? How did the thought of Morgan always manage to soothe her?

Rhea smiled and put the diagram aside. Maybe she should call it a night. A loud crash in the back room had her scrambling to her feet. Every cell in her body hummed with adrenaline. She picked up a crowbar from the nearest shelf and gripped it in her fist. The cold bite of metal against her skin grounded her, and she drew in a deep breath to steady herself. She moved to the back of the workshop and listened for any other sign of an intruder. She stepped up to the storeroom door and took a deep, steadying breath. Her heart pounded against her eardrums, and she fought to focus on the present. Her mind drifted and she was suddenly eight years old, standing at her bedroom door, listening for her father's footfall in the hallway. Her nails bit into the palm of her hand, and she swallowed the panic welling up in her throat.

Rhea shook her head and rubbed her hand across her face.

She couldn't go back there. She had to keep it together. She pushed against the door and winced at the creak of the old hinges.

He's coming.

Rhea stepped through the door and peered into the darkness. She bolted toward the back door when she heard it slam shut. She raced after him. This had to stop. Her knees were weak, and she feared they would give way at any moment, but she was done hiding. If he wanted her, he would have to kill her.

Rhea scrambled around the corner of the barn, careened into hard muscle, and bounced off. She drew back the crowbar and screamed as a cold hand closed around her wrist and a strong arm slammed her against the barn.

"Rhea!"

Rhea fought to free herself. She couldn't let him win, not this time, not ever again.

"Rhea, stop it, it's me."

Rhea struggled and cried. "Stop. Please. Stop."

"Okay, Rhea. Listen to me."

The strong hand wrenched the crowbar from her grip. Rhea waited, her eyes clenched as she tried to shut out what was happening to her. She couldn't look at him. She hated that look in his eyes.

"Rhea, I'm going to let go. I need you to calm down."

The grip on her arms loosened.

"Rhea, look at me. Come on, Rhea, open your eyes."

Rhea drew in a shaky breath and opened her eyes. She frowned, and it took a moment for the past to separate from the present.

"Come on, Rhea, it's me."

Rhea blinked as reality settled the torrent of fear ravaging her mind. "Morgan?" Rhea gasped.

Morgan smiled. "Hey, there."

Rhea's mind raced as she tried to put together the pieces and tried to make sense of what was happening. Morgan's body was pressed against hers and cold rain pelted against her face. Morgan took a step back, and Rhea instantly missed the warmth of her body and wanted to reach out for her.

"What's going on out here? And what's with the crowbar?"

Rhea's gaze settled on the heavy metal bar in Morgan's hand. "Oh God, Morgan, I'm so sorry."

Morgan shook her head. "Just tell me what happened."

Rhea started to shiver. "I heard something in the storeroom. I thought I saw someone run out and I followed them. I didn't realize it was you."

Morgan looked around. "I wasn't in the storeroom. It wasn't me."

Rhea clenched her jaw. "I saw someone," she said through gritted teeth.

"Okay," Morgan said and raised her hand. "I believe you. I'm just saying it wasn't me."

Rhea's legs went weak with relief, and she fought the urge to be sick. She'd almost hit Morgan. She didn't want to think of that. She would never hurt Morgan.

"Whoever it was is long gone now. Let's go see what they were doing in the storeroom."

Rhea nodded.

Morgan flipped the switch just inside the door and light flooded the room. A crate was turned over on the floor and spools of wire and bolts were everywhere.

"Did you do this?" Morgan asked.

Rhea shook her head. "That must have been the crash I heard. That's what made me come back here."

A muscle jumped at the side of Morgan's jaw, and Rhea held her breath. There was no reason for Morgan to believe her. It didn't make sense for anyone to be out there in this weather.

"Are you okay?"

Rhea was stunned. She'd expected Morgan to doubt her, question what she saw. But Morgan didn't do that. "I'm okay." She looked around the room and tried to figure out what someone would want in there. She frowned as a thought occurred to her. "What were you doing out here, this late at night?"

"I couldn't sleep, and I thought I heard something outside. I came out to check on things."

That made sense. If Morgan heard something too maybe someone really had been out there. She wasn't imagining things. She didn't want to admit that she had gotten caught up in the past and lost it. "I'm sorry I almost hit you."

Morgan shook her head. "You didn't expect it to be me. I might have done the same thing."

Rhea laughed. "Right. I didn't see you carrying a crowbar. I can't imagine you hurting anybody."

Morgan stared at Rhea. She wasn't sure what was going on, but Rhea had been out of it, and she was certain Rhea would have clubbed her if she hadn't stopped her. But Rhea was right. "No, I wouldn't. But I'm not going to let someone hurt me either."

Rhea bit her lip. "What do we do now?"

Morgan shrugged. "I guess we check around, take another good look in the morning, and move on."

Rhea frowned. "Aren't you going to call the police?"

Morgan looked away. "No. Not until we find something missing or damaged. This could have just been someone trying to get in out of the weather."

Morgan watched the questions and doubt flicker in Rhea's eyes. She believed Rhea, but she couldn't involve the police. That would just place more suspicion on Rhea after everything else that had been going on. There had been a moment when Rhea wasn't reacting to her, like Rhea was stuck somewhere in her past where her fear blinded her to what was real. Was it possible that Rhea had imagined it all, and the noise she'd heard had been Rhea blundering around in the dark? No. It wouldn't help anyone to involve the police. Not until she had some proof someone had been there.

"Come on. Let's go see about the rest of the farm. I need to see about the studio and the animals. There isn't much more around here anyone would be interested in."

Rhea nodded. "Do you want me to go to the barn while you check the studio?"

"No. I don't want us to split up in case someone is lurking around. Do you have a flashlight in the shop?"

"Sure. Give me a minute."

Rhea retreated into the shop, and Morgan studied the room. She moved the crate aside and found a large muddy footprint. She shifted some things around, but the rest of the mud in the room was scuffed and no patterns stood out. This one footprint was all she had, and there was one thing for certain—this was not Rhea's footprint, not unless she was sloshing around in a pair of size twelve mud boots. She put the crate down. What did it mean?

"Got it," Rhea said as she rushed back into the room.

Morgan smiled to defuse the tension. "Do you mind checking the barn first? I'd like to make sure the animals are okay."

Rhea's smile was uneasy, but she agreed. "Sure."

Morgan took the flashlight and stepped out into the rain.

❖

"Come inside for a bit, there's something I'd like to talk to you about," Morgan said as they closed up the shop.

Rhea was relieved they hadn't found any sign of anyone lurking around, but she was still afraid Morgan thought she was crazy. She paused on the porch uncertain what to expect. "What's up?" Rhea asked.

"Let's go inside." Morgan kept walking. "I'm cold and wet and my bones are starting to ache."

Rhea tensed. She and Morgan had done a lot of work together since her revelation, but they hadn't talked about that night since. She wasn't sure she was ready to play twenty questions with her past. She considered brushing Morgan off with an excuse, but she couldn't think of any reason that made any sense. If she was honest, part of her trepidation was because she enjoyed being with Morgan. She gave up looking for a way out and followed Morgan to the house. She focused on the sound of the rain and timed her footsteps to Morgan's. She was soothed by the rhythm of their strides and the slosh of their boots against the sodden earth.

Rhea stopped just inside the door where the memory of the first time she met Morgan made her stop. She stooped and took off her boots. There was no way she was making that mistake again, no matter how tempted she was by the alluring warmth of the fire.

She waited while Morgan hung their coats by the door.

"Coffee?" Morgan asked.

Rhea shook her head. "No, thanks." She winced at the slight catch in her voice, but Morgan didn't seem to notice and went on into the kitchen. Rhea watched Morgan move around the room and couldn't keep her eyes off her. She recalled the feel of Morgan's body pressed against her when they had run into each other outside the barn. There had been a moment when the fear subsided and she realized she was in Morgan's arms. She had wanted to put her arms around Morgan and bury her face against her.

Morgan must have thought she was out of her mind. First she'd had a complete meltdown after the incident at the diner, and now she'd practically attacked Morgan over some noises in the dark.

"Come on in and have a seat," Morgan said as she sat down in the big chair by the fire.

Rhea jumped at the sound of Morgan's voice. She'd been totally lost in her thoughts and forgotten what she was doing. She took a seat on the sofa across from Morgan.

"There's something I need to talk to you about," Morgan said as she leaned forward and placed her elbows on her knees.

Rhea's stomach lurched, and she automatically expected bad news.

"I've been thinking about what happened in town, and I've received a few calls. The chief of police has let me know there may be trouble brewing."

Rhea closed her hands around her knees until the pain distracted her enough to keep her grounded in the moment. It wouldn't do any good to panic before she heard Morgan out. "What kind of trouble?"

Morgan shook her head. "I'm not sure. But having someone sneaking around the farm at night has me worried. I can't think of anyone who would bother us out here, but people have surprised me before."

"Why didn't you call the police tonight?" Rhea asked.

Morgan sighed. "I wanted to talk to you first. I don't want to bring the sheriff into this if it'll cause more problems for you."

Rhea tried to understand Morgan's logic. "How would that cause problems for me?"

"I'm not sure. I don't really have any evidence that anyone was here, and I don't want anyone looking at you for trouble."

Rhea clenched her jaw. "Isn't that what I am?"

"No, you're not. And I think it's time the people of this town learned that too."

Rhea studied Morgan but couldn't figure out what she was up to. "What does that mean?"

Morgan smiled. "I think it's time you get out there and meet people. Let them get to know you. You've been here on the farm for months with hardly anyone seeing you. It might look like you're trying to hide. I think people only fear what they don't know and what they don't understand."

Rhea shook her head. "You saw what happened at the diner. Do you really want me to walk into a fight?"

Morgan moved to the sofa and sat beside Rhea. She placed her hand on Rhea's knee and met her gaze. "Not a fight, I just think that people will feel better when they see the real you, not some monster they've conjured in their minds."

Rhea blew out a breath. She had promised herself to never be a victim again. Morgan was asking her to stand up and fight for her place in the world, and she wanted to, but someone was already lurking around the farm. What would this mean for Morgan? "What happens when those people out there turn on you? I know what my risks are, but are you sure you understand what you have to lose here?"

Rhea's breath caught when Morgan took her hand, lacing their fingers together.

"It won't come to that," Morgan said.

Rhea's throat went dry, and all she could think of was the feel of Morgan's hand wrapped around hers.

"You don't know that," Rhea whispered. She scanned Morgan's face and was drawn into the tenderness of her eyes and the confidence in her voice. Rhea looked away when her gaze landed on Morgan's lips. She pulled away from Morgan. God, what was she doing? "I'm not someone you need to save, Morgan."

Morgan reached for her hand again and the touch made her look back. Morgan looked sad and the grip around Rhea's heart tightened.

Morgan gripped her hand tighter. "This is as much about saving myself as it is you."

The warmth of Morgan's hand was like a lifeline holding her on course, and Rhea marveled at her need to have Morgan believe she was worth saving. "The world gave up on me a long time ago, but not you. You don't need to be saved. I've seen how people react to you. They love you."

Morgan pulled Rhea's hand into her lap and squeezed.

Rhea stopped breathing. She didn't understand her need for Morgan's trust, her need for her friendship, or this new infatuation with just being near her. As far back as she could remember, she had hated physical contact with anyone. The new craving for closeness was completely foreign, and she had no idea what it meant or what to do about it.

Rhea held on to Morgan's hand and took a steadying breath. "What do you want me to do?"

Morgan smiled. "Just trust me."

CHAPTER NINE

Morgan slid the last box out of the truck and closed the tailgate. She tried to act normal, but her insides were in knots. It was the first week in April, time for the Spring Arts Festival, and she smiled at Rhea as they started toward the crowd. The festival was a local event put on every year to raise money and supplies for the area no-kill animal shelter. Most of the town would be there, and it would be Rhea's first test.

Morgan wondered if this was a good idea. Rhea looked like she was about to climb out of her skin and was more than a little jumpy, but she was handling things better than expected, considering what she'd been through. Rhea had to be worried about how people would react to her, but Morgan was certain this was what they needed to do to let people see the good in Rhea, not the monster they wanted to believe in.

"You ready?" Morgan asked as she bumped Rhea's shoulder with her own.

Rhea pushed back playfully. "No, but that's not going to stop me."

"Hey, Morgan."

Morgan looked up at the sound of her name. Her friend Alex was heading her way with a familiar mischievous grin on her face. Morgan was relieved to see someone she trusted. Having Rhea meet Alex was the first step in her plan.

"Hey, Alex," Morgan replied. She set the box down and embraced Alex with a warm hug. "I'm glad you could make it."

Alex slapped Morgan on the back. "I wouldn't miss it," she said before she let go. "Just promise me I won't have to take any of this year's representatives home with me. If I bring home one more dog, Christian will kill me."

Morgan laughed. "Speaking of Christian, where is she?"

Alex shrugged. "She couldn't make it. She still works part-time out of the New Orleans office and had some things come up."

"That's too bad." It was always good to see Alex, and it would have been comforting to lose herself in their familiar banter, but her attention was on Rhea, who stood to the side, watching with an awkward expression.

"She'll wish she was here after the puppy parade." Morgan slid her arm playfully around Alex's shoulder. "Come here, there's someone I want you to meet," she said as she gestured to Rhea. "Alex, this is my friend and work associate, Rhea Daniels." She turned to Rhea. "Rhea, this is my friend and fellow artist, Alex Moore."

Rhea extended her hand and smiled at Alex. Morgan could see the shimmer of distrust in her eyes but was pleased by Rhea's effort to get to know her friend.

"Ah, you're the new girl in town who's finally made Morgan admit she needed some help." Alex shook Rhea's hand enthusiastically. "I'm very glad to meet you, Rhea, and good job. Maybe with your help, I'll see Morgan more than every three months or so."

Rhea glanced at Morgan and smiled back at Alex. "I'll do what I can."

Morgan picked up her box and grimaced toward Alex. "Please tell me you've already set up the booth."

Alex smiled. "Of course I did. Someone's got to keep your head above water."

Morgan was happy Alex had agreed to work the event with her and Rhea. It would help to have another trusted face around if any problems emerged. Alex was a good friend and no stranger to the challenges of moving to a small town.

An hour later they didn't have time to worry about anything, other than if they had made enough of the custom dog tags Morgan designed for the event. Rhea was in charge of money and packaging, which meant she had to talk to every person who made a purchase. To her credit, she'd managed to win over the majority of the patrons, young and old.

When the crowd began to thin, Morgan took a minute to check on Rhea. "Good job today. How are you feeling?"

"Tired," Rhea answered.

Morgan laughed. "Tired? You work harder than this on the farm."

"Yeah, but I don't have to talk to people all day there. This is exhausting."

Morgan laughed again. "Well, you did great. I think things will die down quite a bit now. The puppy parade is always a big draw."

The puppy parade was the last event of the evening, so they packed up early to enjoy the show. It wasn't long before Alex found a new friend, and Morgan couldn't resist giving her a hard time about the three-legged cat she had adopted, named Tripod. She was the last cat of the day to find a home, and Alex hadn't been able to let her go back to the shelter without any of her feline friends.

"I thought you said Christian would kill you if you brought home another pet."

Alex shrugged and smiled mischievously. "I said she'd kill me if I brought home another *dog*. She didn't say we couldn't have a cat. Besides, look at her, she needs us."

Morgan laughed. "I'm sure that's what she meant."

A wave of unease began to creep across Morgan's skin, and she instinctively turned to find Rhea. She started to panic when she didn't see Rhea close by.

"What is it?" Alex asked.

"Have you seen Rhea?"

Alex looked around. "No. I hadn't noticed we'd lost her."

Morgan peered through the crowd. "I think I'll go back and see if I can find her."

Alex frowned. "I'm sure she's fine."

"I know. I'll just feel better if I know where she is and see that she's okay."

Alex took Morgan's arm. "*Is* everything okay? This isn't like you, Morgan."

Morgan sighed. "Rhea's had a hard time, and there's been a little trouble with some of the folks in town."

Alex's grip tightened on her arm. "What kind of trouble?"

Morgan started walking and pulled Alex along with her. "I can't explain right now. I just need to find her."

"Okay. The last time I saw her, we were at the adoption pens."

Morgan nodded and changed course. She pushed through the crowd to the field behind the parade where the adoption tent was set up. The moment her eyes fell on Rhea the relief was like surfacing for air after being held underwater. Rhea was sitting on the ground in front of a large dog kennel. She looked small and fragile sitting like a child on the ground as she talked to a very large German shepherd. The dog was completely black and its eyes were like glistening black pearls looking back at Rhea. Its long pink tongue lolled in a goofy smile.

"Well, I guess we found her." Alex set the pet carrier down and crossed her arms across her chest and smiled.

"Yeah," Morgan answered.

"She looks okay to me."

Morgan caught the humor in Alex's voice and smiled. Alex was looking at her with that *I know you* look, and Morgan didn't want to answer any of the questions that were brewing in Alex's mind. She turned to Alex and gripped her shoulder with one hand. "Will you look after Rhea for a few minutes?" She held Alex's gaze. "I have something I need to do."

Alex sighed. "Okay, but after this you've got a lot of explaining to do."

Morgan smiled. "I promise. Thanks."

She was surprised this hadn't occurred to her sooner. Without question she knew she was doing the right thing. "Hi," Morgan said as she entered the tent, "can you tell me about the German shepherd you have outside?"

The young girl perched behind the folding table smiled up at Morgan. "Oh my gosh, yes. That's Soldier. We just got him a few days ago. It's sad really. He's a war dog, you know what I mean? He actually went to war. He's retired now, but his owner, a local guy he was with over there, was killed in a motorcycle crash last month. The guy's family tried, but they just can't manage him."

"How sad," Morgan said.

"Tell me about it. He should have a medal for what he's done. He doesn't deserve this."

Morgan nodded. "I agree, and I'd like to do something about that."

Ten minutes later Morgan stepped up behind Rhea and Alex, still hanging out with Soldier. "Looks like the puppy parade is winding down. Are you guys ready to go home?"

Alex was eyeing her with a grin, and Rhea just looked sad.

"Hey, Morgan, where've you been?" Rhea said as she glanced up.

"Around. You ready?"

Rhea sighed and brushed her fingers across Soldier's nose through the bars of his crate. "Got to go, buddy."

Rhea stood up and dusted off her jeans. When she turned around Morgan handed her a leash and tried not to smile at the confused look on her face.

"What's this for?" Rhea asked.

"Well, the farm is a little wild, but the city and the park require you to have your dog on a leash." Morgan waited for the point to sink in.

"What?" Rhea's eyes grew wide. "Are you serious?"

"He's been through a lot and he'll need to be with you almost all the time. I thought you'd be the perfect person to help Soldier out. Do you mind?"

Rhea's mouth fell open. "He's really mine?" she whispered.

Morgan nodded. "You're his."

Rhea instantly transformed from disbelieving to jubilant. She threw her arms around Morgan and hugged her close. The instant Rhea touched her, the world around Morgan melted away, and there was nothing but the feel of Rhea's body against hers. She'd been worried that she might be overstepping by giving Rhea a dog, but Rhea needed Soldier as much as he needed her. Rhea needed to belong to someone, have a connection to another living being, and a dog could give her love without taking, and security that Rhea couldn't trust in a person. Morgan closed her eyes, breathed deeply, and relished Rhea's happiness.

Morgan swayed on her feet when Rhea released her, and she tried to push aside the loneliness that replaced the warmth of her touch.

Rhea kneeled and opened the crate and snapped the leash onto the dog's collar. "Come on, boy, we're going home."

Soldier rewarded Rhea with a gentle head-butt and licked her face in affirmation of their pairing. Morgan's reservations vanished at the sight of the two together.

"Excuse me, but is there something you'd like to tell me?" Alex asked with a sly grin.

"I don't know what you're talking about," Morgan answered.

Alex raised an eyebrow. "That's not what I see."

Morgan frowned and turned to her friend. "There's nothing going on, Alex. I'm just trying to help. She needs it, even if she won't admit it. She doesn't have anyone else."

Alex patted her on the back. "Sounds like someone else I know."

Morgan shook her head. "This isn't about me."

Alex smiled. "However you want to explain this, your heart is in it and that makes it about you."

"Alex…"

Alex put her hands up. "No worries. I like her. And the fact that you like her makes her special. Just be careful, buddy."

Morgan nodded. "Thanks."

Rhea and Soldier looked like the celebration was ready to move forward.

"Ready?" Morgan asked Rhea.

Rhea smiled and Morgan's heart melted. "Yeah, we're ready."

Soldier let out a resounding bark followed by a toothy grin. Morgan laughed. "Let's go home."

❖

Rhea shivered against the cold night air, wondering when winter would finally loosen its grip and the temperature would manage to stay above forty degrees at night. She pulled the blanket closer under her chin and listened to the crackle of the fire as she watched Soldier sleep on the large pillow shaped like a giant doughnut. The instant she'd seen him, she had fallen in love. There was something haunted in his eyes that spoke to her, and somehow she knew this dog understood her.

She marveled at how much her life had changed in just a few short weeks. If she thought about it too much, she found it difficult to imagine either her past or her present was real. Her past and all its pain was a nightmare, and sometimes she wanted to believe she had made the whole thing up in her imagination. But her present didn't feel real either. She felt like an imposter, pretending to be someone she wasn't. She sighed. Where did she belong?

Soldier groaned in his sleep and began to whine. Rhea's heart hurt for him. What terrors haunted him in his sleep? Did he understand what had happened to him? As if reading her thoughts, Soldier opened his eyes, raised one eyebrow and met her gaze as if asking a question.

"It's okay, boy. We're going to be okay."

Apparently accepting her word, he shifted his head onto his paws with a satisfied sigh.

Rhea smiled to herself, pleased that he was there. It was strange to worry about something other than herself and wonder about his thoughts, his feelings, and his happiness. She'd grown up around animals on the farm but hadn't been allowed to have pets. Her mother thought they were too dirty to be inside, and she had learned not to get attached to the farm animals that were often sold or ended up as dinner.

Rhea shuddered at the sudden memory of her father forcing her to kill her favorite laying hen. The chicken was the closest thing she'd had to a friend. Rhea bit down on her tongue, a trick she learned to stave off tears until she could transform her hurt into anger.

She chuckled at the irony of her life. Her father had taught her the cruel truth of life and death and the callousness it took to harm those she loved. In the end it had been that very lesson that had given her the strength to kill him.

Rhea shut her eyes and tried to push the memories away. Her past was a part of her she couldn't escape, but she didn't have to let it determine who she would become.

Soldier groaned again, and Rhea opened her eyes to see him watching her. She got up and went to him. She kneeled and kissed his head and crawled onto the pillow beside him. When she put her arm around him, he lay back against her and stretched his long legs. Rhea curled her fingers into his fur and buried her face in his neck. She liked this new life, and maybe if she pretended long enough, it would become real.

She grinned into Soldier's neck. She had a lot to be thankful for now, and it all started with Morgan. The instant her mind drifted to Morgan, a warm sensation blanketed her as if Morgan's arms were wrapped around her. Rhea smiled to herself and allowed images of Morgan to play across her mind. A slow stir began to tickle her inside until it pulsed low in her belly with each beat of her heart. Morgan had become important to her and made her feel things she'd believed she'd never feel, like trust and friendship. But there was something more that Rhea didn't quite understand. She got excited when she knew she'd be seeing Morgan, and she was lonely when Morgan wasn't around. Rhea sighed and drifted off to sleep, thinking of Morgan.

❖

Rhea woke with a start as a low growl rumbled through Soldier's chest. Instantly she was on alert, all her senses focused in anticipation of danger. She held her hand against Soldier's chest and absorbed the vibrations of his warning. She couldn't hear anything outside, but she trusted Soldier. She glanced around at all the windows. It was light out. She got up, and Soldier stood and went to the door and started scratching at the doorknob. His actions weren't frantic or even aggressive, but he made it clear he wanted out.

Rhea pulled back the curtain covering the small window in the door. She didn't see anything out of place. No one was there. Hesitantly she turned the lock and opened the door.

"Wait," she said in command to Soldier. He stood by her side obediently, waiting as she stepped outside. She still didn't see or hear anything. "Okay, Soldier, come on, boy."

Soldier walked close beside her until they had made a complete lap around the cabin. Rhea was about to go back inside when she heard an ATV engine start, and Soldier began to bark. Rhea ran to the side of the cabin just in time to see someone disappear over the ridge. She was too far away to see who it was, but the familiar uneasy feeling in her gut was back. It could have been anyone this time of year. It could have even been Morgan out checking the property or just out for a ride, but her instincts said no. She was certain she would recognize Morgan from any distance, and she doubted Soldier would have had a protective response to her.

She patted Soldier on the head. "Good boy."

Soldier looked up at her and wagged his tail. Rhea smiled, grateful to have him by her side.

"Come on, let's go for a walk."

Rhea turned toward the barn and Morgan's house. If anyone had been messing around the farm again, she wanted to make sure Morgan was safe.

They found Morgan in her workshop. She wasn't hard to find—Rhea just followed the sound of the heavy hammer hitting metal. She knocked, but there was no way Morgan would ever hear her over all that pounding, so she let herself inside. Rhea stood at the door and watched Morgan swing the hammer over and over against the red-hot metal. She wore a thick leather apron and goggles covered her eyes. The black T-shirt she wore fit tight against the taut muscles that flexed and bulged with each strike of her hammer. Her skin glistened with streaks of sweat and soot that made her look like a warrior.

Rhea didn't want to move. She was mesmerized by the strength and precision of Morgan's body and the intense focus on her face. Morgan was a picture of power and strength, woven together with grace and creativity. For a moment Rhea wondered if Morgan was human. She looked more like a goddess, the embodiment of truth, sincerity, integrity, and raw strength.

Something stirred inside Rhea, and she had the sudden desire to be close to Morgan. Her breath quickened, and she wanted to touch her, feel the raw power in her muscles and the tenderness of her skin. To her dismay her idol worship was interrupted when Soldier decided to announce their presence with a bark hello, as he ran over to lean against Morgan's leg.

Morgan put the hammer down and removed the goggles. When she looked up at Rhea, the flickering light from the flames danced in her eyes. For just a moment, Rhea imagined there was a flash of the devil in the angel's eyes.

"Hey," Morgan said as she wiped sweat from her brow. "What are you two up to?"

"Patrol," Rhea answered seriously. She was still trying to shake the spell she had been under and hoped Morgan hadn't noticed her fluster. "We saw someone on an ATV heading over the back ridge, and we came down to check on you."

Morgan frowned. "Hmm. I can see Soldier here has gone right to work. Any idea who it was?"

Rhea shook her head. "I didn't get a good look, but after the other night, I thought it'd be a good idea to look around."

Morgan took off her apron and wiped her face with a towel. "Good idea."

Rhea squared her shoulders, proud Morgan trusted her. She still expected Morgan to discount her fear, but she surprised her every time. "You don't have to stop your work. Soldier and I can look around."

Morgan smiled and laid her hand on Rhea's shoulder. "I know you could, but I'd like the break and the company."

It was like butterflies had just hatched in Rhea's stomach. She focused her attention on Morgan's hand on her shoulder and was surprised that she didn't want to pull away. She liked the feel of Morgan's touch. So much so, she didn't want Morgan to take her hand away.

But Morgan did move away, and the disappointment morphed into a craving that obliterated all other thought. Rhea shivered at the loss of the connection.

Morgan stepped closer. "Are you okay? I'm sorry. I don't mean to hurt you, I just don't think sometimes."

Rhea grabbed Morgan's hand without thinking. "You didn't. I liked...I mean, it's okay."

Morgan stared at her with a curious expression that made Rhea wonder if Morgan could read her thoughts. Her gaze was questioning, and Rhea caught a glimpse of something vulnerable with a touch of fear, and she wanted to know what Morgan was thinking that could cause so much emotion in just one look. Rhea looked away, effectively breaking the spell. It was like she'd been caught peering at Morgan through the window of her private world and had seen too much. Morgan stepped away and Rhea's fingers slipped through her hand.

Morgan whistled and called Soldier to her.

Rhea's mind swam with questions as she followed Morgan to the barn. She was confused about her feelings for Morgan. She had never wanted to touch anyone the way she wanted to touch her. She had never wanted to know things about anyone the way she wanted to know Morgan, and she had no idea what this meant. She had no idea what was happening to her, but she hoped she figured it out soon.

The moment they stepped into the barn, Rhea knew something was wrong. There was horse feed scattered across the floor, and by what she could count, every bag they had in storage had been opened.

Morgan leaned down and scooped up a handful of feed. Soldier sniffed the ground vigorously and promptly sat in front of the tack room door.

Dread filled Rhea as Morgan pushed the tack room door open and gasped. The room was trashed. Morgan pushed through the scattered papers, bridles, and trash and stepped into the room. Her gaze landed on a pile of black pellets in the center of her desk, and she pinched the metal balls between her finger and thumb and held them up to the light. Rhea watched the muscle at the side of her jaw jump.

Everything had been ripped from the walls and thrown on the floor. Red paint covered everything. Morgan picked up a spray can from the floor, and Rhea's mouth went dry. She recognized the paint she had bought at the hardware store when she'd gone into town for the feed order.

Morgan turned to Rhea. "I think you need to tell me everything you remember about that ATV you saw earlier. We've got a problem."

❖

Morgan fell onto the sofa and covered her eyes. Not only was her entire supply of feed ruined, she had been forced to call the police. It was like handing the sheriff Rhea's head on a stick. He'd been very emphatic in his explanation that all the evidence pointed to Rhea. She had access and was the last one to handle the feed or go into the barn, and she was the only one who had seen the alleged intruder on both occasions. His mind was made up, and she doubted much would be done other than making trouble for Rhea.

She pulled a handkerchief from her pocket and unfolded it so that the contents she had gathered earlier wouldn't be lost. A small mound of tiny metal beads rested like eggs in a nest in the palm of her hand. She cringed at the thought of the metal mixed with the wasted animal feed, but she had a feeling the pellets weren't meant for the animals. This was a message, and it pointed directly at Rhea. Why else would anyone leave behind shotgun pellets? Rhea had shot her father with a shotgun, but what was the point in all of this?

Morgan's head hurt. She needed to get smart fast if she was going to help Rhea and put a stop to this mess. After today she wouldn't blame Rhea for leaving. Morgan groaned. Rhea had answered everyone's questions, but her tone had been flat and Morgan had felt the distrust radiate from her. By the time it was all over, Rhea's eyes had been stone cold, and she would barely look at Morgan. The sheriff had read that defensiveness as Rhea hiding something, but Morgan knew better. There was no way Rhea was behind any of this. But after the way the sheriff had talked to her, would Rhea believe she was still on her side?

Morgan got up and went to the kitchen. Desperate times called for desperate measures. She opened the freezer and dug around behind the frozen peas until her hand closed around her prize. She drew out the container and smiled as she removed the lid. Nothing settled a bad day like triple-chocolate fudge brownie ice cream, her favorite sin.

She didn't bother with a bowl. In a situation like this all she needed was a fork. She'd learned a long time ago that for serious ice cream, a fork was the best tool for the job. She scooped out a bite and groaned as the rich chocolate coated her tongue and the smooth cream began to melt away her stress. She returned to the comfort of the sofa and was lured by the mesmerizing flickering fire. Was she doing the right thing for Rhea or was she getting caught up in her own agenda? Rhea had become important to her, but she wasn't Ashley. How could Morgan expect the community to support a stranger like Rhea when they had turned so completely against one of their own?

Morgan took another bite of the ice cream. The difference was that Rhea wasn't asking for and didn't need their acceptance. She just needed to be left alone. Given time, Rhea would carve her own place in the town's eclectic landscape. But it was clear that someone was determined to make sure that didn't happen. The only way to end this was to figure out who was doing these things. *Seeing is believing.*

"Hmm. Maybe that's it. I need to see him." Morgan took another bite and set the container on the coffee table. She had a plan that might put an end to all of this. She'd have to call in a favor from a friend, but at least it was someone she trusted. But she'd have to tell Rhea her plan. She couldn't run the risk of her thinking she didn't trust her or that she was spying on her.

Morgan worked a frozen bit of brownie between her teeth and tried to imagine what all of this was like for Rhea. She couldn't imagine what it would feel like to have so many people judge her and condemn her, the way people had for most of Rhea's life. The similarities between Rhea and Ashley became clearer when she thought of how Rhea's family had turned against her. Ashley hadn't been able to see beyond the opinions and beliefs of her parents, and when the church rejected their relationship, she'd let their hatred destroy her.

Morgan got up and pushed the ice cream away. Ashley had always been lost. It had been like watching an eclipse as the thin shadow had slowly smothered the light in her heart until she'd disappeared completely. Morgan got up and put the ice cream away. She didn't know what she could have done different with Ashley. Somehow she had always known Ashley would leave her. She'd just never imagined she would do it the way she had.

Maybe this was about *her*. Maybe she was using Rhea to make peace with the ghosts in her past. But what choice did she have? The alternative was to watch Rhea be swallowed up and destroyed by other people's judgments, or let her leave without ever having a chance to prove her worth. The thought of Rhea leaving left a deep hollowness in her heart, and her body tensed. She cared for Rhea, more than she'd like to admit. She not only liked her, she respected her strength and her courage. It didn't matter why she would stand up for Rhea, it just mattered that she did.

Chapter Ten

The next morning Rhea stared out the window at the layer of fresh snow blanketing the ground. It was hard to wrap her head around the contrast between the stark white snow and the yellow daffodils, budding tulips, and smiling faces of the fresh pansies she and Morgan had planted in the flower beds in front of the cabin. It was like Old Man Winter had thrown one last punch before conceding to spring. Rhea cradled a steaming cup of coffee in her hands and took a deep breath and savored the nutty aroma, allowing the comforting smell and warmth to lure her into a dream state. The snow had perfectly hidden the new green shoots that had started to flourish under the longer days and warmer rays of sun. She had watched the land come to life as green grass transformed the gray, desolate landscape into a lush field. Rhea longed for the same miracle in her own life.

She sighed and decided not to get lost in the past again. She glanced down at Soldier and smiled. It was time to play. "Come on, Soldier, let's go out."

Soldier pressed his big head into her palm and leaned against her leg. She looked down into his big brown eyes and was certain he could read her mind. She rubbed between his ears and put on her coat. She was curious how he would react to the snow.

The instant he stepped into the snow he froze and then jumped back onto the porch. Cautiously he sniffed the snow until his nose was buried. She could hear his loud sniffs and snorts as he explored this new phenomenon. A moment later he brought his head up and had a two-inch pile of snow on his snout. Rhea laughed when he shook his head and snapped at the offensive clump as it fell. The next instant Soldier dived into the snow and jumped into the air and lunged into the snow again, until he finally ended up rolling around on the ground. When he stood, he looked like the abominable snow-dog.

Rhea made a snowball and threw it. She laughed until her sides hurt when Soldier ran after it, and came up from the snow looking totally confused when he couldn't find the ball.

"That sounds good," a familiar voice said from behind Rhea.

Rhea spun around just as Soldier bolted past her and jumped circles around Morgan. A flash of heat burned her face and warmed her deep inside the instant her eyes fell on Morgan.

"What's that?" Rhea asked.

"You were laughing. I don't think I've ever heard you laugh before. It sounded good."

Rhea smiled and stuffed her hands into her pockets to keep from fidgeting. She didn't know what to say.

"Would you and Soldier like to go sledding with me?"

Rhea's heart jumped with excitement. Her inner child screamed to play. "For real? You're going sledding?"

Morgan smiled and shrugged her shoulders. "I figure it's one of the reasons God made snow. It just calls for us to come out and play. Besides, snow in April is rare and this will melt fast. We better take advantage of it while we can."

Rhea grinned. "Is that so?"

"Yep. And I'm not one to disappoint the big guy."

Rhea's smile widened. "Well, in that case I guess I could help you out."

Morgan laughed. "Exactly. I'm sure it's meant to be a shared experience."

Rhea shook her head. "I can't believe I'm encouraging this." She walked closer to Morgan. "Where's the sled?"

Morgan pointed to the hill leading to the highest part of the ridge. "I left it over there. I was headed there when I saw you and Soldier playing. Come on, you'll see."

Rhea followed Morgan to the top of the hill as Soldier ran ahead, playing in the snow. The snow was only about three inches deep in most places, but drifts had formed along the path that made the walk feel more like a cross-country hike.

"I can't believe you actually have a snow sled," Rhea remarked.

"Well, to be honest, it isn't really mine. My nephews left it here last winter." Morgan dropped the plastic sled and steadied it with her foot. "Front or back?"

Rhea's jaw dropped. "What?"

Morgan pointed to the sled. "Do you want to be in front or in the back?"

Rhea stared at the sled, the image of Morgan's body wrapped around her stirring a tangle of emotions. She pictured herself in front of Morgan with Morgan's arms wrapped around her, and her shoulders stiffened. "I'll take the back."

"Okay," Morgan said with a mischievous grin, "just try not to fall off. You do remember what's under all that snow, right?"

Rhea wrinkled her nose as it occurred to her what Morgan meant. Cow poop.

Morgan sat on the sled and adjusted the rope. Rhea took a deep breath and sat down behind her. She stopped breathing when Morgan grabbed both her boots and pulled her feet in until their legs were intertwined.

Rhea gripped the sides of Morgan's coat, and Morgan wrapped her fingers around her hands and tugged them around her waist.

"You're going to have to lean in to me or we aren't going anywhere."

Rhea scooted forward and felt light-headed when she pressed against Morgan's back. Her heart raced, and she felt a surge of warmth between her legs.

Morgan pulled Rhea's arms around her and patted her hands. "Hold on."

Rhea leaned closer to Morgan, her breasts pressed against Morgan's back. Her nipples hardened and she was suddenly unseasonably warm. She brushed her chin against Morgan's shoulder and had the urge to press her face against Morgan's neck.

The thought unsettled her and part of her wanted to push away from Morgan and the current of want coiling in her center.

Morgan kicked the ground and gave the sled a push with her foot. An instant later they were soaring down the hill. Rhea was giddy from the rush. She tightened her grip and laughed when they hit a bump that almost tipped them over.

Soldier ran after them, barking as he bounded through the snow and nipped at the sled. Morgan let out a whoop of joy that made Rhea laugh even harder. She couldn't remember ever having so much fun.

Morgan pulled the sled to a stop at the bottom of the hill. Before Rhea could pull away, Morgan wrapped her hands around Rhea's and tilted her head back. Their faces were only inches apart, and Rhea could feel the warmth of Morgan's breath on her cheek. She looked at Morgan and was mesmerized by the shape of Morgan's lips as they curled into a smile.

"That was great," Morgan said. "Let's go again."

Rhea smiled and nodded her agreement.

"Great. Let's go," Morgan said as she stood and effortlessly pulled Rhea to her feet.

Rhea was caught off guard by Morgan's strength, and she stumbled into Morgan as she tried to regain her footing.

Morgan laughed. "Sorry." She held Rhea's hands close to her chest, their thighs touching. "Isn't this fun?"

Rhea couldn't help but laugh at the playfulness in Morgan's voice. "Yes."

Morgan's expression clouded and grew serious. "I'm sorry about yesterday."

Rhea swallowed and looked away. She was unsettled by the sudden change and could feel her defenses slam into place.

"I hate it that the sheriff gave you such a hard time." Morgan placed a finger under Rhea's chin and lifted until Rhea had no choice but to meet her eyes. "I know you didn't do it. I had to call them so it was on record that something is going on here, but we're going to figure this out."

Rhea took a deep breath and nodded. She hadn't blamed

Morgan for calling the police, and she wasn't surprised when they treated her like the enemy, but it still hurt. "It's no biggie. You did what you had to do. I get it."

Morgan gripped Rhea's hands together in hers. Something in Morgan's touch was uncertain and hesitant, as if Morgan was about to deliver bad news. Rhea was worried now, and she braced herself.

"What are you trying to tell me, Morgan?"

Morgan didn't just look at her—she looked into her as if she could see through to her soul. "There are going to be some people around here later. I'm acting as if they're having some work done on a horse trailer that we'll pull into the main barn, but that isn't the real reason they'll be here."

Rhea was confused. "Okay, do you want me to get lost or something?"

"What? No, of course not."

"What is it then? You're freaking me out."

Morgan smiled. "My friends will be installing cameras around the barn and maybe some other places. I thought it would be a good idea to keep an eye out and see if we can figure out who's been lurking around. I don't want anyone knowing about this besides you. Maybe we can catch this guy if he comes back again."

Rhea was starting to understand. "Why are you telling me?"

"I told you." Morgan cupped Rhea's cheek in her hand. "I know you didn't toss the horse feed and trash the tack room. And I don't want you to think I'm spying on you. The police aren't going to do anything, so it's up to us."

Rhea nodded. It was a smart plan, and she was relieved Morgan believed her. "What do you need me to do?"

Morgan's gaze on her was so intense Rhea shivered. Morgan cradled her face in her hand as if she was something fragile. Morgan brushed her thumb across her cheek, and Rhea had the sudden urge to lean in to her touch. She wasn't used to the closeness and tried not to let her imagination get the best of her. Morgan was only trying to reassure her.

"Thanks for understanding. Just do what you always do. Nothing changes."

Morgan stared at her for a moment as if struggling with something. Rhea was frozen in place, unable to move. Morgan was so close, their lips only inches apart. Rhea could feel the warmth of Morgan's breath on her skin, and she licked her lips to taste the heat between them. Was Morgan about to kiss her?

Morgan squeezed her hand and stepped away. Rhea instantly missed her touch and craved the closeness between them. She had been so afraid Morgan would kiss her but was disappointed when she didn't.

Morgan reached down for the sled, but just before her hand closed around the rope, Soldier blundered past and snatched it away. He ran toward the hill with the sled bouncing along behind him.

Morgan looked shocked before the corners of her mouth lifted into an amused smile.

Rhea laughed. "I guess we better let him ride this time."

"I guess so."

Rhea took off at a run. "Race you to the top."

"Hey, no fair," Morgan called after her.

Morgan watched Rhea sprint ahead, and a heavy weight lifted from her heart. She hadn't realized how empty her life was until Rhea's laughter filled the barren space. She tried to calm the stir of desire that had kindled in her the moment she touched Rhea. A storm of emotions brewed in Rhea's eyes, and she had wanted to fall into them. She'd almost given in to the luring temptation of Rhea's lips. She had wanted to kiss her, and for a moment she'd thought Rhea wanted her to.

Morgan swallowed, the taste of regret lingering on her tongue. She might have initiated sledding as a way to ease the blow of her plan and the problems they were facing, but she was surprised to find herself having fun. It was a strange feeling, but she wouldn't mind more times like this when she could get lost in Rhea.

Rhea stopped a few feet ahead of her. "Hey, are you coming?"

Morgan smiled up at her. "Yeah, I just figured you could use the head start."

Rhea put her hands on her hips. "Really? All right then, let's see what you've got, slowpoke."

Morgan ran, and despite Rhea's efforts to outrun her, she caught up to her before they were halfway to the top. As she passed Rhea, she scooped up a handful of snow and rubbed it against Rhea's neck.

Rhea yelled, "Oh my God, you are so going to pay for that."

Morgan could hardly run for laughing. She turned around to boast of her win, and just as she shifted her head, a snowball caught her square on the nose. Her eyes stung and instantly filled with tears and she instinctively covered her face with her hands. An instant later Rhea ran into her and pushed her to the ground and fell on top of her.

"Ouch, nice shot." Morgan groaned. Her breath caught as Rhea's thigh slid between her legs and pressed against her tender sex. Instinctively she slid one hand around Rhea's waist pulling her closer.

"Oh, come on, you big baby, it was just a little snow," Rhea teased.

Morgan laughed and tried to pry her eyes open. She pulled her hand down and squinted at Rhea.

Rhea froze. Morgan blinked hard to clear her vision so she could make sense of the look of shock on Rhea's face. "What?"

Rhea pushed up on her elbow, causing her weight to shift and press even harder against Morgan. Morgan's brain was in complete meltdown as she tried to control the sudden surge of arousal. Rhea wiped her finger across Morgan's upper lip and held it up in front of her. It was red with blood.

Morgan stared at Rhea's finger in disbelief and wiped her mouth. She peered at Rhea with her best scowl and a slow grin began to curl at the edges of Rhea's lips. Morgan pinched the bridge of her nose between her thumb and forefinger. "What are you laughing at?"

Rhea shook her head and gripped Morgan's chin in her hand, turning Morgan's face from side to side as she inspected her with a crooked grin.

Morgan attempted another scowl, but her focus shattered when Rhea reached up and brushed a lock of hair off her cheek. Rhea was still smiling but looked like she had just discovered something.

"What?" Morgan asked softly.

Rhea chuckled. "You are human after all."

"Huh?" Morgan said, confused by the remark.

"It's nothing. Are you okay?"

Morgan touched her nose to see if the bleeding had stopped. To her relief it had. She stared into Rhea's eyes. They were soft and unguarded, brightened by joy and sunlight. Morgan was mesmerized by the deep pools of blue now void of the storm that usually clouded them. She licked her lips. "Looks like I'll live."

Rhea smiled. "I guess you will."

Morgan didn't want to move. Rhea felt wonderful lying in her arms. Their bodies fit together perfectly, and Morgan imagined what it would feel like to have Rhea naked against her, skin against skin.

For a moment Rhea looked as if she wanted to say something, and a slight frown creased her brow. Her lips parted slightly, and her gaze shifted to Morgan's mouth. She tensed and pushed away from Morgan as if she was suddenly afraid.

Morgan knew she should have moved away sooner, but she had been so lost in the closeness she didn't think of what Rhea would think if she realized how much the touch was affecting her.

"Hey, look," Morgan said as a distraction. She pointed to Soldier, who was lying in the snow with his chin on his paws, watching them with his best pound-puppy expression.

Rhea went and kneeled beside him. "It's okay, Soldier, she's all right."

Soldier wagged his tail and shifted his eyes to Morgan. Morgan sat up, scooted next to Rhea, and rubbed Soldier's head. "Sorry, boy. I didn't mean to scare you."

Soldier stood and bumped her chest with his head, then rested his paw on her shoulder. Morgan was touched by how attached he had become, and she was thankful he had found his way to Rhea. Morgan ruffled his fur and sighed as she met Rhea's eyes and smiled. It was as if the air around her had grown too thin, and the want brewing inside her threatened to boil over. If she didn't get a handle on her feelings, she was going to kiss Rhea.

Rhea stood and held out her hand to Morgan. Morgan took her

hand and pulled herself up. Rhea was so close their thighs touched, and Morgan swayed on her feet.

Rhea brushed her thumb across Morgan's cheek. "You still have a little blood on your face. We should go clean that up."

Morgan leaned in to Rhea's touch, unable to stop herself. She didn't want this time with her to end. "Rhea," Morgan whispered. Rhea's lips were so close all she had to do was shift forward and taste them.

Rhea pulled away, and it was as if all the warmth had been sucked out of Morgan's body. She longed for her. She cleared her throat and tried to regain her composure. "How about some hot chocolate?"

Rhea shrugged and shook her head. "Sorry, boss, I've got work to do."

Morgan grinned. "Right." She nodded toward the sled. "You might as well ride back down since we climbed all the way up here. Soldier's expecting his ride."

Rhea hesitated, and Morgan wondered what she was thinking. Rhea had been relaxed and playful, and now Morgan could feel the distance pushing between them again.

"I think it's safer for me to walk back. The bleeding could start up again if I get jarred around too much. Go on, let him have his ride."

Rhea glanced at the sled again. "Are you sure?"

"Of course. I'll see you at the bottom."

Rhea smiled and shrugged. "Okay then."

Morgan helped Rhea and Soldier settle onto the sled and gave them a push. She watched them streak down the slope, feeling the distance between them grow with each second. Soldier barked all the way and Rhea's laughter filled the air like musical notes drifting on the wind.

Morgan laughed. It had been a long time since she'd been so drawn to a woman or had so much fun.

CHAPTER ELEVEN

It was late and a full moon lit up the farm with an ethereal glow. Rhea liked working at night. It was easier to work than lie awake and will the memories away. She flipped on the light as she stepped into the shop and a few minutes later had the kerosene heater going. Soldier got comfortable in his shop bed after completing his usual circle dance and locating his favorite bone.

She picked up a wire brush and went to work, scraping away years of dirt and rust from one of the big tractor wheels. She went over the rough spots with sandpaper until they were smooth to the touch. Some of the damage was deep and took more time, but she loved this kind of work. The more tedious the task, the more lost she became in the detail. When she worked, the fear and hurt receded and she was able to feel like something she did made a difference.

Rhea focused on a particularly damaged area. She worked the edges of the wire brush along the curve of the wheel with more force than usual. Her grip slipped, and the brush crashed into her other hand and stabbed into her thumb.

"Ouch, dammit." She popped the injured thumb into her mouth and let the brush fall to the floor. She grabbed a paper towel from a roll on the workbench and looked at her thumb to survey the damage. There was a thin gash in the side where the skin had been peeled away and blood welled up from it as fast as she could wipe it away. As she stared at her thumb, the image of her brushing it across Morgan's lip flashed in her memory. Morgan's skin had been cold, and Rhea was surprised by how soft and smooth it was. Her skin had tingled and heat spread through her hand and up her arm. Rhea rubbed her finger and thumb together but couldn't replicate the sensation of touching Morgan's skin. She lifted her hand and touched her own lips, but it wasn't the same. Why had she felt the need to touch Morgan? It wasn't like her to touch anyone, but she had reached for Morgan without thinking.

Rhea thought back on their morning. Morgan had been playful and thoughtful, and Rhea had had fun, but there was more to what she was feeling. At first she had been afraid of getting on the sled with Morgan. She'd decided that being in the back would help her feel in control of what was happening, but the moment Morgan had pulled her legs around her and Rhea had wrapped her arms around Morgan, she had felt far from safe. But she hadn't been afraid of *Morgan*. She was afraid of how she felt about being so close to her. She was confused by how comfortably her body had fit against Morgan and intrigued by the contrast of strength and softness of Morgan's body. Mostly she had been mesmerized by the feel of her own breasts pressed against Morgan's back.

Rhea shook her head. Thank God, Morgan hadn't noticed what a mess she'd been. She wasn't herself when she was with Morgan. Rhea looked around the room for a first-aid kit as she wrapped her thumb in the paper towel. The best she could come up with was a roll of electrical tape, which she used to secure the paper towel in place. That would have to do for now.

She picked up the brush and tried to go back to work but her body was humming with energy, and she couldn't think about anything but Morgan. What was happening to her? Was this normal? Did women always feel this drawn to each other? Maybe she was just learning to be close to someone. She knew Morgan was a lesbian, but Morgan hadn't done anything to suggest any sexual interest. She had been relieved by that, but she'd also been a little disappointed. There had been a moment on the hill when she'd wanted Morgan to kiss her. Morgan wasn't like anyone she'd ever known. Morgan didn't treat her like she wanted something from her or she was trying to fill some agenda. Morgan was caring and honest and trusting and incredibly beautiful.

She thought of the sled again and how it felt to touch Morgan. *Am I a lesbian?* She'd known women who were with other women in prison, but she didn't know if that was because they were locked up or because they were gay. She'd never had any interest in any of them, so what was it? She'd assumed she hadn't been interested in the boys at school because of what her father did to her, but she'd never considered the girls either. She'd been content to stay hidden in her solitude, and her energy had been spent pretending her life was normal and protecting her secret. She'd never allowed herself to get close to anyone, for fear they would find out what she was hiding.

Rhea tossed the brush on the workbench in frustration. Whatever was happening, she had no idea what to do about it. Maybe she didn't have to do anything about it, and it would just go away. She liked her life the way it was and there wasn't anything else she needed. As long as she kept her feelings to herself, she didn't have anything to worry about.

She just needed to stop thinking about Morgan.

Rhea turned off the heater and put away her tools. It was clear she wasn't going to get much done tonight, so she might as well head home.

"Come on, Soldier." Rhea tapped her hand against the side of her leg. Immediately Soldier came to her side, ready to go.

She stepped out into the chill night air and saw Morgan walking across the yard toward the barn and instantly felt a thrill of excitement.

Soldier ran to Morgan before Rhea could think. Morgan changed her direction and headed toward her. Rhea's heartbeat sped up, and she was suddenly nervous. Rhea stuffed her hands into the pockets of her coat and waited.

"Hey," Morgan said.

"Hey," Rhea replied.

"You're up late."

Rhea shrugged. "I lost track of time. I should have the tractor ready in a couple of weeks, I think."

"Wow, that's fast. I didn't think it would be possible before summer."

Rhea swayed from foot to foot, uncomfortable but happy Morgan was pleased. "Yeah, it was in better shape than we thought, and I've had a lot of time to put in on it." She looked toward the house and back to Morgan. "You making a round?"

Morgan nodded. "Yeah, one last check on the animals for the night."

"I get it. Do you need some help?" Despite her earlier desire to shut Morgan out of her thoughts, she was looking for any reason to be with her, now that she was so close.

"No. I'll just give a quick look and head back in."

Rhea shrugged, trying not to let her disappointment show. "Okay." She took a step away and waved. "I'll see you tomorrow then."

"Good night," Morgan said, staring after her.

Rhea walked away even more confused than before. She was disappointed that Morgan hadn't wanted her to stay or hadn't wanted to talk more. But since when did she care about things like that? She kicked a rock with her boot and watched it skitter across the lawn. She wasn't sure why she was in a bad mood all of a sudden, but seeing Morgan had stirred her up again, and she was more confused than ever. She stopped to wait for Soldier, who was unusually interested in an old oak tree that stood between her house and Morgan's.

"What is it, Soldier?"

Soldier twitched his ears in her direction but kept his nose to the ground.

She was curious and followed him, trying to figure out what he was trying to tell her. He'd never shown any interest in the squirrels before—maybe it was an opossum or a raccoon.

Rhea circled the tree but didn't see anything on the ground. It was a full moon, and she could see through the branches clearly, but she moved the beam of her flashlight through the branches just to be sure and didn't see anything unusual.

Soldier put his nose to the ground and began tracking a scent. Rhea was curious, so she followed him. They made it to the edge of the yard that edged the woods when a loud crack shattered the silence. Rhea flinched and looked around, trying to figure out what had happened. Another crack, and this time dirt and rocks scattered across the ground in front of her.

"What the hell?"

A third crack, and Soldier yelped and fell to the ground. An instant latter he jumped up and was biting at his front leg as if something had a hold on him.

Rhea ran to Soldier and grabbed the scruff of his neck. He whined and fell onto his side. A line of blood trickled from his shoulder. Panic rose in Rhea's chest making it hard to breathe. "No!" She grabbed Soldier up in her arms and ran. He was surprisingly heavy, and she stumbled more than once and almost fell.

"Morgan." Rhea yelled into the night. She had to get help. Soldier needed help. *Oh God, I can't lose him.*

"Morgan. Help." Rhea's lungs burned, and her arms were getting weak. She didn't think she could go much further.

❖

Morgan burst out of the barn and looked around, trying to locate the sound of the cries. Rhea was running toward her with Soldier in her arms. Morgan broke into a run when Rhea stumbled. She grabbed Rhea and Soldier together, holding Rhea so that she didn't drop him or fall to the ground. "What happened?"

"I think he's been shot."

Morgan stiffened with shock and looked around. "What? How?"

Tears streamed down Rhea's cheeks, and her eyes were wide with fear. Morgan didn't understand but there was no time to figure it out. "Sit down," she said as she pulled Rhea and Soldier to the ground. "Let me look at him."

Soldier's shoulder and front leg were wet with blood. She prodded the area around the wound, and Soldier yelped and whined and licked her hand as if trying to tell her to be gentle.

"What do we do?" Rhea asked.

Morgan looked up and her heart broke at the sight of pain and fear and grief marring Rhea's face. Morgan pulled her cell phone out of her pocket and hit speed dial. After the second ring a craggy voice came on the line. She spoke frankly and explained what had happened. "I'll be at your clinic in fifteen minutes." Morgan hung up and scooped Soldier into her arms. "Let's go."

Rhea didn't hesitate. The calm command in Morgan's voice demanded obedience and gave her an anchor to cling to. She jumped to her feet and ran to Morgan's truck. She held Soldier in her lap as Morgan sped down the long gravel drive and onto the main road through town. Despite their speed it seemed like hours before they pulled in to the parking lot of the animal hospital. The lights were on inside, and a slight woman with gray hair pulled back in a ponytail and rimless glasses stood outside, waiting for them. She wore jeans and work boots and a faded and stained sweatshirt with the sleeves pushed up to the elbows. Morgan pulled the truck only feet from where she stood. The woman reached for the door before the truck stopped. Morgan jumped out and ran to Rhea's side. She slid her arms around Soldier and carried him inside.

The woman opened the door and ushered them in.

"Thanks for meeting us," Morgan said tightly.

"Give him to me now, Matt's already in the back getting us ready. I'll let you know something in a few minutes."

"I want to go with him," Rhea said, fear strangling her words.

"I'll take good care of him. Now I need to you let go and trust me."

Morgan put her arm around Rhea and walked her to a chair in the waiting room as the vet carried Soldier away. She knew how hard it was for Rhea to trust anyone, and Soldier was the one thing she cared for in the whole world. She couldn't lose him now.

"Come on, let Dr. Stevens do her job. She's good. You can trust her, Rhea."

Rhea looked down at her hands and rubbed at the blood staining her skin.

Morgan wrapped her hands around Rhea's and rubbed her thumbs across her wrists, wanting so much to absorb Rhea's pain. She picked at the electrical tape wrapped around Rhea's thumb. "What's this?"

Rhea glanced at her hand, but her eyes were unfocused. "It's nothing. I scraped it on a wire brush earlier and couldn't find a Band-Aid."

Morgan feathered her fingers across Rhea's skin. She needed to know what happened but wasn't sure Rhea was in any shape to talk about it. Morgan took a deep breath. "Can you tell me what happened?"

Rhea shook her head and closed her eyes against the images flashing behind her eyelids over and over again. "We were just walking home and he got distracted up by the old oak. I thought he was tracking an animal or something, so I followed him back to the tree line. I heard a noise like a pop, but I didn't realize what it was. Then it came again, and this time rocks and dirt flew up from the ground between us. A second later it came again, and Soldier cried out and fell. I grabbed him and ran."

"Three shots? That's what you heard?"

Rhea closed her eyes tight, trying to remember. "Yeah. I'm sure it was three." Rhea opened her eyes and looked at Morgan. "Why would anyone shoot him? He doesn't bother anyone. He's a good dog."

Morgan wrapped her arms around Rhea and hugged her. "I don't know." Morgan rocked her in her arms and Rhea focused on Morgan's touch and allowed the warmth to penetrate the cold fear around her heart. She couldn't think about losing Soldier. He had to be okay. Morgan would make sure they were okay.

Morgan ran through Rhea's description and was certain what Rhea described was gunfire. But what troubled her most was how deliberate it seemed. No one could accidentally shoot at Rhea three times, and no one would be out hunting at that time of night, that close to the farm.

"Did you see anyone, hear anything?"

Rhea pulled away and stood up. She paced back and forth across the room, wringing her hands together as if she could rub the fear and worry away. "Nothing. It was quiet. I didn't see anything. It was so dark beyond the tree line, I couldn't see anything."

Tension rippled through Morgan until her muscles were so taut they felt like they would turn to stone. She didn't know what to do, and her helplessness was making her crazy, but she couldn't let Rhea see her fear. She had to keep it together and figure this out.

"How long do you think this will take? It's already been too long. Something's wrong."

Morgan leaned back in her chair and tried to sound calm. "We've only been here a little over an hour. Dr. Stevens will tell us something as soon as she can."

Rhea bit her lip and stared at the closed door dividing them from the treatment room as if trying to see through the walls. Her body was hard and unwavering, and a muscle jumped at the side of her jaw, but her eyes were soft and pleading.

Morgan stood and placed her hand on Rhea's back. "Why don't you come over here and sit down for a while?"

Rhea glanced at Morgan as if considering the invitation.

The door opened, and Dr. Stevens came out. Rhea jumped and Morgan gripped her shoulder.

Dr. Stevens smiled. "He's going to be fine." She held up her hand and showed a misshapen piece of metal. Morgan took it and rolled it in her palm. It was a small-caliber bullet that had been flattened on one side from impact with something hard.

"My guess is it ricocheted off something before hitting the dog. Good thing too, it took a lot of the punch out of the impact and the bullet didn't shatter the bone. We sewed him up, and he should be good as new in a few weeks. But he'll need to stay off the leg, of course."

Rhea gasped and Morgan felt a tremor run through the muscles in Rhea's shoulders. She was relieved to hear Soldier would be okay, but she was even more relieved that Rhea didn't suffer the loss.

"That's great news, Doc. Can we go back now?" Morgan asked.

Dr. Stevens smiled. "Of course."

Morgan walked with Rhea to the recovery room. Soldier was lying on his side asleep, his big red tongue hanging out of his mouth. His shoulder had been shaved and bandaged and he still had an intravenous line in his leg. Morgan watched Rhea tentatively run her fingers over his thick fur and kiss his head. She was so used to Rhea being tough and stubborn and strong. It was hard seeing her so vulnerable and exposed. Morgan felt something inside her shift and had a sudden fierce desire to protect her.

"How did this happen, Morgan?" Dr. Stevens asked.

Morgan shook her head. "I don't know. Rhea says the shots came out of the woods at the farm. She didn't see who did it."

"Hmm. That's odd. I didn't think you allowed hunting on your land."

Morgan sighed. "I don't. And I don't think this was a hunter." Morgan held up the bullet they'd pulled from Soldier's shoulder. "This looks like a .22 slug to me. No one hunts anything at night with a gun that small. Rhea says she heard three shots."

"Damn."

Morgan nodded again. "Yeah, I think I need to give the sheriff a call."

Dr. Stevens nodded. "Go on, I'll stay with her. It'll be a while before he comes around enough to go home anyway."

"Thanks," Morgan said and stepped out of the room.

❖

Two hours later Morgan walked outside with the young officer who had taken their statements. He had a light, easygoing turn to him and didn't seem to think the incident was a big deal.

"I'm sure this was just one of the local kids out messing around looking for opossums and other varmints after getting his first gun for Christmas. I can come out and take a look around, but to be honest I don't think I'll find much in the dark, and whoever it was is surely long gone by now."

The young officer looked like he was fresh out of high school, and Morgan got the feeling he had better things to do than tromp around her farm in the dark. "Just the same, I'd appreciate it if someone would come out and take a look anyway. I'm not ready to accept this as an accident. This is the second incident I've had in just a few days."

The officer nodded and made a few notes on a small notebook and checked his watch. "All right, Ms. Scott, I'll have someone check your place." He paused as if he'd just thought of something. "I'm sorry about your dog. I hope he's okay."

Morgan smiled. "Thanks." She watched him leave and went back to the treatment room where Rhea sat with Soldier.

Rhea looked up at Morgan and sighed. The look in her eyes hardened. "Do you think they'll do anything?"

Morgan shrugged. "I don't know that there's much they can do. I have to agree that there won't likely be anything for them to find."

Rhea frowned. "We have the bullet."

Without thinking Morgan slid her arm around Rhea's shoulder and gave her a squeeze. "I'm afraid that won't help us much. And I don't like it either. First it was the thing with the horse feed and now this. I get the feeling somebody is trying to tell me something."

Rhea shivered. "That's a pretty strong message, if you ask me, and what makes you think the message is for you?"

"My farm, my horse feed, my friends," Morgan answered.

Rhea shook her head. "Yeah, did anything like this ever happen before I showed up?"

Morgan didn't have to answer.

"I didn't think so." Rhea turned her head and stared at Soldier, lying on the table, unmoving. "In prison something like this would be a clear sign that your days were numbered."

Morgan was surprised by Rhea's revelation. She didn't talk about prison often, and it still caught Morgan off guard when she did. She didn't like to think of that part of Rhea's life. "You mean that they were going to be killed?"

Rhea shrugged. "That or beat down. It depends on why someone was being punished."

"So why send a message, why not just act and get it over with?"

Rhea laughed. "The message is to make you sweat. They like to get under your skin and make you live with the fear of not knowing when you're going down or who's going to do it."

Morgan tried not to think about it. Things didn't work like that in the real world. People were mostly good, and she had no reason to believe anyone would want to hurt her. But what if Rhea was right? What if the message wasn't for her? What if all of this was about Rhea? All the trouble had started after Rhea had come to the farm, and people had expressed their dislike of having her around. Morgan's gut twisted at the thought of anyone wanting to hurt Rhea. "Well, around here it's more likely some kids messing around who got carried away."

Rhea pulled away from Morgan. "Trust me, being a kid doesn't make you innocent."

Morgan flinched at the reminder of Rhea's past. "That's not what I meant."

Rhea blew out a breath and glared at Morgan. "You can pretend all you want, Morgan, but the world isn't all love and cotton candy. People do bad things, they hurt other people, and most of the time they don't even feel bad about it. Maybe all that time in the church sheltered you from what people are really like, but I'm not that naïve. I know exactly what people are capable of." Rhea got up and walked out of the room.

Morgan stared after her. Rhea was right about one thing. At one time she had thought there were two camps of people, those who were good and those who were bad. The more she learned about Rhea's story, the more she came to realize that sometimes a person could be both. Maybe if she'd learned that long ago, things in her own life would have been different. Ashley had had clearly defined ideas of what she needed to be in order to be good, and it was an expectation she hadn't been able to live up to, and she'd turned on herself. Maybe if Morgan had understood her better, she could have helped her. Maybe Ashley would still be alive.

Morgan sat on the stool beside Soldier with her shoulders

slumped under the weight of her failure and the helplessness to do anything to stop what was happening to them. Perhaps Rhea was right. Maybe she had been living in a fantasy world and had been kidding herself that she could help anyone.

CHAPTER TWELVE

Rhea and Soldier sat in the field overlooking the farm. She rested her arm around his back, comforted by his warm presence. He was getting better, and she'd started letting him sit outside and watch the sunset every day. She'd barely left him alone since the shooting and was still uneasy about being away from him. Morgan had been by to check on them every day, but they'd hardly talked. Rhea had been angry, and it was easier to shut Morgan out than face what was really bothering her. She'd let Morgan get to her. She'd gotten under her skin, and Rhea cared way too much already. She'd almost lost Soldier, and she couldn't imagine what it would feel like if that had been Morgan. She had pulled back into herself and was determined to keep Morgan at a distance.

She had known better than to believe she could stay and have a life here. Morgan didn't deserve to have everything she'd worked for destroyed because of her. She'd called her parole officer and talked to her about moving. J.J. didn't think it was a good idea to move but left it up to her, as long as she kept in contact. Rhea had barely ever been more than a few hours' drive of her family home, except for the time she was in prison. It wasn't like she had friends to visit or any idea what it was like to be anywhere else. She could always get in her Jeep and drive until she landed someplace for a while. Maybe if she didn't put down any roots and didn't stay long enough for people to start to talk she'd be okay. She still had another year of parole hanging over her head, and that limited her options even more.

She wasn't sure how she was going to tell Morgan she was leaving. She already knew she'd try to talk her out of it, but no matter how she looked at it there wasn't any other answer. Things had gotten out of hand, and she couldn't keep putting Morgan in danger.

The fading light of the sun lit up the sky with streaks of orange and turned the delicate wisps of clouds to dark masses of purple that looked like they had been painted to mirror the roll of the mountains below. Wildflowers danced on the breeze, turning their heads to drink in the last lingering kisses of the sun. The air was full with the smell of cherry blossoms, and a symphony of frogs called out to each other in a well-timed rhythm that was like music to Rhea's ears.

This was the picture she had waited for from the first moment she had climbed this ridge when she'd first arrived at the farm. She had dreamed of spring, all those years she had been imprisoned and shut away from all that was pure and wild. It was cruel to be here now, surrounded by all that she had dreamed of, only to have it tainted by such a heavy heart.

She sat there long after the sun had set and watched the farm fall asleep. Soldier lay with his head in her lap, content. Movement caught her eye, and she looked toward the barn and saw Morgan making her way back to the house. Rhea watched the way Morgan moved. Every step was made with purpose and hinted of the power of her strength and the grace of her tenderness. Once again Rhea had the strange feeling that Morgan wasn't real, that she was so much more than she appeared. Rhea was mesmerized, completely captivated by this infatuation with Morgan, and her heart ached at the thought of leaving.

The light of the moon seemed to follow Morgan across the yard as if the heavens too were drawn to her radiance. Morgan stopped and looked around as if listening to something. Rhea looked around, trying to find the source of Morgan's distraction, but couldn't hear anything at that distance. Morgan turned and took a few steps toward the studio. A second later a bright flash burst through the night and a terrible boom struck Rhea like a fist to the chest. Morgan was thrown back as flames and wood leaped at her. Rhea screamed and jumped to her feet. Soldier was already moving toward Morgan as fast as he could manage and his commanding barks were frantic in the surrounding silence.

Rhea ran as fast as her feet would carry her, desperately hoping Morgan was all right. The studio was on fire and there were oxygen tanks and fuel nearby. God, the whole place could blow. She skidded to a stop at Morgan's feet and fell to the ground at her side. She was facedown on the ground and her thick flannel jacket was on fire. Rhea jerked off her own jacket and used it to smother the flames.

Morgan groaned and tried to roll to her side.

"Morgan, are you all right?" Rhea pulled the collar of Morgan's coat aside. Blisters and red burns crossed Morgan's neck and along her jaw. "Oh Jesus," Rhea whispered. She managed to turn Morgan over. Morgan had a large gash on her head just above her left temple. Panic swelled in Rhea's belly like a raging creek during a spring flood, and she wasn't sure what to do.

Soldier grabbed the shoulder of Morgan's jacket in his mouth and started to pull. Rhea followed his cue and dragged Morgan away from the burning building. She rifled through Morgan's pockets, found her cell phone, and managed to call 911.

Morgan groaned and started moving around as if she was going to get up.

Rhea grasped her hand and pressed against her shoulder to keep her still. "Don't move. Help is on the way."

Morgan kept moving, and Rhea noticed blood in her ears. She wasn't sure Morgan could hear her. She leaned down and pressed her hands against the sides of Morgan's face. Morgan's eyes flickered and she looked up at Rhea with fear and pain in her eyes. Her gaze was unfocused and confused.

Rhea leaned closer until she was certain Morgan was looking at her. "Don't move. Help is coming."

Morgan frowned. "I'm burning."

Rhea nodded. "I put the fire out, but it got you pretty good."

Morgan closed her eyes tight, and when she opened them again they were wet with tears.

Rhea's heart broke. She wanted to help, but there was nothing else she could do to stop Morgan's pain.

"The studio," Morgan rasped.

Rhea nodded. "I'll do what I can. Just don't move, do you hear me?"

Morgan's eyes widened, and she shook her head. "Not safe."

"I'll be okay. I promise."

Rhea looked up at Soldier. "Watch her." She patted his head and ran to the machine shop. She grabbed the thick rubber hose and connected it to the outside faucet. She doubted there was much she could do with a garden hose, but maybe she could keep the place from going down before the fire department arrived.

Rhea tried her best, but the blaze was too hot to put out alone, so she focused on the back of the building and tried to keep the fire from spreading farther. Most of the building was brick and stone and heavy steel, so it was worth a try. Rhea set the hose on full blast, focused it on the back door, and wedged it into a small metal statue Morgan had in the yard. She waited a minute, then ran inside.

❖

Morgan's head rang, but she could hear the sound of sirens growing in the distance. She swallowed and let out a breath of relief. The fire department was on the way. She tried to sit up to see where Rhea went, but the instant she moved, a searing pain shot through her neck and hand and her head felt like it would burst. A solid paw thumped down on her chest, making the final point that she should stay still. She squinted up at Soldier. He looked worried. How many times had he seen scenes just like this or worse?

"It's okay, Soldier." She pulled her hurt hand to her chest. The pain was so intense it was as if her skin was still on fire, but there were no flames. She pushed Soldier aside and rolled to her side so she could sit up. She could see an ambulance barreling down the long dirt road that served as her driveway. The fire engine was close behind and a line of police cars were scattered in the mix. The cavalry was coming.

She looked around but couldn't find Rhea anywhere. She tried to get up, but the world spun beneath her, and she was afraid she would pass out. Finally Rhea came out of the back door of her workshop carrying one of the fuel tanks. Primal fear overtook her the moment she saw Rhea carrying the equivalent to a bomb through the fire. What the hell was she doing?

"Rhea!" Morgan screamed.

Rhea's head jerked in her direction, and she dropped the tank next to three others she had deposited on the ground away from the fire. She ran back to Morgan.

Morgan was amazed by what she saw. Rhea had managed to remove the tanks without getting herself blown up. But her skin and clothes were covered in smoke and soot, her hair was singed, and her eyes were red from the smoke and fumes. Morgan didn't know if she should hug her or kick her for her stupid bravery.

"Are you crazy? You could have gotten yourself killed," Morgan said the instant Rhea was by her side. "Are you okay?"

Rhea coughed, and it sounded like she was having trouble getting in enough air. "I'm okay. It looks like the fire is only in the studio. I got the tanks out before it could reach the workshop." Rhea coughed again. "The walls are keeping it from spreading through the rest of the building."

Morgan let out a sigh of relief. "That was still a crazy thing you did."

Rhea moved around behind Morgan. "Lean on me," she said as she pulled Morgan against her. "What else can I do?"

Morgan rested against Rhea and was grateful for the comfort in her embrace. At least she wasn't alone. "Call J.J."

"Okay." Rhea brushed the hair back from Morgan's forehead and pressed something against her head.

"Ouch."

"Yeah, ouch, you have one hell of a cut on your head, be still."

Morgan shivered and gripped Rhea's arm with her good hand.

"You're going to be all right, do you hear me? You're going to be just fine."

Morgan could hear the fear in Rhea's voice, and she wondered which one of them Rhea was trying to convince. "Okay," Morgan agreed.

The ambulance stopped only feet from where they lay huddled on the ground. A few seconds later two very large men jumped out and pushed a gurney toward them.

Rhea pulled away so the two medics could work on Morgan. She brushed the sting of smoke and tears from her eyes with the palms of her hands and felt the reassuring nudge of Soldier's body pressed against her thigh. She slid her fingers through his thick fur, pulled him against her, and stroked his head. She watched as Morgan was moved onto the gurney and the medic worked on Morgan's burns.

Rhea was lost. She wanted to go with Morgan. She wanted to see to it that she was cared for and kept safe. But she couldn't leave Soldier and the farm.

The second medic came to Rhea. "Are you okay, miss? Can I check you out now?"

"I'm fine," Rhea said dismissively.

"I'm sure you are, but I'd still like to check. At least take a little oxygen. It looks like you took in a lot of smoke."

Rhea nodded and followed the young man to the ambulance. She sat beside Morgan and watched the medic insert an intravenous line.

"Hey," Morgan said.

"Hey, boss."

Morgan smiled, but Rhea could see the pain and fear swimming in her eyes.

The medic handed Rhea the oxygen mask, and she held it to her face for a moment as she watched Morgan. "I want to come with you, but I need to see to Soldier first."

Morgan nodded. "Take my keys out of my coat pocket. You can take my truck. Will you lock the house and call J.J.?"

Rhea nodded. She was relieved to have a direction to go,

something she could do to help, and most of all that Morgan wanted her there. "I'll be right behind you."

Morgan nodded and closed her eyes.

Rhea handed the oxygen mask back to the medic. "Thanks."

"You sure you don't want to ride with us?"

"No, thanks, just take good care of her."

Rhea jumped out of the ambulance and watched the big doors slam shut.

❖

Rhea raced to the hospital as soon as she locked up the house and put Soldier in the cabin and changed his bandages. She decided against driving Morgan's truck because of its size and drove her Jeep instead. It had been weird calling her probation officer in the middle of the night, but J.J. was Morgan's sister and had been grateful she'd called.

Rhea thought of her own sister and longed for that connection. She wished there was some way her sister could understand, but they hadn't spoken in fifteen years and any hope for a connection with her family was a futile dream. Morgan was the closest thing she had to family, and she was hurt and suffering. Rhea clenched her teeth and gripped the steering wheel to keep her hands from shaking and tried to keep her fear from overtaking her.

The ER was bright and the lights made Rhea feel exposed, as if the light magnified her vulnerability and weakness.

"Excuse me, an ambulance brought in Morgan Scott a few minutes ago, can you please tell me where she is?" Rhea asked the woman seated at the reception desk.

The woman looked up at Rhea over small square reading glasses. "Are you a family member?"

Rhea was confused. "She's my boss, and she's hurt. She's expecting me to be here."

The woman sighed. "I'm sorry, but we can't release any information to anyone but direct family members without the patient's consent."

"But I promised her I'd meet her here. She's expecting me to be here with her."

The nurse removed her glasses and looked pointedly at Rhea. "I'm sorry, but those are the rules."

Rhea was frustrated. "Can't you go ask her? You can get her permission."

"I'm sorry. You can have a seat in the waiting area if you'd like."

Rhea could hear the blood rushing through her ears with each heartbeat. Desperation was beginning to get the best of her, and she considered charging past the nurse to find Morgan herself. She'd lived by the rules for years, having to ask permission to go to the bathroom, to read a book, or even to speak. She was tired of rules.

"Look, lady, I know you have a job to do, but my friend is back there somewhere, and she's hurt and scared, and she needs me. I don't give a shit about your rules. Now someone needs to take me to Morgan."

"Ma'am, you need to calm down."

The security guard headed in Rhea's direction, and she braced herself for a fight.

"Is there a problem here?" he asked, as he rested his hand on a Taser on his belt.

Rhea was about to unleash on the security guard when J.J. rushed through the doors.

"Oh, thank God." She ran to Rhea and gripped her arm with the strength of a gorilla. "How is she?"

"I don't know. The secret service here won't tell me anything, and they won't let me see her," Rhea said through clenched teeth.

J.J. squared her shoulders, and Rhea was amazed by the command in her voice when she spoke. "I'm Morgan's sister. Now what the hell is going on?"

"Just a moment and someone will be out to speak with you." The nurse immediately picked up the phone, and a minute later a tall, thin woman in scrubs stepped out from a set of automatic doors and motioned to them. "You can come with me, J.J. I'll take you to Morgan."

Rhea felt relief as sweet as a spring rain when J.J. took her arm and led her down the hall. She was a little light-headed and struggled with the torrent of emotions she'd been through in the last hour. They rounded a corner and stopped outside a thin curtain that closed off a section of the room. The woman turned to J.J.

"She's a little banged up, and she has some burns on her hand, shoulder, and neck as well as on the side of her face, but it isn't too serious. The burns to her neck and face are the worst, but it looks like flash burns. She had a nasty bump to the head, and we stitched up a laceration on her forehead. We took an X-ray of her hand and she has a fracture to her wrist. We gave her something for the pain, so she'll be a little out of it for a while."

"That's good, right?" Rhea asked. "She'll be okay?"

The woman looked at Rhea for the first time, but there was no emotion in her eyes. "Yes, she's going to be fine, but she was damn lucky."

Rhea had the feeling the woman didn't like her much but couldn't figure out why.

"Let me know if you need anything, J.J."

And just like that, the woman walked away.

"Friendly," Rhea said sarcastically. "Do you know her?"

J.J. smiled. "Don't worry about her, she means well. We went to high school together, but she and Morgan weren't close."

Rhea looked down the hall where the woman had disappeared. Something told her there was more to the story, and she couldn't tell if the woman was being protective of Morgan or disdainful, but it was clear she didn't like Rhea being there.

"You ready?" J.J. asked and touched Rhea's arm.

Rhea jumped at the unexpected connection. "Yeah, let's go."

J.J. pushed the curtain aside, and Rhea followed her in. Rhea wasn't prepared for what she saw. Morgan was asleep and bandages covered her neck and part of her face. The skin across her forehead was black and blue, but the rest of her skin was pale. She wore a thin hospital gown and she'd been covered from the chest down with a thin sheet. Her arms were bare and her right hand was wrapped in a brace.

Rhea stared. Morgan looked so frail she could hardly believe it was her. J.J. went to Morgan's side and brushed her fingers through her hair and kissed her cheek. Rhea was touched by the tenderness and looked away. Now that she'd finally gotten to Morgan, she had the feeling she didn't belong there.

"How did this happen? She was always so careful with those damn tanks. She always made sure her lines were clean. She knew better," J.J. muttered.

Rhea wasn't sure what J.J. was talking about. "What do you mean?" she asked.

J.J. looked at her with a wounded expression that tore at her heart. "Metalwork was always her passion, and she loves welding, but I don't know how she let this happen. She was always so careful."

Rhea shook her head. "Morgan wasn't welding when this happened. She was just walking to the studio when the place blew."

J.J. frowned. "But if she wasn't working, what caused this?"

Rhea shook her head and sighed. "I don't know."

The curtain was suddenly pulled back and Rhea jumped to the side as if someone was about to attack her. The explosion and the situation with Morgan had her on edge, and she felt like she was about to climb out of her skin. Two officers walked into the room, and Rhea had the sinking feeling things were about to get much worse.

The younger of the two officers nodded to J.J. "How is she?"

"They said she's going to be fine."

He nodded and turned to Rhea. "Are you Rhea Daniels?"

Rhea's muscles tensed. Here came the part where things got worse. Rhea nodded. "That's me."

The officer focused on Rhea. "I'm Officer Jones and this is Officer Sims," he said, motioning to his partner. "We'd like to have a word with you."

Rhea studied the young officer and tried to gauge the level of crap she was in. His cheeks were red as if he had been standing too close to a fire, and he smelled of smoke. He must have been at the farm during the blaze.

"Can't this wait?"

"I'm sorry, ma'am. We just have a few questions." Officer Jones nodded toward the hall and motioned for her to step outside. "Please."

Rhea sighed and turned to J.J. "I'll be right back. If she wakes up, tell her I'm here."

J.J. nodded. "I will."

Rhea followed the two officers a few steps down the hall. It was Officer Sims's turn to take the lead. He was older, and Rhea could see the faint shadow of hair that ringed his head where he hadn't shaved it to match the bald top. His belly was a little too big to fit comfortably beneath his heavy belt, but he had strong, broad shoulders that suggested he'd been a big man in his younger years. He ran his eyes up and down her body and raised one eyebrow as if he was surprised by something.

"Ms. Daniels, can you tell us what happened tonight?"

Rhea met the officer's gaze. "I don't know. One minute everything was normal, and the next, the studio exploded and Morgan was on the ground."

"How do you suppose that happened?" Officer Sims asked.

Rhea gave him a defiant glare. "How am I supposed to know?"

"I understand you do a lot of work for Ms. Scott. Surely you have some idea how this happened."

Rhea ground her teeth together. It was just as she expected. These guys had already made up their mind that she was behind all of this. "All I can tell you is that the place blew up, Morgan was hurt, I called 911, and here we are. Now if that's all, officers, I'd like to get back to Morgan."

Sims sucked his teeth and continued his assessment of her. "Afraid not, not until we get some real answers."

Rhea crossed her arms over her chest and took a deep breath to make herself appear bigger and cocked her head to the side. "Then I suggest you ask me some real questions. I don't have time or the patience for this."

"Um…" Officer Jones interrupted. "I was wondering what Ms. Scott was doing that late at night."

Rhea turned to the young officer and started to give him another sarcastic answer, but there was no malice in his eyes. She considered him a moment. He looked concerned. This guy might actually care about what really happened.

"Morgan is in and out of that studio all hours of the day and night. She says she likes to work when inspiration hits her."

"Was she working tonight?"

Rhea sighed. "No. She was just checking on things."

"And what about you, Ms. Daniels, what do you do? And why were you out there in the middle of the night?" Officer Sims interjected.

Rhea didn't take the bait. "I work in the engine shop and help out with keeping the farm running. I was just hanging out with my dog, enjoying the night air, when everything happened."

"Now you said Ms. Scott was out checking on things. Why would she need to do that in the middle of the night?" Sims asked.

Rhea counted silently to ten. "I was out with my dog. And if you've done your homework, you know Morgan had some trouble at the farm in the last few weeks, and we've both been keeping a close eye on things. There's a police report and everything."

Sims sucked his teeth again. "Right. Some alleged intruder messed up the horse feed or something like that. And then there was a complaint about someone shooting your dog."

Rhea was losing her patience. "Exactly what is that supposed to mean?"

"Just seems a little strange to me. Ms. Scott's never had any trouble at all until you showed up. And you don't exactly have a stellar record, now do you, Ms. Daniels."

"You know what, I can see you've got this all figured out. It takes a special mind to be able to keep your thoughts inside such a small box. I did my time, and you can't arrest me for my past, so unless you've got something to charge me with, officers, I'm done here."

"A word of advice, Ms. Daniels." Officer Sims stopped her. "This is a small town and someone's always watching. I'd go easy on building that list of enemies if I were you."

Rhea smiled. "I'm very familiar with how things work in a small town. There's no end to how deceitful and traitorous people can be."

Rhea walked away with her head up and her shoulders squared. There was no way she would show these wannabe heroes an ounce of fear.

Chapter Thirteen

It wasn't until Rhea stepped back behind the curtain that her world righted itself. Morgan was awake, and although her eyes were tired and weak, she still managed to give Rhea the feeling that she could see right into her soul.

J.J. was sitting in a chair next to the bed holding Morgan's hand. When Rhea entered she looked up with a relieved smile. "Look who's awake."

Rhea smiled. "Hey, boss, how are you doing?"

"I'm okay, thanks to you." Morgan's voice was coarse and dry as if it hurt her to speak.

Rhea shook her head. "Not me, I think Soldier is the one who deserves the credit."

"Thank you both then."

Rhea shifted on her feet and stuffed her hands into her pockets. She wasn't sure what to say next, and she wasn't sure what she was supposed to do.

"Do either of you need anything?" Rhea asked.

J.J. stood. "Now that you mention it, I need to step outside and make a call. I need to let everyone know she's okay. Will you stay with her for a few minutes?"

"Sure. Take your time."

On her way out J.J. placed her hand on Rhea's shoulder. "Thank you. I'm glad you stuck around a while longer. I can't imagine what would have happened if you hadn't been there."

Rhea swallowed a lump of doubt and nodded. Maybe if she'd left this never would have happened.

She looked over at Morgan. Now that they were alone, a torrent of emotions began to bubble to the surface at once. The fear and anger Rhea had been trying to contain coalesced into overwhelming gratitude and relief that Morgan was okay.

"Hey," Morgan whispered, "are you okay?"

Rhea shook her head, but the words were stuck in her throat.

"Come here." Morgan patted the side of the bed with her good hand.

Rhea stepped closer and filled the chair J.J. had vacated moments earlier.

"Tell me what's going on inside that hard head of yours."

Rhea rubbed her hands up and down the length of her thighs until her jeans were warm and moist from the sweat of her palms. "I was really scared," Rhea finally managed. Her voice was rough and hoarse, and she hardly recognized it. Her throat was raw from inhaling the smoke from the fire, but the hardest part was holding back the tears that pushed at the back of her eyes and made her throat swell.

Morgan motioned for Rhea to take her hand.

Rhea slid her fingers around Morgan's and some of her courage returned. Even injured Morgan was able to anchor her.

"You were on fire and bleeding, and I didn't know what was happening or what to do."

Morgan squeezed Rhea's hand. She could feel the slight tremor as Rhea talked. Rhea was clearly shaken and Morgan had the feeling she was afraid for more reasons than the immediate danger and shock. She knew the police were suspicious of Rhea, and she had to admit they had good reason, but they were wrong. Rhea had saved her.

"I hear a little self-blame going on there. You cut that out."

Rhea shook her head. "Maybe if I'd left before now, none of this would have happened."

Morgan tightened her grip on Rhea's hand. "That's not true. If you'd left, I'd just be alone to figure this out by myself. I won't give up on you if you don't give up on me."

When Rhea didn't answer, Morgan was afraid she was already gone. "I'm asking you to stay, Rhea. I need you to stay."

Morgan wanted to pull Rhea to her and hold her. She needed Rhea more than she could explain. The thought of Rhea leaving left a hollow, sick feeling in her chest.

Rhea chewed her lip and nodded. "Okay."

Morgan let out a sigh of relief. She knew it might only be temporary, but for now she had a chance. "How bad was it...the fire?"

Rhea shrugged. "Hard to say. I left before the fire department was finished putting it out. But it looked like it was holding to the studio."

Morgan nodded and then grimaced when the throbbing in her head intensified. "Makes sense. The explosion came from there, and the brick should have held the fire back for the most part. I guess it depends on how much roof I lost."

Morgan's throat hurt, and the more she talked the more it burned. The taste of smoke was still thick in her mouth and filled her nostrils making her feel sick. "Could you get me a drink of water?" Morgan asked.

Rhea jumped to her feet. "Sure. Hang on a sec."

She stuck her head out of the curtain and asked a nurse for water. The nurse returned a few minutes later with a pitcher of water, and a Styrofoam cup and a straw.

Rhea filled the cup and leaned over Morgan. She cradled the straw between two fingers to keep it steady. Morgan wrapped her hand around Rhea's and met her gaze before taking a long drink. The cold water was soothing and she held the water in her mouth for a moment before swallowing and taking another drink. She took her time so she could watch Rhea and savor her touch. Rhea's expression was serious, and worry lines furrowed her brow. Morgan took one last deep drink and drained the cup. She let go of the straw but held on to Rhea's hand, even when Rhea tried to pull away.

Rhea paused, as if captured by Morgan's gaze. For a moment Morgan forgot about her pain. The moment their eyes met, there was a connection between them that made Morgan feel more alive than she had ever felt. She wanted to pull Rhea closer and search her eyes for a sign that she felt it too.

Rhea frowned.

Morgan let go of Rhea's hand and smiled. *Great, if I keep this up, I'll just scare her again.* Obviously the connection was all in her mind, a foolish hope born of fear, loneliness, and gratitude.

"Thank you," Morgan whispered. She reached up and tugged at a tuft of Rhea's hair. "Your hair is growing out. I think the singed look suits you."

Rhea didn't laugh, but she didn't move away either, and the way she looked at her now made Morgan worry. "What is it?" Morgan asked.

Rhea continued to frown as if she was trying to figure something out. She brought her hand to Morgan's face and brushed her fingertips along her cheek. The touch was tender and left warm trails across Morgan's skin. Rhea leaned closer and slid her fingers through a strand of her hair. Morgan was afraid to move but focused on the delicate look in Rhea's eyes and the gentleness in her touch.

"You confuse me," Rhea answered.

Morgan swallowed. "What do you mean?"

Rhea shook her head. "I just—"

The curtain opened, and the doctor stepped inside, with J.J. only a couple of steps behind.

Rhea pulled away, and Morgan groaned at the sudden loss of contact.

The doctor was a tall thin woman with serious eyes that Morgan was sure didn't miss anything. She looked like a runner or maybe a cyclist. She looked as if she took fitness seriously, whatever it was she did to stay in shape.

"Ms. Scott, I'm Dr. Lewis, how are you feeling?"

"Tired."

Dr. Lewis nodded. "I bet. You've had a tough night. I've looked over your tests, and I've decided it's a good idea to keep you overnight. Normally I wouldn't recommend an overnight stay, but I understand you lost consciousness for at least a few seconds, is that right?"

Morgan nodded. "I think so." She looked to Rhea.

"Yeah, she was out for a bit. I'm not sure how long though," Rhea said.

"Well, you were a little disoriented when you arrived here, and in the case of an explosion, I'd like to be on the side of caution. You have a pretty nasty concussion, and it won't hurt for us to make sure there aren't any infections setting up in those burns. They are superficial partial-thickness burns, so of course they hurt like the dickens, but the scarring will be minimal. You were lucky."

Morgan didn't want to stay, but she was exhausted, and by the look on J.J.'s face, she wouldn't win this fight. "Overnight, huh?"

"As long as nothing else comes up and you're doing okay tomorrow, we can send you home."

Morgan looked at Rhea. "Can you take care of the farm?"

Rhea grinned. "Don't I always?"

Morgan nodded and smiled. "I guess it's settled then." She lost sight of Rhea when the doctor leaned over her to check her bandages.

"Everything looks good. We should have you a room shortly." The doctor placed a hand on Morgan's shoulder. "Try to rest."

"Thanks, Doc."

As Dr. Lewis left, J.J. plopped down in the chair again. Morgan looked around the room but Rhea was gone. What had Rhea wanted to say to her before she was interrupted? She would have given anything for one more minute alone with Rhea. It was obvious she had wanted to tell her something important.

"Are you feeling okay, sweetie?" J.J. asked.

"I'm fine, just tired," Morgan said and closed her eyes. "You don't have to stay here. I really am okay by myself."

J.J. rested her hand on Morgan's. "I know how tough you are, but how about you let me play the worried big sister, just this once."

Morgan squeezed J.J.'s hand. She had to stop pushing J.J. away. "Just this once, but you can't tell anybody."

J.J. laughed. "Who are you trying to impress?"

Morgan immediately thought of Rhea. "I just don't want you getting the big head."

"Mmm-hmm, whatever you say."

Morgan didn't have the strength to argue anymore and drifted off to sleep.

❖

Rhea was relieved to see most of the emergency crew had left when she arrived back at the farm at dawn. There was only one fire truck and a car that said *Fire Chief* on the side, and all of the cop cars were gone. She pulled her Jeep beside the car and got out. She looked around and surveyed the damage. The smell of charred wood still permeated the air and coated the back of her throat when she breathed. As she looked around in the growing light of morning, it became painfully clear how bad things had been, and she started to shake inside.

Rhea walked up to a line of yellow tape that had been put up around the building. She watched an older man in dark pants and a white shirt sift through some of the debris and take a few pictures of the walls and the remains of what was left of Morgan's studio. She guessed this guy must be the fire chief. "Hey, how do things look?"

The man looked at her and nudged a piece of twisted metal with his boot. "Are you the one that pulled those tanks?" he asked.

Rhea was too tired to be defensive, and it wouldn't do her any good to be evasive if she wanted answers. "Yes, sir."

"You must be crazy," he said and grinned at Rhea.

"So I've heard."

"Good thing. This whole building would have been a complete loss if those tanks had blown."

Rhea shuddered. "Any idea what caused this?"

He walked across the rubble to a twisted and charred hunk of metal in the corner. "Do you know what that is?"

Rhea tried to make out what the misshapen mass might have

been. It didn't match any of the pieces she remembered Morgan displaying in the studio.

Rhea shook her head. "No. What is it?"

"That there used to be a kerosene heater."

Rhea tried to put the pieces together but couldn't make sense of what it all meant. "Do you think that's what started the fire?"

"That's what it looks like."

"How can you tell?"

The chief pointed to the blackest part of the wall behind the heater. "See that V shape on the wall? That's a burn pattern. It tells me this is where the fire started and burned the hottest."

Rhea thought for a minute before asking her next question. "What would cause it to blow up like it did?"

The chief scratched his chin and eyed Rhea. "Well now, that's the million-dollar question, isn't it? I have some more tests to run, but it's possible someone put gasoline in the fuel."

Rhea had a bad feeling about where this was going.

"I'll have a report ready in a few days. You need to be careful using these old stoves—just a little gasoline in those can be disastrous."

Rhea thought about the explosion and something didn't add up. "Chief, wouldn't the heater have to be on for this to happen?"

"Under the right circumstances, this thing could blow just from the ignition switch turning on, but yes, there would have to be contact with a spark."

"Well, this can't be right then. The heater wasn't on. Morgan was just coming into the building when the place blew."

The chief scratched his chin again and looked thoughtful as he studied the area around the stove. "Hmm. I guess I'll do a little more digging around. We're just looking for hot spots right now to make sure the fire doesn't start up again. I'll stick around for a while and look around more when things cool off a bit and the light is better."

"Okay," Rhea said, but something was telling her there was more bad news to come. She waved good-bye and headed toward the cabin. She was eager to get home and check on Soldier. He had been through just as much as she had, and she wanted to make sure he was okay. He'd put a lot of stress on his wounded leg, and she was afraid there would be more damage. She smiled when she heard his bark long before she reached the cabin. The sure, strong sound of his voice was like a beacon bringing her home. It had been a long night, and she was mentally and physically exhausted.

Soldier met her at the door. As soon as she came inside, he stood on his hind legs, put his good paw on her shoulder, and sniffed every inch of her face.

Rhea was certain she knew for the first time in her life what it was like to be loved. After the reunion, Soldier wanted to follow her every step as she went through the morning chores and made sure all the animals were fed, but she could tell his leg was bothering him. She could tell he was tired, but she didn't have the heart to leave him alone in the cabin, so she put him in the ATV and rode him around so he didn't have to walk. When she was finally done, he lay beside the tub while she showered.

Rhea sat on the bed exhausted. She thought of Morgan in the hospital and imagined how hard it must be for her to be away from home and the animals she loved and cared for like they were her family. Morgan had trusted her with everything that was dear to her. She was grateful for that but wondered what it cost to have that kind of trust in another person.

Rhea patted the bed with her hand. "Come on, boy."

Soldier jumped onto the bed and stretched out beside her as if he always slept in her bed. She sighed and rested her hand on his head for comfort. She couldn't stop thinking of Morgan and how fragile she looked in that hospital bed, covered in only a hospital gown and bandages and a thin sheet. The image had shaken her and in that moment she had realized how fragile life was and how much she had grown to care for Morgan.

A troubling thought needled at the back of her mind. How would gasoline get into the kerosene heater? There was no way Morgan would be careless enough to let anything like that happen. Rhea groaned and sank farther into the bed and closed her hand into a fist. The same way lead pellets got into a locked office and horse feed got scattered across the floor. Someone put it there. Her gut twisted. But who would want to hurt Morgan? She rubbed her hand through Soldier's fur. Maybe the same person who shot her dog.

Rhea was frustrated and scared. She wanted to ask Morgan about what had gotten her attention moments before the explosion. If her gut was right, someone was out to get Morgan, and so far they were doing a good job of making it look like it was her. The bad feelings she had about the situation were getting worse, and she had learned a long time ago to listen to those warnings. In prison her gut had been as good as an alarm system, and right now it was on full alert.

Rhea looked at the clock. How long would it be before Morgan would be home? She rested her hand across Soldier's chest and focused on the beat of his heart and the rhythm of his breathing, allowing his warmth and presence to lull her to sleep.

CHAPTER FOURTEEN

Morgan crawled out of J.J.'s car and stared at the carnage of what used to be her studio. She was numb, as if something inside her was broken. She'd lost a lot in the fire. Her drafting table, display tables, and most of the artwork she kept on display were all destroyed. Many of the tables had been passed down to her by her grandfather and those could never be replaced. The brick walls and heavy metal doors she had made did a good job of keeping most of the fire confined to the studio, so she hadn't lost her forge or her tools. That was a relief at least. It would have taken forever and more money than she wanted to think about to replace all that. As it was, it would take months to get the studio rebuilt.

How had this happened? Why?

J.J. slid her arm around Morgan's waist. "I can't think about what would have happened if you'd been in there."

Morgan nodded. "Yeah."

"Come on, sweetie, let's get you inside."

Morgan sighed in resignation. She'd have plenty of time to look around later. Right now she didn't need to give J.J. any more reason to worry.

"Good idea," Morgan said as she slid her arm across J.J.'s shoulders. Cheerful barking drew her attention, and she looked around to see Soldier hobbling toward her and Rhea coming out of the barn. Soldier's tail was on high speed and swirled in circles as he did his best to wag his tail and keep his balance on three legs. Morgan smiled. It was good to be home.

Soldier went to Morgan but didn't give her his usual hug, choosing instead to lean against her leg. As if he could sense her injuries, he sat in front of her with his big tongue lolling to the side of his mouth in a toothy grin. Morgan laughed and reached down and rubbed his ears. "Hey, buddy."

Rhea arrived a moment later. She looked at Morgan with an uncertain smile and stuffed her hands in the pockets of her jeans. She looked as if she didn't know what to do. She looked innocent and concerned and awkward. She looked beautiful.

Morgan drew in a deep breath as if she could draw Rhea into herself. She wanted to touch her. She wanted to hold her until all the pain in her eyes melted away. She wanted her. "How's everything?" she asked.

"Good," Rhea answered. "Everyone's been fed, the stalls are clean, and I put the goats in the pen."

"Thanks." What would she have done without Rhea? She had no doubt Rhea could handle the farm on her own, but that wasn't what she had been asking about. She wanted to know if Rhea was okay. "And you? Are you okay?"

Rhea shifted on her feet and dug her hands deeper into her pockets, obviously uncomfortable, but she never took her eyes off Morgan. "I'm good. It's good to have you back."

Morgan smiled and nodded. She turned to J.J., suddenly aware she was watching the exchange. "How about lunch? I think they try to starve people at that hospital so they'll leave."

Rhea ran up onto the porch, unlocked the door, and opened it. She stood still as J.J. passed her and went inside. She smiled and handed Morgan the keys.

"Thanks for taking care of everything," Morgan said as her fingers closed around Rhea's hand. Her skin was warm and soft, and the touch was like a lifeline, grounding her. She didn't want to let go. Rhea's cheeks were red from the cool air and hard work, and Morgan wanted to run her thumb across the delicate line of her cheek and brush her fingers through her hair. Morgan let her gaze fall to Rhea's lips and the pull between them was electric, and a bolt of heat shot through Morgan's veins. She wanted to kiss her.

Rhea smiled up at her, and Morgan was relieved she didn't pull away. Instead she held Morgan's gaze with a pleased expression that made Morgan's pulse race.

Morgan sighed and let go.

Rhea took a step back. "Let me know if you need anything."

Morgan frowned. "Aren't you going to have lunch with us?"

Rhea shrugged and glanced inside to J.J. "Soldier and I can grab something at the cabin. I still have some things I need to do, and he needs his meds."

Morgan touched Rhea's arm, letting her fingers slide down the line of muscle in her forearm. "I'd like you to stay. Soldier is welcome too, of course."

Rhea glanced inside to J.J. again. "I'll let you two get settled, but I'll come back in an hour or so."

Morgan was disappointed. She didn't want Rhea to go yet. She needed her close as much as she needed to take her next breath. She couldn't believe how close she'd come to losing her. But she also knew that Rhea did things in her own way, and Morgan respected her needs. "Okay, but I really need to talk to you later."

Rhea nodded and turned away. Morgan watched her bound down the steps and walk across the lawn with Soldier limping dutifully by her side. She didn't take her eyes off Rhea until she disappeared inside the workshop. The instant she lost sight of her, loneliness pinched at her heart. She sighed. She'd been kidding herself for weeks about her feelings for Rhea and now the truth stared her in the face.

Morgan closed the door and slid the jacket J.J. had lent her off her shoulders. She tried to wiggle her fingers in the cast, but the resulting pain signaled that wasn't a good idea. She kicked off her boots and turned to find J.J. watching her, her arms folded across her chest. Morgan imagined this was the same look she gave the boys when she discovered them doing something, and she didn't approve.

Morgan ignored J.J. and walked into the kitchen. "What's for lunch? I'm starving."

J.J. followed her. "What's going on?"

"What do you mean?"

J.J. scowled. "Don't give me that innocent crap, you know what I'm talking about. What's going on with you and Rhea?"

Morgan rummaged through her cupboards, putting bread and cheese on the counter and selecting a can of tomato soup. "Nothing's going on."

J.J. took the can of soup out of Morgan's hand. "Sit down, and I'll cook while you tell me what's up with you."

"I told you, nothing's going on. We're friends. Didn't you expect that when you pushed me into letting her stay and work here?"

"Don't try to put this off on me. I'm not talking about you being friendly. I saw the way you were looking at her and I know you, Morgan, and that was a little too friendly." J.J. put the pan down on the stove with a clang and turned on Morgan. "I like Rhea. I wouldn't have suggested she stay here if I didn't, but that doesn't mean it's a good idea for you to get involved with her."

Morgan sat down at the island and cradled her injured hand close to her chest. Her head was starting to hurt again, but it had nothing to do with the lump on her head. "I already told you, I'm not involved with her, but what's the big deal if I was?"

J.J. sighed and shook her head. "I just don't want to see you get hurt again. You're just starting to come around again and with all that's happened...I just don't want to lose you."

Morgan grimaced. She didn't want to talk about Ashley, but she knew where J.J. was going. "This isn't like before."

"So there is something going on with you and Rhea."

Morgan was getting frustrated. "J.J., I love you, but I'm not having this conversation with you."

J.J. plated a grilled cheese sandwich and a bowl of tomato soup and placed them in front of Morgan. "You never talk about what happened with Ashley, and now you won't talk about Rhea, and you expect me to believe I shouldn't worry?"

Morgan bit her lip to keep from saying something she would regret. "There isn't anything to talk about."

J.J. placed her hand over Morgan's. "There wasn't anything

you could have done to save Ashley. Her death was tragic on so many levels, but it wasn't your fault."

"Make your point, J.J."

J.J. sighed. "Rhea's troubled. Her past isn't something anyone can go through and not have some serious issues. She's already thinking of leaving. I know you, and I know you'll want to save her. But this isn't your battle, Morgan. She has to do this on her own."

Morgan drew her hand away and pushed her chair back. What did she mean Rhea was thinking of leaving? Morgan couldn't think straight. "Don't worry, I have no illusions about saving anyone. That's not my job anymore, remember? I'm tired. Why don't you go home and get some rest and spend some time with the boys. I'm fine here."

"Morgan…"

"Go home, J.J.," Morgan said and walked out of the room. She knew she was being harsh, and J.J. didn't deserve her anger, but she didn't want to hear any more about Ashley or any of the many reasons why her feelings for Rhea were a bad idea. J.J. wasn't telling her anything she didn't already know.

❖

Rhea stomped her boots on the mat outside Morgan's door and tried to calm the nervousness in her stomach. Her hands were sweating and she was jittery like when she drank too much coffee, only she hadn't had any coffee all day. She took a deep breath and knocked on the door. She just wanted to check on Morgan. She'd been relieved to see J.J. leave earlier, making it easier for her to keep her promise. She didn't know why, but J.J. made her nervous. They got along well enough and J.J. had been awesome at the hospital, but she was still her parole officer. Besides, if she was honest, she just wanted to see Morgan alone. She soothed herself by playing with Soldier's ear while she waited.

Morgan looked frustrated when she answered the door. Her face was red and her brows were drawn together in a frown. "Hi, Rhea, good timing. I could use a little help."

Rhea was surprised by the greeting and was immediately on alert. Was Morgan hurt? Was she sick? Had something happened? "What's wrong?" Rhea stepped inside and looked around for any sign of a problem. Soldier was immediately on alert at the sudden change in her mood and pushed in front of her with his hackles raised.

Morgan blew out a breath. "Nothing, really, I just can't get this sling off to change this bandage."

It took a minute for Rhea to register what Morgan said and to accept that there was no danger.

Morgan smiled sheepishly. "Sorry. I'm not usually so dramatic."

Rhea laughed, completely disarmed by Morgan's apparent embarrassment and frustration. She guessed it wasn't often Morgan admitted she needed help for anything. She was so relieved Morgan was okay that she went to her without thinking and began undoing the buckles that strapped her arm in place. "Tell me what else you need me to do." Morgan tried to help with the straps, and Rhea pushed her hand away. "I've got this. Let me do it or you'll just end up hurting yourself."

Once the straps were loose, Rhea helped Morgan shift out of the sling, careful not to bump her hand or brush the bandages covering her burns.

Rhea let out a sigh of relief when the sling was finally off. "What now?"

Morgan shrugged. "I need to get this shirt off."

Rhea blinked. Had she heard right? She watched as Morgan tugged at her shirt with her one good hand. Rhea stared as the buttons snapped open one at a time as Morgan pulled against the fabric. Rhea's mouth went dry, and she couldn't move.

Morgan struggled to get the shirt off her shoulder. Rhea snapped out of her dream when Morgan winced in pain.

"Sorry. Let me get that." Rhea slid the shirt off Morgan's shoulders and slowly worked the fabric over the cast covering her hand. When she was done, she took a step back, clutching the shirt in her hands, relieved to see Morgan wore a dark gray tank top. Her heart lurched at the sight of the bandages covering Morgan's nec' and part of her shoulder. The surrounding skin was red and swollen, and Rhea remembered Morgan's coat on fire.

Morgan pushed tentatively at the bandages and hissed. "Ouch. That's tender."

"Stop poking it then," Rhea snapped. She hated seeing Morgan in pain. "Just tell me what you need me to do already."

Soldier whined from his spot on the floor at Morgan's feet.

Morgan took a deep breath. "I need to take these off and clean the burns. I have some ointment I have to put on, and new bandages."

"Okay. I can do that." Rhea looked up at Morgan. Morgan's gaze was gentle, but she could see the pain swimming in her eyes. "You should sit down. Give me a minute to wash my hands. Do you need anything?"

Morgan shook her head. "No."

Rhea smiled. "Sit. I'll be right back."

When she came back, Morgan was lying on the sofa with her broken hand against her chest and her good arm thrown over her eyes. She looked tired. Rhea moved her eyes over Morgan's body and took in every inch of lean muscle. Morgan had always been a rock, and since the fire Rhea realized how much she relied on that strength. Now it was her turn to be strong for Morgan. She owed Morgan, not because she had played her, or run some scam on her, but because she had been a good friend. Morgan had faith in her when no one else would have. Morgan trusted her.

Rhea kneeled by the sofa. "Morgan," she whispered.

Morgan moved her arm and looked at Rhea.

"Are you ready?" Rhea asked.

Morgan groaned. "I have to admit I'm not looking forward to it, but I guess it's best to get it over with."

Morgan shifted to sit up, and Rhea put her hand on her arm stopping her. "Just stay there. Roll to your side, facing me. I think it will be easier that way."

Morgan shifted to her side, and Rhea sat on the sofa beside her. She took Morgan's hand and laid her arm across her lap for support. "How's that feel?"

Morgan swallowed hard. "Fine."

Rhea brushed the hair away from Morgan's neck and studied the bandages. Thankfully the hospital hadn't used the sticky tape, and the bandages came off easily enough.

Morgan stiffened and the muscle at the side of her jaw jumped with each tug of the tape. Her eyes were closed tight and her mouth was pressed into a thin line. No matter how gentle Rhea tried to be, she could tell she was hurting her.

Morgan was so beautiful, that Rhea's heart ached. She brushed a damp strand of hair from Morgan's forehead. "Do you need a break?"

Morgan opened her eyes and looked at her tenderly as if she was the one that needed comfort. "I'm okay. You're doing great, it's just tender." She closed her eyes again when Rhea went back to work.

Rhea licked her lips and her hands trembled as she removed the last piece of tape. The blisters were sickly white and gray as if the flesh beneath them was dead. A thin black line traced the burns in areas, and the surrounding skin was red and swollen. Rhea cleaned the area and applied the medicine. The instant the ointment was in place, she felt Morgan relax. Whatever was in that stuff, it was working. She studied Morgan's face as she worked and was mesmerized by the curve of Morgan's cheekbones, the strong angle of her jaw, and the soft lines at the corners of her eyes.

Morgan's breathing slowed and the tension around her eyes softened. Rhea wondered if she'd fallen asleep.

Rhea took her time. This was the closest she'd ever been to another human being without fear or pain. It was a strange feeling to be so drawn to another person the way she was to Morgan. She held her breath as she reached out a shaky hand and slowly ran her fingers along the edge of Morgan's shoulder and down her arm, tracing the contours of muscle. Morgan's body was hard muscle and smooth skin as soft as satin. Rhea was light-headed and intoxicated with curiosity and wonder. She was desperate to touch Morgan again. She played her hand through Morgan's hair, letting the strands bathe her fingers like rivers of silk. She was lost, completely captivated by the feel of Morgan. She was consumed by new emotions, new wants, and new needs beyond anything she had ever dreamed.

Morgan sighed and her arm tightened across Rhea's lap. Rhea was afraid to move. She knew Morgan was awake and aware of her touch, but she couldn't bring herself to withdraw.

Rhea felt a jolt of trepidation as Morgan slowly moved away. When Morgan looked up at her, her gaze was questioning and cautious. There was none of the hunger or lust Rhea had expected. Instead she found concern and hope staring back at her.

Rhea started to pull away, suddenly embarrassed by her boldness, but Morgan stopped her.

Morgan took her hand. "It's okay," she whispered. Morgan placed Rhea's hand against her cheek and held it against her face for a moment. She traced her fingers along the back of Rhea's hand before letting go. She lay still as if waiting for Rhea to move.

"You can touch me."

Rhea's heart pounded wildly against her ribcage and her ears buzzed with the rush of blood filling her veins. Her skin tingled and her muscles vibrated from the pent-up energy that coursed through her. She drew in her breath and held it as she played her thumb across Morgan's lower lip the way she had done the day they went sledding. Morgan's lips were even softer than she remembered. Emboldened by Morgan's encouragement, she touched her lips tenderly with the tips of her fingers, relishing the softness as her finger dipped into the moisture of Morgan's mouth. Morgan's lips parted with a sharp intake of breath. Rhea's stomach fluttered and she was pleased by Morgan's response to her.

She watched as Morgan's lips darkened and appeared to swell beneath her touch. Heat emanated from Morgan's body, and a thin sheen of sweat formed on her brow and down her throat into the hollow at the base of her neck. Rhea traced the line of sweat with her finger, playing along the line of collarbone that jutted beneath the thin fabric of Morgan's tank top. She watched the rise and fall of Morgan's chest as her breasts swelled with each intake of air. A vein danced in Morgan's throat with each steady beat of her heart, and Rhea had the overwhelming desire to place her lips over the throbbing point of flesh and taste Morgan.

Morgan watched the emotions play across Rhea's face as her fingers explored her lips. It was like watching the sun rise. Rhea was awash with the newness of the connection between them, and Morgan didn't want to do anything that would scare her away. Rhea's touch was amazing. She made Morgan feel like a treasure being discovered for the first time. Rhea was tentative and reverent but courageous, as she pushed the boundaries of her comfort. Morgan was careful not to move, not to let her growing desire show. It felt good to be touched. Rhea made her feel alive in ways she never had, and her body responded so fiercely she feared she wouldn't be able to control herself.

Morgan's heart stopped when Rhea's hand stilled on her chest. She placed her hand over Rhea's, hoping she wouldn't pull away. Rhea was studying her and Morgan knew Rhea's decision would change her forever. She imagined this must have been what it was like the moment before Eve bit into the apple. "What is it?"

Rhea licked her lips nervously. She leaned forward until Morgan could feel her breath on her face, their lips only inches apart. Morgan parted her lips, opening herself to Rhea as she slid her fingers over her lips again.

Slowly Rhea lowered her head until their lips brushed so lightly, Morgan thought she'd imagined it. Bells rang in her head and desire surged through her body, but she remained still. Rhea pulled away and stared at Morgan's lips. She brought her fingers to her own lips as if she could hold the kiss in her hand.

"Rhea?" Morgan said softly.

Rhea looked up, her eyes swimming with uncertainty.

"Could you please do that again?"

The corner of Rhea's mouth lifted in a faint smile. She moved closer. She claimed Morgan's lips again, this time with more certainty as her mouth melded to Morgan's.

Morgan moaned as Rhea pulled away. She knew this would change things between them, but she didn't care. She wanted Rhea had wanted her for months. She wanted her more than anything.

"Don't leave," Morgan whispered.

Rhea stared down at her with a curious expression, and Morgan saw confusion flicker in her eyes as the faintest crease furrowed her brow.

"Close your eyes and rest," Rhea said.

"I don't want you to leave."

Rhea sat up. "I'll stay, just go to sleep. You look beat." Rhea brushed her fingers across Morgan's cheek. "Go to sleep."

Morgan wanted to protest, but she was tired and the medication was doing a number on her. She closed her eyes and focused on the feel of Rhea's fingers gliding across her skin and the heat between them where she lay against Rhea's leg. Morgan drifted to the edges of sleep with Rhea's voice calling to her, like a whisper through fog. She strained to hear, but the words were lost to her dreams.

CHAPTER FIFTEEN

The sun wasn't up yet, and the room was dark. Rhea turned on the reading lamp on the small table by the door where Morgan kept her mail. Rhea sat in the chair and watched Morgan sleep. There was something ethereal in the way she slept, and once again Rhea had the strange feeling that Morgan was too good to be true. But Rhea knew Morgan wasn't the celestial immortal she had seemed to be when they first met. She had seen Morgan bleed and knew too well how easily she could have lost her forever.

Everything had happened so fast. She had kissed Morgan. She had wanted to for weeks but had been too afraid of what it might mean. Now she couldn't take it back and didn't want to. Everything she'd experienced since meeting Morgan was surreal. Maybe she would wake up in her cell the way she used to and find that Morgan and her freedom had only been a dream. At least that would make her feelings for Morgan and the kiss they shared make sense. There was no way any of this could be real.

Rhea trailed her eyes across Morgan's body and rubbed the tips of her fingers with her thumb. The mere thought of touching Morgan had her heart thundering like the primal beat of a bass drum. She was losing her mind. She knew better than to let anyone get that close, but no matter how she rationalized it, no matter how much she heard the warning voice in the back of her mind, she couldn't walk away. She watched Morgan sleep and hung on every breath as if the dream could somehow come true.

Soldier got up and stretched his long legs as best he could in a bow and yawned. He came to her and raised his paw.

"Is that foot hurting again? Don't you worry, you'll be good as new in no time." Rhea smiled. This had to be real. She couldn't bear to wake up to a world without Soldier. She sat up and rubbed his face and placed a kiss between his ears. He was better than wearing a watch for keeping her on task and in the moment. Soldier always knew when she was drifting into the shadows of her past and just how to bring her back. He always knew when it was time to feed the animals or put them in the barn, and he especially remembered when it was time to eat. This was one time she was thankful for the distraction.

"Good boy."

Rhea was torn. She needed to take care of the farm, but she didn't want to leave Morgan. What if she needed something? What if something happened? Rhea shook her head. She had to get a grip. Whatever was going on, she couldn't lose her head. She'd spent enough of her life waiting for something to happen, and she wouldn't let one kiss make her soft.

Rhea placed Morgan's meds and a glass of water on the coffee table, gathered a blanket from the back of the chair, and covered Morgan. She had to get moving. She wouldn't be gone long and she could check on Morgan in a few hours.

Soldier bumped her leg teasingly and mouthed her hand. She swore he could read her mind. "Stop it," she whispered and smiled to herself.

Soldier tugged playfully at the hem of her shirt.

"Cut it out, it's no big deal." She shook her head. *Good grief, now I'm being teased by a dog.* Maybe this was a dream after all. She rubbed Soldier's face and got out his pain medicine. "I know you want to go with me, but I need you to stay here and watch over Morgan."

He took the pill she had wrapped in a little ball of cheese and went to his pillow.

"I'll be back later," she said as she placed a kiss on his head.

Soldier laid his head down on his paws and licked his lips a if he was already on his way to sleep. Rhea went to the door and slid on her boots. She stepped onto the porch and watched Morgan slowly disappear as she pulled the door closed. The air was crisp and clear and the confusion in her mind slid away. She was free. She no longer had to live by the rules of her father or those imposed by the state penitentiary. Her choices were her own, and whatever she did or didn't do would be on her terms.

Rhea stepped off the porch into the dark. The sun still wasn't up yet, but she didn't care about the time. She felt as if she was walking on air, her first kiss resounding through her memory, breaking the bonds of her fear. She had all the time in the world.

❖

Morgan woke with a start, not certain where she was. She looked around the room frantically. The room was bathed in sunlight and the only sound was Soldier's rumbling snore. Rhea wasn't there. The room was chilly, having lost the fire sometime during the night. She shifted and the skin on her neck tightened. She sighed, frustrated by her situation and disappointed that Rhea was gone.

She sat up and noticed the water and pills on the table. She smiled as the memory of Rhea's kiss rippled across her lips. Oh boy, what was she going to do now? After months of denying her attraction for Rhea, the gate had been opened and there was no way to put this horse back in the barn.

Morgan didn't bother with the fire. The sun would warm the house soon enough. She was restless and the house was too quiet. She doubted she'd be able to see much of the damage from the fire yet and didn't want to disturb the scene until the investigation was over. Maybe she would feel better if she visited the barn. She looked at the medicine Rhea had left her. More pills meant more sleep, and she'd had enough lying around.

Soldier was asleep on his pillow, out like a light. Rhea must have seen to it that he had his medicine too. Morgan watched him leep, remembering the pain in Rhea's eyes when he'd been shot. She d the feeling that all the weird things that had happened around the farm were connected, she just couldn't prove it. She rubbed her hands on her jeans, frustrated by her helplessness. She had to get out of the house or she'd drive herself crazy.

The barn smelled of cedar chips and hay, and Morgan listened to the sound of hooves rustling against the stall floors, the occasional murmur from a horse, and the scurrying of rodents in the hidden crevices. As she listened, she imagined the movements of each animal as clearly as if she had them in her sight. The barn had been her favorite place to play as a child. She'd imagined herself as an adventurer, traveling from town to town, visiting villages in foreign lands and taming wild animals. She smiled at the memory.

A sound at the back of the barn caught her attention. This wasn't one of the animals shifting restlessly—there was someone in the barn. Rhea? What would she be doing in here at this hour? Morgan crept down the corridor, glancing nervously into each stall as she passed. She could hear a faint rustling as if someone was moving things around in the storage room. Her gut twisted. What if the intruder was back? What should she do?

A wave of anger bolstered her courage. She wouldn't let anyone hurt her animals. She'd already lost enough. Morgan gripped the handle of the door so hard she felt the edges of iron dig into her palm. She counted to three and threw the door open.

There was a moment of complete chaos. Someone screamed as something hurdled past her head. Morgan ducked to avoid the projectile. She cried out as her injured hand slammed against the wall. She looked around the room, expecting someone to attack or at the very least run away. She was shocked to find Rhea pressed into the corner of the room. She was shaking, and she looked like a trapped animal about to be slaughtered.

"Rhea?"

Rhea didn't move. Morgan straightened and stepped into the room. "What are you doing in here?"

Rhea glanced around the room as if looking for a way out or maybe looking for something…but what? It was clear Rhea wasn't registering what was happening. Morgan remembered the night Rhea told her about her father and decided not to push.

"You scared me. I thought the intruder was back." Morgan looked around. "Good thing I left Soldier in the house or we'd both be in trouble."

Rhea blinked. "Soldier?" Soldier was her dog. She looked around beginning to understand. This was Morgan's barn. She was so scared her insides vibrated. Her legs buckled, and she slid down the wall and sat on the floor.

"I...I was looking through the supplies to make the order at the Co-op." She gripped the legs of her jeans at her knees to keep her hands from shaking.

Morgan looked around and retrieved the clipboard Rhea had thrown at her. Rhea sighed. When would she stop confusing the present and the past? "Sorry about that. You scared me."

Morgan smiled and some of Rhea's fear melted away.

"I guess we're both a little jumpy." Morgan moved over to Rhea and extended her hand. "We've got to stop running into each other like this."

Rhea laughed and took Morgan's hand. She was effortlessly pulled to her feet so fast her head buzzed. Morgan had a way of doing that to her, catching her off guard. The instant she registered the ground under her feet, she was aware of Morgan's thighs pressed against hers and the pulse of Morgan's heart against her hand, pressed to Morgan's chest.

Rhea looked up at Morgan expecting more humor but was met by concern and understanding and something else simmering beneath the surface.

"Are you okay?"

Rhea nodded and pressed her body against Morgan's and wrapped her arms around her.

Morgan pulled her close. She drew in a deep breath and pressed her cheek against Rhea's head. "Do you want to tell me what happened when I startled you?"

Rhea stopped breathing. She should have known Morgan had been aware of what was happening to her. She didn't miss much.

Rhea sighed. "When I was in prison, they would toss our ells to look for contraband. They would storm the block and lock everyone down. They'd throw everything we had on the floor and go through our stuff. Nothing was private. Sometimes it was routine, but sometimes they did it because they wanted to make a point. For a moment there it was like I was back in my cell. You can put the rest of it together."

"I'm sorry. I can't imagine."

Rhea stiffened. The memory of prison and the fear made her defensive, and having Morgan close made her feel vulnerable. She had to put some distance between them. "It's not your problem."

Morgan leaned down and kissed Rhea lightly. "Yes, it is."

The instant Morgan's lips were on hers, Rhea was flying. Her body hummed with energy that coiled in her center and grew into a red-hot ball of need. Rhea let go and gave in to her desire. She pushed against Morgan until she felt hard muscle against her middle. She pressed into the kiss and slid her tongue against Morgan's lips and pushed into her mouth. Morgan seemed to melt against her and was completely submissive to her touch. All thought left her. Rhea was completely going with her feelings and her feelings were telling her she wanted more of Morgan.

Rhea pushed Morgan against the wall and felt her groan against her mouth. She pushed her hands into Morgan's hair, amazed by the silky smoothness. The contrast between the fear and concern and desire she had experienced in the last few minutes had her grasping for reason, but her body had completely surrendered, and she no longer had the strength to run away anymore. Rhea's hand grazed Morgan's neck. Morgan jerked back with a wince. Rhea pulled away, gasping for breath.

"Shit. I'm sorry. I didn't mean to hurt you."

Morgan reached for her before she could break the connection between them. "It's okay. I forgot about the burns until just now. I wasn't thinking."

Rhea was tense and struggled to hold back the torrent of fear and want that warred within her. She gritted her teeth. "How do you do that?"

"Do what?" Morgan asked.

"Make me lose control."

Morgan smiled. "It felt like a good thing to me."

"See, you say things like that, but what's the catch? What's your game?"

Morgan frowned. "There's no game, Rhea." Morgan brushed a finger along Rhea's hairline across her forehead. "I think you are captivating and beautiful."

Rhea pushed Morgan away. "Don't say that. Don't ever say that."

Morgan slumped down onto a stack of crates. "Okay. I don't know what's happening right now, but I'm sorry I upset you."

"You don't get it. I'm bad for you. I'm bad for everyone. I lost control and hurt you." Rhea's pulse was racing. She wasn't sure whether to run or surrender. She'd managed to turn the best moment of her life into just another bad thing.

Morgan put her hands up. "Will you stop that already? You didn't mean to hurt me. I'm very much aware of how bad this hurts and I didn't care. I wanted to kiss you. You didn't do anything wrong."

Rhea stared. "I don't know what's happening. I don't know if I can handle this." Her voice trembled. She felt so defeated and lost. She'd never experienced anything like this before. She looked at Morgan, and some of the pain surrounding her heart eased. Morgan looked just as scared as she was.

Morgan shrugged. "It's okay. You can make all the moves, and I'll follow. We'll figure it out as we go. There aren't any rules to this. Even if you don't want anything at all between us, it's okay."

Rhea wanted to believe Morgan, but she wasn't sure she could try. Morgan was giving her control, something she'd never had before. Morgan was willing to trust her. Maybe she could take a chance.

She stepped closer. "I'm not sure."

"Okay," Morgan answered and pulled her into her arms.

Rhea focused on the tenderness in Morgan's touch and slid her arms around Morgan's waist and rested her head on Morgan's shoulder. Morgan was warm and strong and comforting, and for the first time Rhea let herself trust. There was no pain, no fear, no struggle, when she was in Morgan's arms.

❖

Rhea put away the last of the tools and checked the clock. It was time to feed and close up the barn for the night. She hadn't seen Morgan since their talk earlier that morning. Morgan was keeping her promise and giving her space to make her own decisions about where things would go. She closed up the shop and headed to the barn. After the chores were done, she'd go to the house to get Soldier and visit with Morgan. Putting the two of them together to mend was the best way she could think of to keep them both out of trouble. Soldier had been more protective of Morgan since the fire, and he was more willing to stay put if he was watching over her.

Rhea nuzzled the ears of the old mare and slipped her a slice of apple. Her stomach rumbled and she took the last bite for herself. "Sorry, girl, I guess it's time for my dinner too." As she closed the stall door, a strong arm came around her and a hand clasped over her mouth. In an instant she was pulled off her feet. She tried to scream, but his hand was over her mouth. She kicked wildly against the legs of her attacker but couldn't break free of his hold.

A rough voice chuckled and hot breath blew against her hair. "I knew you'd be feisty. I like that, but you'll stop if you don't want Morgan to have the same little accident as that dog of yours."

Rhea stilled. Oh God, not Morgan. Rhea closed her eyes and gritted her teeth. She took a deep breath and tried to take her mind to a distant place she'd created as a child when her father hurt her. It was like putting a part of herself away in a safe place where the pain and horror couldn't reach. It was the only way she'd survived the years of his abuse, and she used that skill now to protect her from a new threat.

The man pushed her against the wall, and a knee slammed into her back so hard it knocked the breath out of her. Her lungs screamed for air and pain shot through her back like an electric shock. Rhea struggled to draw a breath as black spots danced in her vision. She gasped as air suddenly filled her lungs, and she swallowed gulps of air like water. Her mind cleared, and she realized if this guy was with her, he couldn't hurt Morgan or Soldier. The realization that she could fight bolstered her courage, and when he grabbed her left arm to turn her to face him, she swung her right hand around and slammed her fist into his ear. She'd caught him off guard and he stumbled. As he struggled to regain control, she slammed her fist into his face with all the force she could muster. He grunted but didn't loosen his grip on her.

"You'll pay for that, bitch." He slapped her across the face and lightning shot through her head. He grabbed her by the throat and threw her to the floor. Rhea's head hit the wall and her vision dimmed. *Don't lose consciousness, don't black out now.* She couldn't let this bastard win. Rhea squinted up at her attacker, but before she could see his face, he slammed her to the ground again.

Rhea pushed against the ground and tried to get up when a boot landed next to her. The next thing she knew, his foot crashed against her head. Blood flooded her mouth, and something crunched in her jaw. She spat on the floor, and blood and one of her teeth hit the ground. She growled and tried to push herself up again. He planted his foot against the center of her back, forcing her back to the ground.

Time shifted and Rhea stared at the blank glass eyes of her teddy bear, stuffed under her bed. There was nothing she could do. Hot tears burned her skin as they leaked from her eyes and pooled on the floor. His thick hand clenched around her throat smashing her face against the cold wood. She whimpered against the pain.

"Shut up. I told you to be quiet."

She cried for her mother, but she didn't come. She prayed for God to save her, but he didn't hear her pleas.

He grabbed her by the back of the shirt and pulled her to her feet. Rhea blinked and tried to focus, but it was hard to remember where she was.

"This is how things work," a rough voice said in her ear. "You do what I say and I won't kill you. Try to run or any more of your little stunts and I'll have you watch while I drain Morgan dry."

The sound of Morgan's name snapped her back to the present. The hand holding her was not her father's and she was no longer a helpless child.

"Screw you, you bastard."

He laughed. "Oh no, that's your job, sweetheart."

Rhea kicked again and fought to pull away from his grasp. She had to get away. There was no way she was letting this creep touch her.

He slammed her head against the wall again, and light burst behind her eyes before everything went dark.

Chapter Sixteen

A hammer thundered against the inside of Rhea's skull and the acrid smell of mildew and dirt filled her nose and throat. She tried to move, but her hands were bound behind her back and her head screamed in protest when she moved. The room began to spin, and she felt dizzy and weak. She listened but couldn't hear anything. Maybe she was alone. She opened her eyes and managed to turn enough to get her face out of the dirt. She squinted through the grime, but her eye was swollen, making it difficult to see anything. She lifted her head and tried to force her eyes open. She had to figure out where she was. A sinister laugh echoed through the room and acid rose in her stomach. He was there. He was taunting her, mocking her.

"What's the matter, little girl, can't find your way out of the box?" He laughed.

Rhea jerked. His voice was getting closer, and she could smell his breath.

"You made this too easy. I guess all those years on a prison schedule is a hard habit to break. It's been fun watching this little dance between you and Morgan. Man, how pathetic. I can't believe she thinks she can have what so clearly belongs to a man." He ran his finger along her neck.

Rhea winced at the line of fire that followed his touch and seared through her veins. She couldn't let him see her fear. If he could break her, he would enjoy her suffering, and she wouldn't give him the satisfaction. She drew her knees up to her chest and rolled onto her back, ignoring the pain cutting into her hands and ripping through her shoulders. She ground her teeth together and glared up at him with all the hatred and rage that boiled inside her.

"What do you want?" she asked.

He laughed. "*What do you want? Why are you doing this?* It's always the same questions. Come on, Rhea, you can do better than that."

He leaned over her, and Rhea shifted to keep her feet between them.

"Some things are obvious, aren't they," he sneered and blew her a kiss.

Rhea lashed out with her legs, kicking wildly, but her control was off. Something was wrong with her.

He jumped back, laughing. "See, I knew you'd make this fun."

She needed to get smart if she was going to get out of this. She sized him up. He was at least six feet tall and there was something about his voice she thought she recognized. She replayed what had happened, and the memory of his breath presented the perfect picture in her mind. She pushed herself onto her knees. The plastic zip ties around her wrists cut into her arms and her hands were going numb. She wiggled her fingers to restore the circulation as she glared up at her captor. She wouldn't tip her hand. She sat back on her heels and worked at the leg of her jeans to get to the knife she kept in her boot. With a little luck she'd be able to get her hands free. "What did you give me?"

"Hmm. Figured that out, did you? It's just a little something to loosen you up a bit. We'll have a little more as soon as Morgan joins us." He leaned forward, and Rhea was able to see his face clearly for the first time.

No. Not Morgan. She couldn't let him hurt her. She should have known who was behind all of this all along. All the cards were on the table now, and she knew they were about to play out the endgame.

"What are you waiting for, big man? Do you think you can jus* take what you want and I'll just entertain you? What are you waiting for, Jeff, or do you need an audience to get it up?"

She knew she'd hit a nerve. His face was red with rage, and he chewed the wad of tobacco pressed into his cheek with grinding force.

"Aw, the big bad man can't control his little wiener," Rhea teased.

"There's nothing wrong with my dick"—he spat—"and just as soon as Morgan arrives, I'll prove it."

Oh, damn, he was going after Morgan. But what did he mean by *when she gets here*? Rhea bit down on her tongue and tried to clear the fog out of her head. She didn't want to imagine this man's filthy hands on Morgan.

"This is between me and you. Let's settle this. Leave Morgan out of it."

He laughed at her. "You think this is about you? Oh no, it's about time I teach Morgan a little lesson. She and I have a little score to settle once and for all."

Rhea was speechless. What was it with this guy and Morgan?

"Yeah, you heard me, girly. And don't you worry, she'll be along soon."

"Leave Morgan out of this," Rhea growled.

He laughed again. "Oh, I can't do that. I've waited a long time to teach that holier-than-thou bitch a lesson, and thanks to you, I'll finally get my chance."

Thanks to her? What was this grudge about? Rhea scanned the room. She wasn't sure where she was, but she guessed it had to be somewhere near or inside the studio, by the smell of smoke and ash. The room wasn't very big and had a dirt floor. Maybe it was an old storm cellar or something. She looked around, but no matter where she looked she couldn't see a way out, and there was no way she'd be able to get past him with her hands tied. She had to figure a way out of this before he involved Morgan. Everybody had a game, and she needed to figure out his.

"So what's your beef with Morgan? Did she steal your

girlfriend or something, and your little-boy ego can't handle it?" He didn't answer. "Ah, that must be it. Morgan showed you up, and you lost the girl. Dude, accept it, she's better than you." Rhea chuckled. "I can't believe you think this can end well for you. You'll rot in prison, and trust me, a little pissant like you will be very popular on the inside."

He turned and spat on the ground in front of her. "Got you again, sweetheart. I won't be going to prison. When I'm done, everyone will believe it was all you." He laughed. "My little ex-con scapegoat. Are you getting the picture yet, sweetheart? The police already know you're up to no good. All I had to do was give them a little incentive. Everyone already knows you're a murderer, and when you and Morgan have a little falling-out, you lose it again and kill her too. Morgan never did know when to leave things alone. When she's dead, everyone will believe it was you."

Rhea's mind was racing. She knew his plan, but she didn't understand why. What drove this guy to want to kill Morgan? If she could just find out why, she could play the game.

❖

Morgan walked the perimeter of her property and looked out over the fields. Spring wildflowers dotted the landscape with a rainbow of color. Wild orchids grew along the stone wall and pink lady slippers graced the edge of the back field like an invasion of ballerinas. Morning dew dotted the fresh leaves, and blades of grass filled the air with the crisp fragrance of spring. She took a deep breath and gave thanks for her life. She looked down across the field to Rhea's cabin. The windows were dark, and she hadn't seen any sign of her since the day before. She wanted to see Rhea, she needed to see her. She missed her. But she'd promised Rhea the chance to decide for herself where things would go between them.

She looked at her watch. It was strange that Rhea wasn't already up and moving about the farm. The goats hadn't been let out for the day, and it was past time for feeding. Morgan walked past the cabin on her way to the barn, but there was no sign of Rhea there either. She went ahead and got started on the chores. Maybe Rhea was sleeping in. After the events of the past few days, she wouldn't be surprised if she needed a little rest.

Morgan played with the goats and moved on to the horses. She felt good despite the nagging burns and the cast on her hand. The lights were on in the barn and the horses were restless as if they'd been spooked. She tried to soothe them, but nothing worked. Even the old mare refused to come to her despite the offer of a treat. Morgan had an uneasy feeling. Where was Rhea? She looked around and spotted something odd on the wall. She ran the tip of her finger through the dark smudge staining the old timber. Morgan's heart stopped when she realized it was blood. Fear gripped her heart and smothered her soul. Rhea?

Morgan took a step back and looked around. Something had happened here. There were drops of blood and something else on the floor. Morgan bent down and picked it up. Her stomach revolted, and she yelled out when she realized she was holding a tooth. "Oh, dear God," Morgan yelled and covered her mouth with the casted hand. Tears filled her eyes. Oh my God, what had happened? Morgan turned in a circle, scrutinizing everything around her. There was no doubt now that something was terribly wrong. Something had happened to Rhea.

Morgan ran back to the house. She needed to check the video footage from the barn. Why hadn't she done this earlier? She'd been too wrapped up in herself and too medicated to think clearly. Why hadn't she paid attention to the warnings? This should have been the first thing she did as soon as she'd gotten home. She threw open the door and Soldier jumped to his feet. She ran into the office and worked her way through the video footage. Soldier laid his head in her lap, and she mindlessly rubbed his ears. "It's going to be okay, we're going to find her. I promise we'll find her."

Morgan sped through the video recordings, beginning with the last time she'd seen Rhea. She slowed the tape when she saw Rhea enter the barn the night before. Her heart sank when she saw a dark figure lurking in the background. Whoever it was, he was waiting for her.

Morgan's phone rang. She ignored it, irritated by the interruption. Nothing was more important at that moment than finding out what had happened to Rhea and getting her back. She watched Rhea step out of the mare's stall.

"Look out," she screamed when the large figure dressed all in black with a hood pulled over his head grabbed Rhea. She watched in horror as he slammed Rhea to the floor and kicked her. Rhea tried to fight but she was no match for the big man. There was a moment when Rhea looked right into the camera. Morgan recognized the look of terror on her face, and the moment when Rhea shut down.

Morgan's phone rang again and she grabbed it in irritation. The number was blocked. She ignored it. She was just about to push the button to call the police when a text message appeared. Morgan opened the text and couldn't believe what she saw. Oh God, no. She stared at the message. Her body went hot as if she was on fire again, but this time it was her rage fueling the flames. She steadied herself and tried to think of a way out of this. She needed to call the police, but by the time they arrived it could be too late. She swallowed the knot of fear and rage swelling in her throat and knew what she had to do.

❖

"Looks like your girlfriend doesn't want to answer the phone. I wonder what we could do to change her mind."

Rhea snarled, "She isn't my girlfriend."

He grinned at her and shrugged. "It doesn't matter what you think, I'm betting Morgan thinks different." He pulled a syringe out of a small black bag he had sitting on an old crate that looked like it had been there since before she was born.

"Yeah, why's that?"

He leaned in front of her and she held her breath to ward off his stench. She flinched when the needle bit into her skin.

"You think I'm the bad guy here, but you just think you know Morgan. I know the real Morgan, and before this is over, you will too. She likes to make you think she's all perfect and devoted and pure, but when it counts, she won't be there when you need her. She's a coward."

"You know so much, enlighten me. Tell me what she did." Rhea blinked as a sudden rush hit her and she was flooded with a feeling of euphoria that made her want to forget everything. She closed her eyes tight and fought the wave of nausea that hit, as if her stomach had been flipped. Her veins burned as if liquid fire coursed through her blood, and her vision dimmed. Her skin tingled, and she had the desperate need to go to sleep.

"He's talking about Ashley."

Morgan's voice came out of the darkness and Rhea's heart jumped. She was so grateful to hear Morgan's voice and know she had come for her, but then fear and sorrow washed over her. Morgan shouldn't have come. But she couldn't have known what she was getting into.

Morgan stepped into the dim light. Her face was calm and her jaw was set with determination. Morgan's strength and unwavering conviction never faltered even when she looked at Rhea. There was compassion and sorrow and anger in her eyes but not fear. Rhea let out her breath and hoped Morgan had a plan. She fought to keep her mind clear. She had to figure a way out of this, or she was going to lose everything.

"Ah, Morgan, glad you decided to join us. I was beginning to think you were just going to let our little friend here die alone. That's your thing, isn't it, like the way you let Ashley die?"

"You're right. I failed Ashley. And I'll never forgive myself for not being there. That's something I have to live with every day."

"Damn right, it was your fault. She was fine before she met you," Jeff growled.

Morgan shook her head. "We were only kids when we met. Ashley didn't start using drugs until after your parents sent her away ·o we couldn't be together."

"You're the reason she had to leave. You corrupted her and filled her head with filth."

Morgan shook her head. "I failed her. I wasn't enough to save her, but I wasn't the one that broke her. You have to forgive yourself for that. We all made mistakes."

"You're the reason she's dead," he shouted.

Morgan looked at Rhea as if she was saying good-bye. What was she up to?

"Well, you have my attention, Jeff. Leave Rhea out of this."

He laughed. "Oh, but Rhea has a very important part to play. You took something I loved, and I'm going to take everything from you."

"Ashley loved you, Jeff. All she needed, all she ever wanted was for you to accept her and love her for who she was. She was hurt and confused and she needed her family."

"Stop it. You made her think she was queer. She wasn't like that before you started putting that crap into her head."

Morgan shook her head. "I understand your need to believe that, but I wasn't the first girl Ashley dated. Ashley started using drugs to try to drown out her feelings because your family wouldn't accept who she was. They kicked her out and she had nowhere to go. She was lost and lonely and afraid. It doesn't matter how much you punish me. It won't undo what you did and it won't bring her back. You have to forgive yourself."

"Shut up. You don't know what you're talking about."

Morgan took a step toward Rhea.

Jeff pulled out a gun and pointed it at Morgan. "Move away from her."

Morgan stopped. "You're not going to shoot me, Jeff. You didn't go through all this just to shoot me. I know you're angry and hurt, but this won't take that away."

Jeff grinned. "You're right. After what you did to my sister, I've got a lot planned for you."

He motioned for Morgan to move with a quick flick of the gun. "Over here."

Morgan did as she was told but never took her eyes off Rhea

Her face was swollen and bruised and blood crusted at the corner of her mouth. She had to get Rhea out of this.

"Sit down," Jeff demanded.

"No," Morgan replied. She wouldn't let him think for a minute that he had control.

Jeff pointed the gun at Rhea. "Sit down or I'll shoot her."

Morgan's stomach lurched, and she fought the urge to scream. She shook her head. "No, you won't. If you shoot her, it's all over."

Rhea had gone pale and Morgan knew she was scared. She needed to do something, send some signal that she wouldn't leave her, that she would be all right.

"You never did know what to do with strong women. Did you really think you could just come here and wave a gun around, and I'd just do anything you want?"

Jeff grabbed Rhea by the shoulder and pulled her to her feet. He wrapped his arm around her throat and squeezed until she whimpered. He licked his tongue up the side of her face and sneered. The look of horror and disgust on Rhea's face almost broke Morgan. She'd beg if he wanted her to, anything to make this stop.

"Come on, Jeff, we both know she's not what you want. She's a good soldier. She shouldn't have to pay for our sins."

Rhea's eyes brightened and Morgan was certain she'd understood the message.

"You were the one who destroyed the horse feed and the tack room and set the fire. You blew up my studio, didn't you?"

Jeff grinned. "That was fun. I didn't expect you to be there, though. That was a bonus." He laughed. "You flew through the air like a rag doll. Man, that was a rush." He planted a kiss on Rhea's cheek. "I thought it was all over right then, but our girl here had to swoop in and save you. But not this time, no one's walking away this time. I've had a lot of fun around here these last few months. I thought for sure you'd drown your fool self after I lured that calf into the mud. You actually thought he just wandered out there all by himself. I knew then I had to send a better message, play with you a little bit. Then Rhea here gave me the perfect idea. It was easy making everyone think it was her after that little stunt she pulled at the diner and everyone found out about her. Everyone already knows what a hothead she is. It won't be hard to believe when she snaps and kills you."

"So what's your plan? What is it you want from me that you think will atone for what you did to Ashley?"

Jeff pushed Rhea down in the dirt and closed the distance between them in two swift strides. His fist caught Morgan in the jaw, and her head snapped to the side. She took a staggered step back, then straightened.

"Is that all you've got? If you wanted to hit me, you could have done that a million times in a million places. I would've thought you would've wanted someone to see that."

He shoved Morgan against the wall and pointed the gun to her face. "I'm going to watch you die, Morgan. I'm going to watch the last breath bleed from you. But first I'm going to show you exactly how Ashley died. And this time you're going to be there. You're going to watch the whole show."

Morgan clenched her jaw and stared into his soulless eyes as the realization came to her and she understood what he planned to do.

❖

Rhea slid the knife open with a flick of her thumb and worked the small blade along the plastic gripping her wrists. She was having trouble focusing and she didn't have much time before he got tired of playing with Morgan and moved on with his plan. She focused on the feel of the blade sliding between her wrists and felt the plastic give with a faint snap. The rush of relief nearly took her breath away, and she almost fell over. She steadied herself the best she could. She couldn't tip her hand yet. She had to play this smart.

He held the gun to Morgan's head and pressed the barrel against her cheek. "Your little girlfriend and I have already started. I didn't give her too much to start though. I didn't want you to miss anything."

"I'm okay, Morgan. Don't listen to him," Rhea said in her most defiant tone, but despite her attempt to control her voice, the words came out slurred.

Jeff laughed. "Oh, she's okay all right. And a little more of this and she'll let me do whatever I want and won't even care."

Morgan prayed the police would be there soon. She didn't know how much longer she could draw this out without him hurting Rhea any more than he already had.

Without warning, Jeff punched Morgan in the gut and pushed her to the ground.

All the air exploded out of Morgan's lungs when he hit her. She clutched her injured hand to her chest as she gasped for air.

"Morgan," Rhea cried. "Leave her alone, you stupid fuck."

Jeff grabbed another syringe, fisted Rhea's shirt in his hand, pulled her to her knees, and reached for her arm. The instant his focus shifted, Rhea struck out and slashed the back of his hand with her blade. He let her go, and before he could react, Rhea drove the knife into his thigh.

Morgan ran at Jeff and threw her shoulder into him the moment he released Rhea. They crashed into the wall and searing pain lashed through Morgan's neck and shoulder as the tender skin was ripped open. She heard a grinding crunch, and Jeff wailed and hit the floor.

"Soldier, attack," Morgan yelled.

Soldier leaped out of the darkness and hit Jeff in the chest. He closed his powerful jaws around Jeff's hand and shook his head as if wrestling one of his chew toys. Jeff screamed and let go of the gun.

Morgan scrambled to her feet and stomped the syringe into the floor.

Jeff wailed. "Get him off me. Oh God, make him stop."

"Down, Soldier," Rhea muttered.

Soldier stopped and moved to Rhea's side.

Rhea stood over Jeff and Morgan holding the gun pointed at Jeff's face, but she didn't see him. Time had shifted and she stood in her father's study, shaking with fear and rage. She just wanted him to stop. She couldn't let him hurt them anymore. She gripped the gun in her hands so hard she couldn't feel her fingers. All she had to do was pull the trigger and all the pain would stop. He wouldn't hurt them anymore.

Morgan crawled to her feet. "Rhea," she whispered. "Give me the gun, sweetheart."

"I have to make him stop. I can't let him hurt you."

Jeff held his bloody hand to his chest and whimpered. He scooted backward on the floor, trying to get away from Rhea and the gun pointed at his head.

Morgan stepped closer to Rhea but didn't touch her. "He won't hurt either of us anymore. You can let go now."

A sob gathered in Rhea's throat. "I can't."

"Yes, you can. I've got you. I promise you, he'll never hurt you again."

Morgan gently wrapped her hand around Rhea's on the gun. "Give me the gun, Rhea. It's okay now."

A tremor ran through Rhea, and her finger ached from not pulling the trigger. She wanted to believe. She wanted the nightmare to end. The hand on hers was tender and comforting and Rhea wanted so much to trust. She was so tired of being afraid. She shifted her gaze and found the gentlest eyes she'd ever seen, staring back at her with promise and hope and love. Morgan? How did Morgan get here?

"You don't have to do this, Rhea. Trust me. I won't let him hurt you."

Perhaps it was the tenderness of Morgan's touch or maybe Rhea's own willingness to let the past go, but something inside Rhea changed. It was as if the past lost its grip on her soul and she was able to let go. Rhea nodded and released her grip on the gun.

Morgan swallowed hard and took the gun.

Jeff laughed. "Bad move, girly. Didn't I tell you Morgan's a coward?" He pushed up and stumbled to his feet. Blood oozed from the wounds ripped in his flesh by Soldier's teeth and trickled from the stab wound in his leg. When he stood up his hand was clenched around a steel rod. "I told you you'd know the real Morgan before this was over." He sneered at Rhea.

Soldier growled.

"What are you going to do, Morgan? Can you shoot me? You should have let Rhea do it. We both know you don't have the balls."

"I don't want to hurt anyone. It's over," Morgan answered.

Rhea's hand slid into Morgan's and their fingers entwined as much as the cast around Morgan's hand would allow. Morgan felt some of the tension around her heart lessen.

"Don't do this, Jeff."

Jeff drew back his arm and lunged forward.

"Morgan," Rhea screamed.

Morgan drew the gun and fire erupted from the barrel. Jeff hit the floor.

Morgan stood with the smoking gun in her hand. Her head rang and her body was rigid as stone. She stared at Jeff lying on the floor and felt something settle inside. She felt no pleasure for what she'd done, but there was no regret.

Rhea threw herself into Morgan's arms and cried.

Morgan wrapped her arms around Rhea and held on as if her soul depended on it. Rhea was all that mattered.

Rhea looked up at Morgan. "I can't believe you did it. You stopped him."

Morgan stroked Rhea's hair and kissed her head. "Sometimes if you don't fight back everyone loses."

Rhea smiled up at her. "He was wrong about one thing. I do know the real you."

Morgan pulled Rhea closer and took a deep breath. She closed her eyes and gave thanks to heaven for their lives and her new understanding of the thin line between right and wrong.

CHAPTER SEVENTEEN

Rhea heard the sirens as soon as they stepped outside. "You called the police?"

"Yeah. But I was beginning to think they weren't coming." Morgan frowned. "This might take a while to clear up. You should probably put Soldier in the house."

Rhea nodded. "Come on, Soldier, nap time."

Morgan swallowed the lump of dread growing in her throat. This wasn't going to be easy. She placed the gun on the ground and waited. She motioned the police and EMTs into the wine cellar and explained what had happened. The young officer she'd talked to at the vet clinic escorted her to a patrol car and asked her to wait. A few minutes later Rhea was back, and the tight feeling of dread squeezing her heart eased.

"Is Soldier okay?" Morgan asked, sliding her hand into Rhea's.

"Yeah, he seems to be."

"Good." Morgan tightened her grip on Rhea's hand. "I don't want you to be afraid. Everything's going to be okay now."

Rhea clung to Morgan's hand as she watched the medics and two police officers pull Jeff out of the old wine cellar on a gurney and put him in an ambulance. He might not be able to get his hands on her now, but she knew the threat wasn't over. Her skin itched and the hairs at the back of her neck stood on end. She looked around to find Officer Sims eyeing her suspiciously, and she knew it was only a matter of time before he came to question her. She knew no one would believe her story even with Morgan's account of what happened. She'd been through this before. People would believe what they wanted to believe. She was the outsider, and she was certain Jeff was spinning his own story to put doubt in everyone's mind about her. This was far from over.

As if reading her mind, Officer Sims walked toward her. His voice was cold and his words clipped when he spoke. "Ms. Daniels. Ms. Scott. I have a few questions."

"Sure," Morgan answered.

Rhea didn't say anything. She didn't trust Sims. He was the kind of guy who made up his mind about someone and then built a case around his theory. He had an agenda and it didn't involve the truth.

"Ms. Daniels, if you'd come with me please."

Rhea tensed, and Morgan's hand instantly tightened around hers.

"Is that necessary?" Morgan asked.

"It'll only take a few minutes. Officer Jones will be over to take your statement in a moment."

"Can't you just talk to us together? We haven't done anything wrong." Morgan kept her tone light, but she was uneasy. She didn't want Rhea to be put through questioning like she was a criminal.

Officer Sims rested his hand on his sidearm and sniffed. "Well, a man's been shot on your property, Ms. Scott. I'd say that's a bit out of the ordinary, and we need to put together what happened here."

"What happened here is that Jeff was trespassing on my property, abducted Rhea, and was going to kill me and Rhea too, and have her blamed for everything."

Morgan was losing her patience. Officer Jones approached just as Sims stepped up and pointed his finger at Morgan.

"That's what you've told us," Sims said, "but we have Jeff telling us a different story, a much more likely story. See, we have to assume the possibility that Rhea invited Jeff here, maybe they had an argument, and things got out of hand. Then again, maybe she lured him here with plans to kill him. You see, Ms. Scott, there's still a lot of unanswered questions, and we need answers." He shifted h weight and spread his legs, broadening his stance as if preparing for a fight. "Now if you have a problem with that, we have to assume you have something to hide. At the very least, I can charge you with impeding a police investigation."

Rhea stepped in front of Morgan, putting herself between her and the officer. "It's okay, Morgan." She turned to face Sims. "I'll go."

Sims grinned at Rhea as if he'd just won a game. Morgan knew if he got Rhea alone he'd be pursuing her as the perpetrator of a crime and not as a victim. Morgan pulled out her cell phone and hit play. Jeff's voice blasted from the speaker.

Sit down.

No.

Sit down or I'll shoot her.

No, you won't. If you shoot her, it's all over. You never did know what to do with strong women. Did you really think you could just come here and wave a gun around and I'd just do anything you want?

There was the sound of scuffling and a whimper.

Come on, Jeff, we both know she's not what you want. She's a good soldier. She shouldn't have to pay for our sins. You were the one who destroyed the horse feed and the tack room and set the fire. You blew up my studio, didn't you?

That was fun. I didn't expect you to be there, though. That was a bonus.

Jeff laughed.

You flew through the air like a rag doll. Man, that was a rush.

Rhea stared at Morgan, her mouth slightly ajar.

Sims took a step toward Morgan so fast that she flinched and clenched her hand tight around the phone.

"What's that?" Sims demanded.

Morgan shrugged. "This is Jeff's confession. I taped the whole thing."

"Well, I'll be damned," Jones said.

Sims glared at Morgan. "She's not off the hook yet. She could have been in on the whole thing."

Morgan shook her head. "I don't think so. I have a video in my office that shows Jeff attacking and abducting Rhea from my barn." Morgan pulled something from her jeans pocket and held out her hand, palm up. "I found this on the floor where he kicked her in the face."

Rhea and the officers stared at the tooth in her hand.

Morgan glanced at Rhea. "I think that's more than you'll need to have a very clear understanding of what happened here, officers. Rhea and I will be more than happy to answer your questions, but Rhea isn't going anywhere without me."

Rhea reached for Morgan's hand. She'd never been more grateful, more surprised, or more amazed with anyone in her life.

"Holy hell," Jones said.

Sims glared at him.

"Oh, give it up, Dave."

Sims cursed and stomped off.

"Sorry, ladies"—Jones nodded toward Sims—"we'll have to get your statements separately, that's protocol. But it can wait until a medic checks Ms. Daniels out." He held up a hand and motioned the paramedic over.

"Thank you," Morgan said. "We'll be happy to answer any of your questions as soon as our attorney is present."

"You aren't being charged with anything at the moment, Ms. Scott."

"Just the same, I want to make sure there aren't any misunderstandings."

A medic set a large bag down on the ground in front of them. "Mind if I take a look?" he said, pointing to Morgan's bandages.

"In a minute. She needs you first."

"I'm okay," Rhea argued.

Morgan cupped Rhea's cheek in her hand and kissed her lightly on the lips. "Humor me. I know how tough you are, but I'll feel better, and it's more evidence."

Rhea nodded. "You'll stay with me?"

Morgan smiled. "Every minute."

Rhea slid her arms around Morgan. "Thank you," she whispered.

Morgan circled her in her arms, and Rhea knew without a doubt that she was safe.

"I told you I wouldn't let him hurt you, and I'll keep that promise," Morgan said firmly.

Rhea tightened her arms around Morgan. She had no doubt in her mind that what Morgan said was true.

❖

Would this day ever end? Rhea rubbed her eyes with the heels of her hands and yawned. She and Morgan had answered every question the police had asked, explained every detail of what happened, and turned over the audio and video recordings. They had been to the hospital and been poked, prodded, and photographed. Rhea had given blood for a drug test because of the stuff Jeff had given her, but didn't seem to be in any danger. Rhea wanted to go home and crawl into bed and sleep the memories away. But before anything else she needed to see Soldier. He'd been cooped up in the house for hours, and she needed to check his leg and feel his reassuring warmth.

Rhea shoved her hands deep into her pockets and watched Morgan say good-bye to Officer Jones. She shivered at the thought of how things could have gone if Morgan hadn't set up the video surveillance. Without that evidence, it would have been easy for everyone to believe she had been behind everything. She closed her eyes and shook herself. Going back to prison was unthinkable. After having these months of freedom, she could never again survive being put in a cage.

"Hey, are you okay? You looked a million miles away."

Rhea jumped at the sound of Morgan's voice. "Yeah, just tired."

"Well, I think they have everything they need for now. I think it's time we take care of something you need."

Rhea squinted at Morgan, confused by her meaning. "What I need?"

Morgan smiled and nodded. "Come in the house, someone's waiting for you."

Rhea's heart swelled.

Morgan put her arm around Rhea's shoulders. "You know, I'm not sure he's a normal dog. He seemed to sense what was happening. I could have sworn he could read my mind. He's very special."

Rhea smiled. "I know."

Morgan nodded and opened the door for Rhea. Soldier was lying on a giant pillow in front of the fireplace. His giant ears were up and he wagged his tail happily, but he didn't get up.

"See what I mean, even now it's like he's waiting for us to tell him you're okay before he'll move."

Rhea ran to him. She fell to her knees and hugged him. Soldier put his paw on her shoulder as if hugging her back. Rhea ran her hands all over his body, checking for injuries. She scrutinized the sutures on his shoulder and was happy to see the incision was closed and there was no new tearing. He licked her face as if trying to tell her he was okay. He yelped and whined and moaned and barked as if he was telling her his story. Rhea laughed and burrowed her face in his neck and hugged him.

Morgan smiled and sat down on the floor beside them. Rhea laid her head on Soldier and Morgan leaned down and wrapped her arms around them both. Tears filled Rhea's eyes. Morgan and Soldier had become her family, more than the one she'd been born into. Morgan had risked everything for her. She'd risked her life for her. It was too much, and she couldn't hold back her feelings anymore as everything came flooding in at once and she began to sob.

Morgan rubbed her back. "What is it?"

Rhea took a deep breath and tried to put words to her feelings. "Being here with you and Soldier has been the best time of my life and I almost lost you both."

Morgan's arms tightened around her. "We aren't going anywhere. You're safe here."

Rhea raised her head and looked at Morgan. She focused on the feel of Morgan's touch and the steady strength in Morgan's eyes. Despite everything she'd been through, Morgan was able to soothe the fear and reach beyond her armor and truly touch her.

"How did you know to record everything?"

Morgan sighed. "After I saw you on that video, I knew what I had to do, and after the way the police treated you after the fire I wanted proof. I couldn't let the system fail you again."

Rhea lowered her gaze and took a deep breath. "And how are you with what happened?"

Morgan's jaw tensed. "I don't feel good about shooting a man, but I'm very happy you're okay. I still don't think violence is the answer, but I realize that sometimes there's no other way."

Rhea nodded, understanding that Morgan was talking about more than what happened that night.

"I thought I'd killed him, and I thought a part of me would die too. I'll never understand why people hurt each other, but I couldn't allow him to hurt you either. My choice was clear, and I don't regret what I did."

"All that stuff about Ashley must have been hard for you," Rhea paused and sat up to face Morgan. "You aren't the reason she's dead, you know."

"Maybe," Morgan answered.

"You gave her choices. You loved her. But sometimes people can't accept a different life."

Morgan nodded. "I know. What about you? Can you accept a different life?"

Rhea smiled. "Does that life include you?"

Morgan grinned. "I hope so."

"Then I'd like to try."

Morgan reached out and cupped Rhea's face in her hand. She meant everything she'd said to Rhea, and as long as Rhea would let her, she'd spend the rest of her days giving Rhea that new life. She brushed her thumb across Rhea's swollen cheek. "Does it hurt much?"

"Honestly, yes, but it'll be okay."

"Hang on a minute." Morgan got up and went to the kitchen and brought back an ice pack. She held out her hand to Rhea. "Here, this might help."

"Thanks."

Morgan sat down on the sofa and stretched her legs out in front of her. Rhea put the ice pack to her cheek and winced, and Morgan couldn't get the image of Jeff kicking Rhea out of her head. She'd felt rage and desperation and helplessness, standing in front of Rhea as Jeff taunted her. The fear in Rhea's eyes had burned through her, like hot steel piercing though her heart and scorching her soul.

"I think I understand you better now. Until all of this, I didn't really understand what a sacrifice you made for your sister. I can't imagine what that must have been like for you, but I know I would have done anything for him not to hurt you."

Rhea froze. She peered off into space, and Morgan was afraid she'd said too much. Rhea had that faraway look in her eyes that she got when she relived that terrible part of her past.

"I'm sorry. I shouldn't have brought it up."

Rhea lifted her eyes to Morgan's and slowly the sadness faded and she smiled. "We finally understand each other. Maybe the only thing we need for redemption is to forgive ourselves."

Morgan nodded. "Can you do that?"

"Yeah, I think I can now. Can you?"

Morgan reached out and brushed her fingers along Rhea's hand. "I think I did the moment I stepped into that cellar and faced Jeff. Facing what happened to Ashley made me realize that although I couldn't save her, it wasn't my fault. My ego was telling me I should have been enough for her, but it never was about me."

Rhea slid her fingers into Morgan's hand, lacing their fingers together. Something inside her had changed. *She* had changed. She had spent her entire life pushing people away, hiding from intimacy, and blaming her fear on her father. She was done running, done hiding, and although her father was a sick bastard, she had the power to decide not to let him take love away from her.

"Most of my life I've had to fight to survive. I didn't think there was any other way. For years I used my anger and hatred to build a wall around myself so that no one could ever hurt me again. But being here and knowing you, I see there's so much I was missing."

Rhea settled back on the couch and leaned against Morgan. She pulled Morgan's arm around her and laced their fingers together

Morgan's steady breathing and warm touch soothed her, and the exhaustion she'd been fighting slowly won out and she fell asleep.

Morgan felt the tension slip from Rhea's body and heard the subtle change in her breathing. After everything Rhea had been through and the day they'd had, this was exactly what Morgan needed. She leaned down and placed a kiss on Rhea's head. She wasn't sure how long it would take to burn the images of what happened out of her mind, but this was a good place to start. Holding Rhea was exactly what she needed to quell the fear that was still wrapped around her heart like barbed wire. She closed her eyes and thought about what Rhea said. What was she telling her? Was Rhea admitting to feelings for her?

Morgan sighed. *I am hopelessly in love with this woman and there is absolutely nothing I can do about it.* Morgan brushed her fingers along Rhea's arm and watched her sleep. She hoped Rhea would give her a chance, give them a chance, but she knew she would love Rhea no matter what she chose. Morgan offered up her thanks for the woman in her arms and the love in her heart and drifted off to sleep.

CHAPTER EIGHTEEN

Rhea woke to find Morgan sitting across from her, reading. Her hair was damp from a shower, and she looked refreshed in a clean cotton T-shirt and a pair of running shorts. She looked younger without her usual jeans and boots. Rhea studied the firm muscles of Morgan's legs and trailed her gaze up Morgan's body to the soft curve of her lips and noticed a softening in the faint lines around her mouth and eyes. Warmth spread through her, and her stomach fluttered as she slowly took in the beauty of the woman before her. The stir of desire that she had once denied now sent a thrill of excitement rippling down her spine to the base of her belly, and her clitoris twitched.

Morgan glanced up and saw her staring. A quick smile transformed Morgan's face, and she was suddenly radiant. "Hey," Morgan said, leaning forward and putting her book down on the coffee table. "How was your nap?"

Rhea stretched and sat up. "Good. But I think I'll feel much better after a shower."

Morgan nodded. "I already put some clothes and a fresh towel in the bathroom for you. I can tell you from experience, the shower feels amazing."

"Could you be any more perfect?"

Morgan felt her face go hot and dropped her gaze.

Rhea smiled. "I'll only be a few minutes."

Morgan watched as Rhea stood and made her way to the bathroom. She'd awoken with Rhea cradled in her arms, and she'd almost cried from relief and gratitude. She'd watched Rhea sleep, thinking of how much Rhea had changed her life, changed her, and how much she'd grown to need Rhea. She loved her.

Morgan was still lost in her thoughts when Rhea came back, looking fresh and revived from the shower. Her skin glowed from the heat of the water on her skin, and she looked nervous as she fingered her hair into place. Morgan's heart ached as her gaze fell on the bruise along Rhea's face and the swelling around her eye where she'd been kicked.

Rhea walked up to Morgan until she stood in front of her and held out her hand. She wasn't sure what she was doing, but she couldn't stop. She wanted to touch Morgan. She wanted to be touched. She was done hiding.

Morgan looked up at her and narrowed her eyes with a questioning look and took her hand. Rhea pulled Morgan to her feet and wrapped an arm around Morgan's waist and slid the other around her neck wrapping her fingers in Morgan's hair. Morgan's gaze burned into her, but it wasn't the soulless lust of her fears. Morgan looked at her like she was something to be cherished.

Rhea pulled Morgan closer until their lips met. Morgan's mouth was sweet and warm. She could spend hours exploring and tasting Morgan's lips, her mouth, her tongue.

Morgan slid her hands over Rhea's hips and around her back. She spread her fingers over the small curve just above her waist and gently pulled her closer.

Rhea had never felt anything so tender in her life. Morgan didn't just kiss her, she filled her, tasted her, and pulled her desire and need to the surface until she wanted Morgan's mouth everywhere. Morgan promised her a new life, but she was the one who had to claim it. Somewhere along the way she had begun to need Morgan, and after what they'd been through together, she couldn't hide from her feelings any longer.

Rhea pulled away and studied Morgan's face, and this time she recognized her need reflected back through Morgan's eyes. There was fire just beneath the surface, but her need wasn't possession. Her need was about giving, not taking.

"Teach me how to touch you," Rhea whispered. "I want to know what it's like to touch you."

Morgan drew in a deep breath as if she had just surfaced after holding her breath underwater. She pulled Rhea closer and caressed her face. Morgan traced her fingers over the bruise on Rhea's cheek and the swollen spot on her jaw. "Does it still hurt?"

"Not too much. Not you. You heal me."

Morgan leaned down and kissed her.

The instant their lips met, Rhea melted into Morgan and let herself go. She needed to be closer. She wanted to feel Morgan in a way she had never wanted anyone before. Morgan's mouth was hot, and she slipped her tongue inside to lick at the flames of Morgan's desire.

Morgan moaned and trembled. Rhea was amazed how Morgan yielded to her without losing herself. Rhea grasped the edges of Morgan's shirt and the tank she wore beneath and slowly worked it up Morgan's body, taking in every inch of flesh revealed as she pulled the shirt over Morgan's head and let it fall to the floor. She stared at Morgan's bare breasts, and the nipples hardened under her gaze, sending a thrill through Rhea that made her skin burn hot. She had dreamed of this body for weeks. Morgan had perfectly sculpted curves of muscle shrouded in delicate soft skin. Rhea raised her hand and brushed her fingertips across Morgan's breast. Morgan's chest swelled as she drew in a deep breath of air. Rhea pressed her hand to Morgan's chest and felt the strong rhythm of her heart beating against her palm. She had never seen anything more beautiful.

When Rhea raked her fingertip down Morgan's side and across her stomach, Morgan trembled and dug her fingers into Rhea's hips.

"Is this okay?" Rhea asked.

"Yes," Morgan answered, her voice tight and strained. "I'm going to have to lie down soon. My legs won't hold me much longer if you keep doing that."

Rhea's face grew hot, but she didn't let the embarrassment deter her. She was excited by Morgan's response to her. "Show me."

Morgan took her hand and led her to her bedroom, stopping just outside the door. She kissed Rhea again, but this time she didn't hold back. She stroked Rhea's lips and filled her mouth with her tongue, claiming her until it was Rhea who struggled to stand. The kiss was deep yet gentle, delicate yet possessing. Morgan was claiming her.

Morgan moved to Rhea's neck, planting kisses along the sensitive skin, making Rhea shudder with need. Rhea let her head fall back, offering herself to Morgan. Morgan's touch left trails of pleasure along her skin that made her dizzy with want.

Rhea took a step back, leading Morgan into the room until they stood by the bed. Rhea resisted when Morgan tried to guide her down onto the bed.

"No. I can't have you on top of me." She swallowed and felt the first wave of trepidation ripple through her until she was shaking.

"It's okay," Morgan whispered. "We can do this any way you want. We can stop any time you want."

"I don't want to stop. Show me how to love you."

Morgan sat on the edge of the bed and lay back until she was stretched out on her back. Rhea followed her down onto the bed, straddling Morgan's hips. Rhea's heart beat so hard she was certain Morgan could hear. Morgan took Rhea's hands and placed them over her breasts. Rhea instinctively caressed the soft mounds of flesh and raked her thumbs across Morgan's nipples, watching them harden at her touch.

Morgan groaned and lifted her hips. The pressure of Morgan's thigh against Rhea's clitoris was like a bolt of lightning igniting a fire, and she felt herself swell. She sat up and gripped the end of her shirt and pulled it over her head, as another tendril of uncertainty snaked up her spine. Rhea shivered as the cool air hit her skin and Morgan's gaze fell to her breasts.

"You are so beautiful," Morgan whispered.

Rhea started to protest, but Morgan reached up and cupped her face in her hand, drawing her back to the moment. "If you will let me, I'll show you all the ways you are beautiful to me."

Rhea smiled, knowing in her heart Morgan could honor her words. The way Morgan looked at her, the way she touched her, made Rhea believe she *was* beautiful.

"What do I do?" Rhea asked.

"All you have to do is touch me."

Rhea took Morgan's hand and placed it over her breast and felt Morgan's fingers close around her nipple. A flood of heat coursed through her, and she throbbed low in her belly and between her thighs as liquid heat filled her. Morgan sat up and cupped Rhea's breast in her hand as she kissed her. Rhea dug her fingers into Morgan's wrist, holding her to her. Her hips surged and her thighs ached. She needed more. She pushed Morgan back onto the bed and tugged at Morgan's shorts and slowly pulled them down exposing more muscle and honey-brown skin and the soft mound of short dark hair cloaking tender folds of pink flesh.

Morgan reached for her. "Will you take yours off too? I want to feel you against me."

Rhea removed her own shorts with trembling fingers. This was the most vulnerable she had ever allowed herself to be with anyone. She didn't recognize what was happening to her body, but it was a feeling beyond anything she had hoped. She let her guard down and took a chance. She crawled up Morgan's body and settled over her until their nipples brushed and their centers met in a union of heat on heat, wet on wet, skin on skin.

She looked into Morgan's eyes and brushed her fingers through Morgan's hair. Morgan held her gaze as if they were tied to each other's souls. Rhea pushed up with her arms and gasped when Morgan took her breast into her mouth. The heat, the silky wetness, and the smooth, firm stroke of Morgan's tongue sent waves of pleasure coursing through her until the pressure between her legs threatened to burst. She craved Morgan, and every cell in her body cried out for her touch, her mouth.

"Oh God, Morgan, show me now. Show me how to touch you. Show me."

Morgan took Rhea's hand and guided her fingers between her legs through her wetness until Rhea's fingers slid through the slick folds and pressed against her hard clitoris.

Rhea gasped. "You're so wet."

"For you," Morgan groaned.

Rhea moved her hand to her own sex and touched herself lightly. "Oh."

Morgan smiled up at her. "You are amazing."

Rhea slid her hand between Morgan's thighs and slid her fingers through the wet folds of molten flesh. She watched the pulse in Morgan's neck quicken and closed her mouth around it and sucked until Morgan writhed beneath her.

"Please don't stop."

Rhea kissed Morgan and slid into her, feeling the delicate muscles tighten around her fingers. With each stroke she could feel the tension building in her center, and blood rushed to her head until she could no longer think. Morgan's hand brushed through her hair and down her back in gentle strokes urging her forward, drawing her deeper. Morgan's touch was featherlight and warmed her like beams of sunshine. Morgan moved against her, mirroring each stroke of her hand. With each movement, her clitoris rocked against Morgan's thigh. She pressed herself harder against Morgan until she thought her mind would melt and her body would explode.

"Oh, Rhea," Morgan moaned. "That's it, sweetheart. Oh, heavens, I can't hold on much longer." Morgan tensed and groaned against Rhea's neck. She was close. She had dreamed of what it would be like to make love to Rhea, but she hadn't expected to feel so completely consumed. She wanted to touch Rhea, taste her, and explore every inch of her. She groaned and tempered the urge to take Rhea. She wouldn't push. She had to let Rhea set the pace. Rhea was so brave and Morgan wanted to give herself to her in every way, but she couldn't let her want come before Rhea's need.

Rhea's clitoris rubbed against her thigh with every stroke and thrust, and Morgan was lost in the feel of Rhea's heat, and the glide of her wet lips against her sent her to the edge.

"Now," Morgan whispered. Her body tensed and ripples of pleasure grew until she couldn't hold back the orgasm any longer. "Now, I'm coming now."

Morgan marveled at the power surging through her body as she gave herself to Rhea, completely trusting her with her body, her heart, and her soul. Morgan felt both empowered and humbled by the beauty and purity of Rhea's trust, and her heart ached with the love filling her.

Rhea rocked her hips faster, pushing her clitoris into the firm muscle of Morgan's thigh. "Oh yes," Rhea cried out, as the pressure in her clitoris exploded and waves of pleasure pulsed through her like waves crashing against shore. Pleasure erupted inside her until she was beyond reason and the ecstasy spread to her fingertips and the very ends of her toes. She fell against Morgan's chest and held her in her arms, feeling Morgan tremble beneath her, mirroring the shocks of pleasure still pulsing within her.

Morgan stroked her hair and ran her fingers along her spine in long tender caresses. "Please let me touch you."

"I don't know if I can," Rhea answered, her voice barely a whisper.

Morgan wrapped her arms around Rhea and rolled so that they were on their sides facing each other. She cupped Rhea's cheek and kissed her.

"Look at me."

Morgan smiled when Rhea looked at her and began to trace her fingers along the line of muscle along Rhea's neck to the hollow at the base of her throat. She leaned down and took Rhea's nipple into her mouth and sucked until Rhea gripped her hair and she felt Rhea's hips thrust against her.

"I will never hurt you," Morgan said as she slid her hand between them and stroked Rhea's thigh, seeking permission. "I want you to think about what we just did and how wonderful that felt. I want to make you feel that again." She kissed Rhea again and this time slid down Rhea's body, taking her nipple in her mouth again. Morgan teased and kissed Rhea until she groaned and thrust her hips, telegraphing her need.

Morgan smiled against Rhea's breast and began to kiss her way lower. Rhea rolled and Morgan wrapped her arms around her thighs and settled between Rhea's legs.

Rhea whimpered and ran her fingers through Morgan's hair.

Morgan pressed a kiss to the apex of Rhea's sex.

Rhea jerked when Morgan's lips brushed against her clitoris, overwhelmed with pleasure as the heat of Morgan's mouth bathed her. She lifted her hips and surrendered to Morgan's mouth. Rhea gasped when Morgan's tongue brushed against her clitoris again, and the world around her melted away. She looked down into Morgan's eyes, amazed by what was happening.

"Stay with me," Morgan whispered.

The muscles in Rhea's thighs tightened as Morgan licked her tongue up the length of Rhea's clitoris. Need coiled inside her until she couldn't take much more.

"Please, Morgan."

Morgan's mouth closed around her and she shuddered as the tension unraveled, unleashing a flood of pleasure so intense she cried out.

"Oh my God, please, please, don't stop." Rhea gripped Morgan's hair in her hands, holding her to her, and tightened her thighs around Morgan as her hips bucked, and she erupted in Morgan's mouth. Morgan stroked her and kissed her until the last waves of her orgasm subsided, before kissing her way up her body.

Tears of pleasure trickled from the corners of Rhea's eyes, and Morgan kissed each one away with a tender brush of her lips.

"Are you okay?"

Rhea buried her face against Morgan's chest. "I never imagined it could be like this." She cradled Morgan's breast in her hand as Morgan's arms closed around her.

❖

Morgan held a trembling Rhea in her arms and gasped as the last aftershocks swept through her. They had made love through the night exploring and claiming each other's bodies until they were both spent and sated. Rhea had been silent for so long Morgan thought she'd fallen asleep.

She held her breath and tried to plot a course from here. She had no idea how Rhea would feel about what had happened between them. If Rhea turned away from her now, it would break her. She'd held nothing back and had given her heart to Rhea along with her body. Doubt crept into her mind and fear shimmied down her spine.

"Are you okay?" Rhea said in a tired voice.

"Are you?"

Rhea lifted her head and looked at her. Morgan searched Rhea's face for any sign of doubt or regret or fear or hurt. But Rhea's eyes were bright and there was a new lightness in her face that Morgan had never seen before.

Rhea smiled. "I don't know how to describe what I feel. It's like I was trying to find something, but I didn't know what it was until I found you. I never imagined I could feel like this."

Morgan let out a sigh of relief. "You're amazing, and I can't imagine anything more beautiful than making love with you. I could hold you forever."

Rhea stilled and a faint line creased her brow. "Do you mean that?" Rhea asked.

"Of course."

"What if I can't be who you want me to be?"

Morgan took Rhea's hand and kissed the tips of her fingers. "I only want you to be you. You, just the way you are, nothing more and nothing less." Morgan was holding her heart out to Rhea. This wouldn't be the first time she'd wanted to be enough for someone, only to be turned away. She'd been selfish in the past and asked too much. She wouldn't do that to Rhea. She would walk away before she did that.

"If this is too much, Rhea, all you have to do is say so."

Rhea rolled on top of Morgan and kissed her. She took her time exploring every recess of Morgan's mouth until Morgan's doubt was a vague memory.

Morgan groaned. "Rhea?"

"Hmm," Rhea answered, playing her fingers across Morgan's chest.

Morgan swallowed, afraid she was about to say something Rhea wasn't able to hear. "I love you."

Rhea's fingers stilled.

"You don't have to say anything. I just wanted you to know. Just tell me what you need, and I'll do it."

Rhea pulled away from Morgan and pushed up on her elbow so she was looking down at Morgan. "What I need is to have you show me more of the things you like. I need to hear you call out my name until I believe all of this is real. I want you to make me feel things beyond imagining. I want you to show me all the things I never knew about love."

Morgan slid her hand up Rhea's back. "I can do that."

Rhea smiled and wiggled closer against Morgan with a contented sigh and played her fingers along Morgan's cheek. She leaned down until her lips were a breath away from Morgan's.

"Good." She nipped Morgan's lower lip with her teeth. "Because I love you, Morgan, and I never want to stop."

Morgan smiled and kissed her.

About the Author

Donna K. Ford is a licensed professional counselor who spends her professional time assisting people with their recovery from substance addictions. She holds an associate degree in criminal justice, a BS in psychology, and an MS in community agency counseling. When not trying to save the world, she spends her time in the mountains of East Tennessee enjoying the lakes, rivers, and hiking trails near her home and in the Great Smoky Mountains. Reading, writing, and enjoying conversations with good friends are the gifts that keep her grounded. She shares her life with her loving partner Keah and their now three adoring cats and one increasingly crazy beagle. They are her heart and her home and keep life interesting.

She spends much of the summer months traveling to Pride events with other Bold Strokes Books authors, where she enjoys meeting readers and talking about books.

Books Available From Bold Strokes Books

A Reluctant Enterprise by Gun Brooke. When two women grow up learning nothing but distrust, unworthiness, and abandonment, it's no wonder they are apprehensive and fearful when an overwhelming love just won't be denied. (978-1-62639-500-8)

Above the Law by Carsen Taite. Love is the last thing on Agent Dale Nelson's mind, but reporter Lindsey Ryan's investigation could change the way she sees everything—her career, her past, and her future. (978-1-62639-558-9)

Actual Stop by Kara A. McLeod. When Special Agent Ryan O'Connor's present collides abruptly with her past, shots are fired, and the course of her life is irrevocably altered. (978-1-62639-675-3)

Embracing the Dawn by Jeannie Levig. When ex-con Jinx Tanner and business executive E. J. Bastien awaken after a one-night stand to find their lives inextricably entangled, love has its work cut out for it. (978-1-62639-576-3)

Love's Redemption by Donna K. Ford. For ex-convict Rhea Daniels and ex-priest Morgan Scott, redemption lies in the thin line between right and wrong. (978-1-62639-673-9)

The Shewstone by Jane Fletcher. The prophetic Shewstone is in Eawynn's care, but unfortunately for her, Matt is coming to steal it. (978-1-62639-554-1)

Jane's World by Paige Braddock. Jane's PayBuddy account gets hacked and she inadvertently purchases a mail order bride from the Eastern Bloc. (978-1-62639-494-0)

A Touch of Temptation by Julie Blair. Recent law school graduate Kate Dawson's ordained path to the perfect life gets thrown off course when handsome butch top Chris Brent initiates her to sexual pleasure. (978-1-62639-488-9)

Beneath the Waves by Ali Vali. Kai Merlin and Vivien Palmer love the water and the secrets trapped in the depths, but if Kai gives in to her feelings, it might come at a cost to her entire realm. (978-1-62639-609-8)

Girls on Campus, edited by Sandy Lowe and Stacia Seaman. College: four years when rules are made to be broken. This collection is required reading for anyone looking to earn an A in sex ed. (978-1-62639-733-0)

Miss Match by Fiona Riley. Matchmaker Samantha Monteiro makes the impossible possible for everyone but herself. Is mysterious dancer Lucinda Moss her perfect match? (978-1-62639-574-9)

Paladins of the Storm Lord by Barbara Ann Wright. Lieutenant Cordelia Ross must choose between duty and honor when a man with godlike powers forces her soldiers to provoke an alien threat. (978-1-62639-604-3)

Taking a Gamble by P.J. Trebelhorn. Storage auction buyer Cassidy Holmes and postal worker Erica Jacobs want different things out of life, but taking a gamble on love might prove lucky for them both. (978-1-62639-542-8)

The Copper Egg by Catherine Friend. Archeologist Claire Adams wants to find the buried treasure in Peru. Her ex, Sochi Castillo, wants to steal it. The last thing either of them wants is to still be in love. (978-1-62639-613-5)

Capsized by Julie Cannon. What happens when a woman turns your life completely upside down? (978-1-62639-479-7)

A Reunion to Remember by TJ Thomas. Reunited after a decade, Jo Adams and Rhonda Black must navigate a significant age difference, family dynamics, and their own desires and fears to explore an opportunity for love. (978-1-62639-534-3)

Heartscapes by MJ Williamz. Will Odette ever recover her memory, or is Jesse condemned to remember their love alone? (978-1-62639-532-9)

Built to Last by Aurora Rey. When Professor Olivia Bennett hires contractor Joss Bauer to restore her dilapidated farmhouse, she learns her heart, as much as her house, is in need of a renovation. (978-1-62639-552-7)

Girls With Guns by Ali Vali, Carsen Taite, and Michelle Grubb. Three stories by three talented crime writers—Carsen Taite, Ali Vali, and Michelle Grubb—each packing her own special brand of heat. (978-1-62639-585-5)

Murder on the Rocks by Clara Nipper. Detective Jill Rogers lives with two things on her mind: sex and murder. While an ice storm cripples Tulsa, two things stand in Jill's way: her lover and the DA. (978-1-62639-600-5)

Salvation by I. Beacham. Claire's long-term partner now hates her, for all the wrong reasons, and she sees no future until she meets Regan, who challenges her to face the truth and find love. (978-1-62639-548-0)

Trigger by Jessica Webb. Dr. Kate Morrison races to discover how to defuse human bombs while learning to trust her increasingly strong feelings for the lead investigator, Sergeant Andy Wyles. (978-1-62639-669-2)

24/7 by Yolanda Wallace. When the trip of a lifetime becomes a pitched battle between life and death, will anyone survive? (978-1-62639-619-7)

A Return to Arms by Sheree Greer. When a police shooting makes national headlines, activists Folami and Toya struggle to balance their relationship and political allegiances, a struggle intensified after a fiery young artist enters their lives. (978-1-62639-681-4)

After the Fire by Emily Smith. Paramedic Connor Haus is convinced her time for love has come and gone, but when firefighter Logan Curtis comes into town, she learns it may not be too late after all. (978-1-62639-652-4)

Necromantia by Sheri Lewis Wohl. When seeing dead people is more than a movie tagline. (978-1-62639-611-1)

Fortunate Sum by M. Ullrich. Financial advisor Catherine Carter lives a calculated life, but after a collision with spunky Imogene Harris (her latest client) and unsolicited predictions, Catherine finds herself facing an unexpected variable: Love. (978-1-62639-530-5)

Dian's Ghost by Justine Saracen. The road to genocide is paved with good intentions. (978-1-62639-594-7)

Wild Shores by Radclyffe. Can two women on opposite sides of an oil spill find a way to save both a wildlife sanctuary and their hearts? (978-1-62639-645-6)

Soul to Keep by Rebekah Weatherspoon. What won't a vampire do for love... (978-1-62639-616-6)

When I Knew You by KE Payne. Eight letters, three friends, two lovers, one secret. Can the past ever be forgiven? (978-1-62639-562-6)

Love on Tap by Karis Walsh. Beer and romance are brewing for Tace Lomond when archaeologist Berit Katsaros comes into her life. (978-1-62639-564-0)

Whirlwind Romance by Kris Bryant. Will chasing the girl break Tristan's heart or give her something she's never had before? (978-1-62639-581-7)

Tracker and the Spy by D. Jackson Leigh. There are lessons for all when Captain Tanisha is assigned untried pyro Kyle and a lovesick dragon horse for a mission to track the leader of a dangerous cult. (978-1-62639-448-3)

Whiskey Sunrise by Missouri Vaun. Culture and religion collide when Lovey Porter, daughter of a local Baptist minister, falls for the handsome thrill-seeking moonshine runner, Royal Duval. (978-1-62639-519-0)